MAGAZINE

Volume 12, Number 3

*"Deep in each man is the knowledge that something knows of his
existence. Something knows, and cannot be fled nor hid from."*

—CORMAC McCARTHY

From Tin House Books

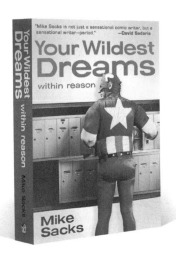

WHY DO FOOLS FALL IN LOVE?
A REALIST'S GUIDE TO ROMANCE

By Anouchka Grose

In this nimble and original exploration of love's hidden motivations and manifestations, Anouchka Grose tries to get to the heart of its hold over us. This straight-talking, sympathetic book sifts through the combined wisdom of philosophers and poets, scientists and shrinks to offer serious solutions to the conundrum of love.

"This is not a guidebook on how to love more successfully—it's more an exploration of the territory. Grose provides a hugely entertaining account that aims to make you think differently about the machinations of love."

—*Time Out,* London

Available January 2011 :: Trade Paper :: $15.95

YOUR WILDEST DREAMS,
WITHIN REASON

By Mike Sacks

Your Wildest Dreams, Within Reason collects Mike Sacks's unique humor pieces into one handsome, convenient volume. Whether it's a groom tweeting his wedding and honeymoon in real time, or a publisher offering editorial suggestions for *The Diary of Anne Frank*, Sacks's work tangles contemporary social satire with his absurdist sensibilities.

"*Your Wildest Dreams, Within Reason* makes you laugh out loud, and at the same time it inspires wonder . . . Mike Sacks is not just a sensational comic writer, but a sensational writer—period."

—*David Sedaris*

Available March 2011 :: Trade Paper :: $13.95

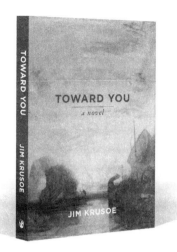

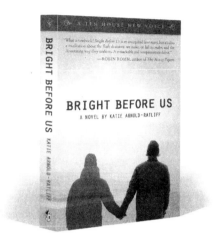

TOWARD YOU

By Jim Krusoe

BRIGHT BEFORE US

By Katie Arnold-Ratliff

Toward You completes Jim Krusoe's bittersweet trilogy about the relationship between this world and the next. Bob has spent several years trying to build a machine that will communicate with the dead, getting more or less nowhere until a couple of surprising events lead him to believe he might succeed after all. *Toward You* is a poignant story of longing, mistakes, regret, disaster, and, above all, hope.

Facing the prospect of fatherhood, disillusioned by his fledgling teaching career, and mourning the loss of a former relationship, Francis Mason is a prisoner of his past mistakes. When his second-grade class discovers a dead body during a field trip, Francis spirals into unbearable grief and all-consuming paranoia. A haunting debut novel, *Bright Before Us* explores the fraught journey toward adulthood, the nature of memory, and the startling limits to which we are driven by grief.

Praise for *Erased:*

"Smart and funny . . . Krusoe is an engaging writer and an acute observer of his own brand of quotidian strangeness."

—*New York Times Book Review*

"A remarkable and compassionate debut. "

—Robin Romm, author of *The Mercy Papers*

Available April 2011 :: Trade Paper :: $14.95

Available May 2011 :: Trade Paper :: $14.00

"Talent is helpful in writing, but guts are absolutely necessary."
—Jessamyn West

Michener Center for Writers

MFA in WRITING

FICTION   POETRY   SCREENWRITING   PLAYWRITING

A top ranked program. Dedicated and diverse resident faculty. Inspiring and distinguished visiting writers. $25,000 annual fellowships. Three years in Austin, Texas.

www.utexas.edu/academic/mcw • 512-471-1601

THE UNIVERSITY OF TEXAS AT AUSTIN

Tin House MAGAZINE

EDITOR IN CHIEF / PUBLISHER
Win McCormack

EDITOR	Rob Spillman
ART DIRECTOR	Janet Parker
MANAGING EDITOR	Cheston Knapp
SENIOR EDITOR	Tonaya Thompson
EXECUTIVE EDITORS	Lee Montgomery, Michelle Wildgen
POETRY EDITOR	Brenda Shaughnessy
ASSOCIATE EDITOR	Brian DeLeeuw
ASSOCIATE POETRY EDITOR	Matthew Dickman
EDITOR-AT-LARGE	Elissa Schappell
PARIS EDITOR	Heather Hartley
EDITORIAL ASSISTANT	Lance Cleland

CONTRIBUTING EDITORS: Dorothy Allison, Steve Almond, Aimee Bender, Charles D'Ambrosio, Anthony Doerr, CJ Evans, Nick Flynn, Matthea Harvey, Jeanne McCulloch, Christopher Merrill, Rick Moody, Whitney Otto, D. A. Powell, Jon Raymond, Rachel Resnick, Peter Rock, Helen Schulman, Jim Shepard, Karen Shepard, Bill Wadsworth

DESIGNER: Diane Chonette

INTERNS: Gabriel Blackwell, Emma Komlos-Hrobsky, Craig Moreau, Daniel Rivas

READERS: Shomit Barua, Deanna Benjamin, Max Ehrenfreund, Brooke Ellsworth, Santi Holley, Hannah Huber, Jonathan Hunsberger, Jake Kinstler, Chris Leslie-Hynan, Kathleen Langjahr, Amy Myer, Dan Oswalt, Sara Phinney, Peter Rawlings, Nicole Rosevear, Jennifer Taylor, JoNelle Toriseva, Allison Werner, Linda Woolman, Rosetta Young, Sean Zhuraw

DEPUTY PUBLISHER	Holly MacArthur
CIRCULATION DIRECTOR	Laura Howard
PUBLICITY DIRECTOR	Deborah Jayne
COMPTROLLER	Janice Carter

Tin House Books

EDITORIAL DIRECTOR	Lee Montgomery
EDITORIAL ADVISOR	Rob Spillman

EDITORS Meg Storey, Tony Perez, Nanci McCloskey, Deborah Jayne (Publicity)

Tin House Magazine (ISSN 1541-521X) is published quarterly by McCormack Communications LLC, 2601 Northwest Thurman Street, Portland, OR 97210. Vol. 12, No. 3, Spring 2011. Printed by R. R. Donnelley. Send submissions (with SASE) to Tin House, P.O. Box 10500, Portland, OR 97296-0500. ©2011 McCormack Communications LLC. All rights reserved. No part of this publication may be reproduced, stored in a retrieval system, or transmitted in any form or by any means, electronic, mechanical, photocopying, recording, or otherwise, without the prior written permission of McCormack Communications LLC. Visit our Web site at www.tinhouse.com.

Basic subscription price: one year, $24.95. For subscription requests, write to P.O. Box 469049, Escondido, CA 92046-9049, or e-mail tinhouse@pcspublink.com, or call 1-800-786-3424. Additional questions, email laura@tinhouse.com

Periodicals postage paid at Portland, OR 97210 and additional mailing offices.

Postmaster: Send address changes to Tin House Magazine, P.O. Box 469049, Escondido, CA 92046-9049.

Newsstand distribution through Disticor Magazine Distribution Services (disticor.com). If you are a retailer and would like to order Tin House, call Dave Kasza at 905-619-6565, fax 905-619-2903, or e-mail dkasza@disticor.com. For trade copies, contact Publisher's Group West at 800-788-3123, or email orderentry@perseusbooks.com.

Albert Einstein, who knew a thing or two about exploring the unknown, said, "The most beautiful thing we can experience is the mysterious. It is the source of all true art and science." Mysteries, be they grand or intimate, fire our imagination and enflame our curiosity, and all great writers aspire to plumb the unknown, at least psychically. National Book Award winner Andrea Barrett has charted a career of exploration marked by meticulous research and deep imagination in books such as *Ship Fever*, *Voyage of the Narwal*, and *Servants of the Map*. In this issue, Barrett chronicles the lives of early-twentieth-century astrophysicists, whose discoveries shake the very foundations of their beliefs. Young terror Benjamin Percy ventures into the dark to converse with horror master Peter Straub, who kindly offers tips on how to grab your reader by the throat. Our own Cheston Knapp probes the bizarre subculture of UFO researchers, where nothing is certain and everything is possible. At the very least, from now on he'll never look at the night sky the same way. We cover the spectrum of spooky stuff, from new ghost fiction to noir, from true crime to psychic memoirs, from poetry that is ineffable to forays into classics by C. K. Chesterton and J. K. Huysmans. There's no mystery as to what you want to read—it's in your hands. Don't be scared. Really. And for an even deeper, darker experience, including an even more in-depth version of the Percy/ Straub interview, please visit our newly revamped and expanded website at www.tinhouse.com.

CONTENTS

ISSUE #47 / SPRING 2011

Fiction

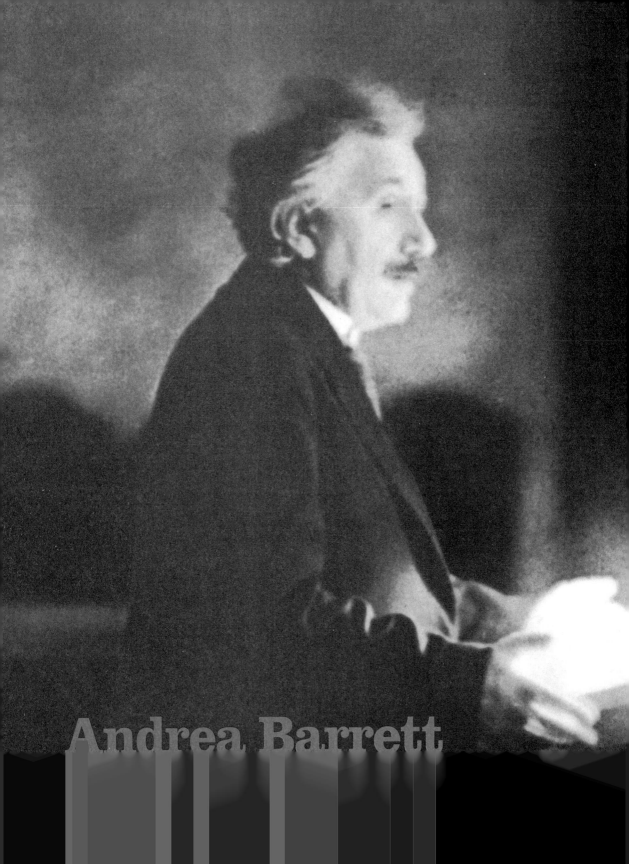

Andrea Barrett

The Ether of Space

There was a lot of chitchat, to start. Some the usual—Owen's health, the weather in London, a tactful acknowledgement of the tenth anniversary of Michael's death—but some not: Owen's sister was heading to Russia with a group of Quaker relief workers; his paper on variable stars would be published in the spring. But where was the crucial news?

Across the ocean, at her desk in her bedroom in her parents' house in Philadelphia, Phoebe Cornelius scanned the pages of her friend's letter impatiently. Last March, after the fighting had stopped, some British astronomers had quickly organized an expedition to view the eclipse. At two different stations along the path of totality, despite clouds in the Gulf of Guinea and a distorted mirror in Brazil, they'd photographed stars in the neighborhood of the sun. The results had been presented in November, at a meeting in London that Phoebe had been in no position to attend, and since then—nearly two months; it was already January, not just a new year but a whole new decade—she'd been waiting for Owen to supplement the sketchy, sensational newspaper articles with some firsthand observations.

We were all squeezed into the meeting room at Burlington House; the pews were packed and there were people standing behind the last row and in the anteroom. The usual eminences from the Royal Society and the Astronomical Society— J. J. Thomson, Fowler, Lodge, Silberstein, Jeans, etc.—but also the philosopher Whitehead, several reporters, and many I didn't recognize: about 150 of us, so many the room was steaming despite the wintry day. Dyson spoke first, summarizing the work of the expeditions and then describing the photographs in the most enthusiastic terms, despite the lack of data. He claimed there was no doubt that they had confirmed Einstein's prediction: the sun's gravitational field had been shown to bend the rays of starlight in accordance with his law of gravitation.

But Dyson's words don't really explain it—it was more the tone, the feeling in the room. I wish you'd been there. Half of us sighed as the other half gasped, some thrilled and some appalled and some split between the two; the older members were really upset. I could feel—well, I'm not sure what that was. Something that shook me. I took notes as fast as I could, trying to get not only the Astronomer Royal's tabulated values but Dr. Crommelin's description of conditions in Brazil during the eclipse and Professor Eddington's comments on the difficult weather. I noticed that Eddington had discarded many observations, but we'll see what's really there when the full report is published a few months from now. I do believe that Einstein's theory is correct, but I'm not sure these results support it as definitively as they're claiming.

The report on the meeting in the next day's Times *was typically muddled regarding the mathematics and said nothing, after these years of denouncing all things German, about the oddity of celebrating the work of a German scientist. In fact an article on the same page announced the king's call for two minutes of silence during the anniversary of the signing of the armistice. I went with my sister to the cenotaph that day, and when eleven struck and the guns went off, the crowd fell silent. The traffic stopped, too, and the trains and the tube, people stood still in the shops, stood up at their desks—I wept like everyone else and for an instant thought: I have never seen anything like this. Although later I realized that, at Burlington House, I'd had a similar sense of being present at a—what do you call these? A discontinuity, a rift? In one case torn by grief and in the other by wonder.*

For some, the meeting itself was a kind of grief. In the midst of the questions, Sir Oliver Lodge stood up abruptly and rushed out without a word. Later he told a reporter he'd left to catch a train, but some of the younger men have been a bit cruel, the old man running from the new theory and so forth. Not easy at that age, I imagine, to find that the world has just become a different place.

I have forgotten to thank you for your report on the Washington meeting, and to say that I read your draft chapter on "The Evolution of the Stars" with real interest. I hope the book is coming along wonderfully, and that you and Sam are both well.

> **The articles trumpeted the impossibility of understanding the theory while at the same time suggesting that it had changed the world.**

An actual report, finally, from an actual witness: how pleasing, to glimpse a scrap of reality! The articles in the *New York Times*, based on cables sent from London, had been as muddled as those Owen described. *Men of science more or less agog*—oh, indeed. *Lights all askew in the heavens.* The articles trumpeted the impossibility of understanding the theory while at the same time suggesting that it had changed the world.

Phoebe rose from her desk, went downstairs, and stepped outside to look at the sky. Nine o'clock and freezing cold, the moon two days past new, the stars giving no sign that they were not as they'd once seemed. The sound of her father's viola waved down from the top of the house, bits of Bach easing through the old glass in the attic windows, spreading from her mother's garden, where in summer the peonies flourished as if fertilized by the sound, through the tiny backyard to the neighbors on all sides. Always her father played at night, retreating from what to him was a world in which everything—business, politics, music, art—grew steadily worse. Yet the house hadn't crumbled around them; the house, in which first he and then Phoebe had grown up, looked the same. So too—she checked again—did the stars above. Where you lived and what you knew determined what you expected to see. Once the moon was a smooth glowing orb, and then it had mountains and seas. Once Jupiter wandered alone, and then he had moons; once orbits were round and the stars stayed still in space. In earlier books, she'd traced those changing perceptions. Now she was trying to write about the universe beyond the solar system. Who first thought those glowing specks were other suns, like ours? Or that some were island universes, far beyond the Milky Way?

Owen was at Cambridge now, a rising young astrophysicist with everything before him.

Back in the dining room, her mother sat at one end of the table, doing something with a heap of cloth, while Sam, at the other end, frowned over his homework. Phoebe stopped in the doorway, next to the long crack that might have appeared to a stranger as part of the molding's design, but in fact had been made when Sam, in a fit of temper after they'd first moved here, had hurled his suitcase at the wood. "I had a letter today from London," she told her mother. "Michael's old student, Owen—"

"Do these look the same length to you?" her mother asked, holding up two white strips.

"She's been cutting out sleeves, for shirts to send overseas," Sam explained without raising his head. He turned the pages of a small notebook and with his pencil added a tiny number to a column.

"Homework?" Phoebe asked her son. *Look up*, she thought. *Talk to me.*

"Sort of," he said.

If she moved his way, she knew, he'd smile and close the notebook, say good night, and a minute later disappear into his room. Door closed behind him, books closed on his shelves, body—he'd suddenly sprouted six inches, and his hair had darkened to Michael's shade—concealed beneath long sleeves and long pants. Instead of reaching for her secretive boy she hung back and watched her mother shuffle paper patterns, pins and chalk, and a formidable pair of scissors.

"Russia?" she asked. "Owen said his sister is headed there with another relief committee."

"Germany," her mother said. "Suzanne's doing the collars and Leila's working on the cuffs. We'll start piecing them together next week. What else did he have to say?"

Briefly, Phoebe explained the meeting in London and the results that Owen had described. Sam's pencil ticked down the numbers while her mother's scissors yawned and then snapped through the middle of a word. "That sounds important," her mother said.

"It is," Phoebe said. "I need to understand it better, for a chapter in the new book. In fact—"

"Of course," her mother said, snipping away. "Don't let us interrupt you."

Back at her desk, back in her room, centered in the house like a plum in a dumpling. Her father above and her mother and Sam below—Sam, who for a couple of years after Michael's death had clung so closely that sometimes, if she stopped or turned quickly, she'd trip over him. He'd liked to balance on a footstool, one hand on her thigh and the other on the frame of the large painting hanging in their tiny rented house in Washington.

"Tell me," he'd demand, until she pointed out the figures that her great uncle, Copernicus Wells, had painted on Pike's Peak during the eclipse of 1878. Then she'd name the instruments—telescope, spectroscope; your father had fancier versions of those—and finally note the flaring corona and the coincidence of her being born, far away, on that exact day. Copernicus had given her father the painting, which her father had given to her—

"Just after you were born," she'd add, pushing away the memory of Michael gazing at his new son, eyes wide beneath his reddish-gold brows. "When you're grown up, I'll give it to you."

Adrift in Washington then, with no idea how to continue her life, she'd imagined that she and Sam would always be close and that when he was older she'd tell him how that painting, along with her love for mathematics, had helped steer her toward astronomy. How her father had bought her a telescope when she was twelve, while her mother, who came from a Quaker family with a long tradition of learned women, had encouraged her studies. Surely Sam would want to know what she'd done before he was born. She'd imagined telling him about her time at Cornell, where she'd been drawn not to the patient collection of data, nor to speculations about the nature of the universe, but instead to the long, complicated, orderly calculations of celestial mechanics. An observant professor had steered her toward a job as a computer at the nautical almanac office in Washington, where she'd briefly imagined that she might be promoted. Instead, she'd met Michael Cornelius, an astronomer with the Smithsonian.

"We fell in love," she'd told Sam beneath the painting. A phrase that usefully hid everything, from the feel of Michael's leg against her own to the smell of his hair warmed by the bedside candle. "We got married, and—your father always appreciated the work I did—I kept my job until you were born. I helped him with his papers."

Sam, not quite four when Michael died, claimed to remember his father's instruments and the scarred wooden desk where he'd bent over maps of the sky—but not Phoebe beside him, plotting points on a graph. What different images they'd kept from those few years! The bed she and Michael had shared, their passionate absorption in astronomy, and their companionable hours of work were invisible to Sam, who remembered only what he saw and heard, and what had to do with him. In the dimly lit room where they worked after supper, Sam sat on Phoebe's chair, his back snugged against her side, tightly held by her left arm—but it was Michael, concentrating fiercely, whom he faced and whose smile lit Sam's eyes. So too had he faced the student visiting from England, a young man with an odd gait who delighted in clowning and liked chanting nursery rhymes to Sam. Tweedledum and Tweedledee: that was Owen, acting out bits from *Through the Looking Glass* while she calculated results from the data he and Michael had gathered.

Owen was at Cambridge now, a rising young astrophysicist with everything before him. Whereas she . . . at least he was polite about her work. Books and articles for the interested ignorant—*Astronomy for the Young*, *Eclipses for Everyone*—mingling what she hoped were sufficient facts with artful descriptions and homely analogies designed to take the place of the mathematics she loved but knew her readers couldn't understand. The Milky Way is shaped like a biscuit. A nebula is like a cloud on the verge of condensing into rain. Donkey work, requiring a certain gift but not, despite what Owen was polite enough to pretend, a valuable one. She pushed herself to try something new each time. For her latest, *The Universe Around Us*, she'd promised her publisher a clear and interesting version of the complicated material often mauled in popular accounts. Until recently, when she'd begun this difficult chapter on gravitation and the ether of space, she'd thought it was going well.

She turned back to Owen's letter, struck again by that image of Sir Oliver Lodge bolting from the meeting. Only a few days earlier she'd seen an article about him in the newspaper. He was on a ship from London to New

York, about to begin a big lecture tour. Some of the talks were already sold out, which wasn't surprising—unusually, for such an eminent scientist, Lodge liked to write for those who had no scientific training, and she'd sometimes turned to his books for help. Remembering that a list of lecture dates had appeared in the article, Phoebe rummaged through the stack by the fireplace until she found the right paper.

"The human personality survives death in a form we cannot see, but which makes communication after death possible."

On the evening of Lodge's scheduled talk, a crowd snaked out between the tall arches of the Academy of Music, and she learned that she'd made up her mind too late: every seat was sold. Reluctantly, she bought a standing-room ticket and entered the stream, carried up the stairs and then up again to one of the galleries on the second tier, where she came to rest behind two women pressed against a fluted column.

"You can fit in here," the first woman said, moving her purse to make room.

"It's Phoebe, isn't it?" said the second. Her nostrils faced more out than down, giving her otherwise pleasant face a slightly piglike air. "Odette," she continued, tapping her chunky throat. "Jenkins—your mother's friend?"

"Of course," Phoebe murmured. One of the scores of well-meaning women who served with her mother on committees to educate the children of China or feed those starving people in the Balkans. Too many to keep straight. They'd cheered her decision to go to college, been delighted when she got her job in Washington, tried to conceal their disappointment when she married young and promptly had Sam.

"There he is!" the first woman said.

Phoebe craned her head but could see the famous old physicist only in snippets. One long leg, one big hand; he was enormously tall. A sliver of his forehead gleamed in the light of the chandelier before a woman's hat eclipsed it. He would speak, he said—he had a fine voice—on "The Reality of the Unseen."

She missed his introduction. His words floated up through the horseshoe-shaped tiers, interrupted when the crowd murmured or shifted in their seats, obliterated entirely when Odette whispered to her friend. There were things known to be real, Lodge said, but impossible to see: atoms, for example. Molecules. She strained to hear, hoping he'd describe the invisible but omnipresent ether. Instead she caught something about the vast distances between the stars and the contrast between that and the minuteness of the atomic world: also unseen, but also real. After a lost chunk that must have contained a vital transition, she heard next a sentence about the reality of mental events, such as thoughts and feelings, which were also invisible. She peered through the crack between the two women's necks.

"Likewise," Lodge said just then, "the human personality survives death in a form we cannot see, but which makes communication after death possible."

> Instead of learning what she needed, she was forced again to confront the unalterable fact of Michael's death.

She pulled her head back and jammed her hands into her coat pockets. What kind of science was this? She knew he was interested in psychical research—he was as famous for this, in circles she avoided completely, as he was for his work on the ether and electromagnetic waves—but she'd assumed his lecture would be about physics. Instead, he was explaining how great discoveries in science have reversed the evidence of the senses: The earth is not flat, but round, and it is not static, but whirls through space at inconceivable speeds. So too will we come to reverse the evidence of our senses with regard to death. Psychic research, the youngest science, deals, like astronomy, with phenomena that cannot be examined in the laboratory. Still, theories can be tested and refined over time. Science will eventually prove the existence, all around us, of former humans; they are not far from us; we are all one family still. To the mothers of boys lost in the war, I would say that they are only separated from us by a veil of sense.

In front of her, both women sighed, and Phoebe remembered that Odette's son had gone overseas to drive an ambulance. Had he returned? All around her, the audience—mostly women, she now realized—listened raptly, while Odette reached back to touch Phoebe's arm, as if they had something in common.

"We should not exalt the senses," Lodge continued. Phoebe drew her arm away. "They have been developed through the necessity for the physical survival of the fittest. But if we did not dedicate ourselves so completely to the daily work of keeping our bodies alive, what organs of spiritual comprehension might we not develop? The space that separates you"—he stretched one hand toward the audience—"from me"—he pressed that hand to his chest—"is not empty. It is the purveyor of light, of electricity, of magnetism; and it may well contain our immortal souls, which persist after matter has disintegrated."

She stepped back before she understood that she was going to, ignored Odette's startled face, and pushed her way through the bodies and down the stairs. Wrong, wrong, wrong. She hated when people spoke of communication with the dead, and it was worse when a scientist did so. Rappings and knockings, scribblings on slates, ectoplasm and all the rest—ancient history, half a century old, most already proven fraudulent and the rest fit only for parlor games but still strangely persistent. When those superstitions had surfaced again, during the thrilling years when the discoveries of X-rays and radium, radio waves and electrons had made almost anything seem possible, she and Michael had simply ignored them, instead reading eagerly about light as waves, light as photons, energy possessing mass. The space between them, Michael said, was filled with energy, the ground of life itself; the question had been what the ether *was*.

She couldn't imagine what he'd have made of the ease by which, once the war began to swallow the young, those left behind were deceived by the resuscitated parlor tricks. By then, left behind herself, she knew exactly how despicable were the turbaned women cracking their joints in code or slipping their feet from specially stiffened shoes to write with their toes on slates. In 1909, not long after Owen returned to England, Michael had welcomed into the observatory a little boy who turned out to have measles. The boy recovered, but Michael's fever soared higher and higher until the morning he closed his eyes and sighed and—stopped, just stopped. In that instant she'd known she would never talk with him again.

The lobby stank of face powder; Phoebe pushed through the doors and into the street, where the snow flickered in the electric lights and a cat streaked by with something squirming in its clamped jaws. Michael had wanted to show off the wonders of the universe and now—she was walking so fast that her cheeks were hot and a woman in a short skirt stared at her—now, because a boy had given him measles, because she had a boy of her own to raise (the church bells chimed the hour; he'd be doing his homework), because, despite working all the time, she couldn't save enough to buy a house of her own, she was, at the age of forty-one, living with her elderly parents and still, despite having published three books and innumerable magazine articles, orbiting so far from the center of the scientific world that she must turn to others for explanations that would, when included in her book, lend it the air of authority she lacked herself.

She must go to a lecture where, instead of learning what she needed, she was forced again to confront the unalterable fact of Michael's death.

———— • ————

I was astonished, she wrote to Owen a few days later.

> *Not to mention disappointed. How does a man like him—a man who has spent his entire life thinking and writing about physics—a man who idolizes Clerk Maxwell and Helmholtz and the rest—end up like this? One thing to bolt from your meeting; Einstein's theories are so abstract that I sometimes wonder if anyone really understands them. But to refuse to accept them on the basis of insufficient proof, while at the same time contending that the survival of human personality has been proved: how does this make sense? The crowd was enormous, though, and seemed to glide right over the holes in his logic.*

What, she thought as she took a new sheet of paper, would Owen have made of that talk? He'd been fresh out of university when he came to Washington, a slim boy with a high forehead, a clubfoot, and a calm faith in the triumph of true science. Not once had he acted surprised by her mathematical skills or questioned her ability to help him and Michael. He'd been Michael's protégé, not hers, but she'd come to think of him as a friend and an equal and still considered him her one stalwart colleague, although they hadn't seen each other since before Michael's death, and she could no longer picture his face. Always—almost always—he responded to her letters. Always, courteously, he asked about her son, although she knew he envisioned not this Sam but the eager, open toddler of their days in Washington. Sam's hair had been blond then, wisping pale curls she could never keep parted; no more like the springy auburn mat he now hid behind than her own sandy dullness was like the shiny chestnut waves Michael had loved. But then Owen himself might be halfway bald, no longer thin; perhaps with a stoop, still with a limp: wouldn't he have told her if he'd had his foot repaired? Maybe not. Ideas connected them, mathematical symbols and diagrams, a disembodied thread of thought divorced from their daily lives. When she wrote him, she shaped her letters around pleasant anecdotes.

There'd been no point describing the details of those first harsh years after Michael's death, when she'd tried and failed to regain her old job and then found that she and Sam couldn't survive on the piecework calculations sent over by the Ephemeris staff. Skipping over the daily humiliations and petty miseries, she wrote lightly about the newspaper editor seated next to her at a dinner party—in her letter to Owen, a casual encounter; in fact, her rescuer—who, after learning about her training, had asked her to explain what actually caused an eclipse. Pleased by her quick demonstration with an apple, an almond, and a candle, he'd suggested she try writing about astronomy for the general public. From the column in his local paper (no examples of which she sent to Owen), she'd moved on to articles for the *Electrical Experimenter* and *McClure's*, then to her *Scientific American* pieces (which she did send), and her first books.

> **Ideas connected them, a disembodied thread of thought divorced from their daily lives.**

She liked the work; she was good at it and pleased when Owen praised her, but it was too painful to explain to him that, even writing all the time and as fast as she could, she could barely pay the rent, and she was sometimes short with Sam. Nor had she wanted to mention that Sam repaid her with temper tantrums, shrieking with anger when she tried to work on weekends, until finally her parents, after several worried visits, had convinced her to move back to Philadelphia—which move she'd presented to Owen as a pleasant choice. No mention after that, of course, of the way Sam at first ignored his teachers and balked at his grandfather's attempts to discipline him; nor about the molding he broke around the dining-room door or the scene he caused, a few months later, that ended with a broken vase and a cut on his scalp. And so, thus, no need to express her huge relief when, after a while, something happened—a teacher was kind, his body changed when he turned eight, who knew?—and he settled down. And no need to admit, except in the most positive and praising terms—*Sam has grown very studious and stays late at school almost every day, working on special projects with his teachers; you'd recognize him instantly as Michael's son*—that now, instead of hanging around her, scowling and demanding her attention, he was completely courteous but as distant as Jupiter.

———— • ————

A series of short magazine articles on the night sky in winter kept her from tackling the chapter she should have been writing, and she felt herself falling farther and farther behind. Behind what? her mother asked, reasonably enough, when she found Phoebe fretting at the window. The same unambitious and pleasant publisher had handled each of her books, approving her rough outlines and then leaving her alone until she returned with a tidy pile of pages, which he exchanged for a check. It was hard to explain that the self-imposed schedule she'd laid out so carefully was as real to her as the demands of her mother's garden.

From the basement came a man, shaken and pale, to report that the gas and water pipes were similarly sparking.

Weary of her own excuses, she was also embarrassed by the way she'd left Lodge's lecture, bolting from a disagreeable idea in the same way that Lodge himself, confronted with the evidence that his beloved ether might be in jeopardy, had fled the meeting in London. At the library, where she went to catch up with the astronomical journals, she instead took out a pile of his books. She read swiftly, voraciously, taking notes. What was she hoping to find? She could not have answered, she was glad no one asked. Nor could she have explained why she expanded those notes into pages describing material that she and Michael, years ago now, had once discussed. She wrote:

> The whirling machine, the massive metal structure bolted into the bedrock beneath the lab: it's difficult for a modern reader to imagine without inspecting the illustrations from Lodge's 1893 paper, "A Discussion Concerning the Motion of the Ether near the Earth." Here you may see the steel discs, a yard in diameter, perched on the central pillar like an oversize hat on a woman's head. In a separate drawing is the optical frame, complete with mirrors, telescope, and collimator; a third illustration shows the whole assembly in action, a man standing beside the pillar, frighteningly close to the discs and caged by heavy timbers supporting the optical apparatus. It looks like a sketch for Mr. Wells's Time Machine, an utterly improbable device on which Sir Oliver Lodge made the experiments he has called the most important of his life.
>
> During the 1890s, he performed a series meant to supplement the Michelson-Morley experiments, which he felt could not be right. Electromagnetic waves, including light, moved through the luminiferous ether; a wave must have something to wave in, and the ether, whatever its mechanical structure, was the needed medium. That medium must be detectable, flowing past the rapidly orbiting earth as a kind of wind, but the two scientists in Cleveland had failed to find it. Their results suggested that a layer of the ether must be carried along by the earth, but that hypothesis offered another set of problems. To test it, Lodge designed his pair of huge steel discs,

clamped together with an inch of space between them, rotating at high speed while
light traveled round and round between them with and then against the discs' motion,
which might determine if rapidly moving matter could drag the ether with it. The
machine was enormous, and very expensive. All the experiments failed. But he con-
tinued to define and extend the properties of the ether in his 1909 book, The Ether
of Space, *and still defends his concepts despite the absence of confirmatory evidence.*

The Smithsonian's copy of that book was one of the last that she remembered Michael reading, and indeed the instant she opened the library's cheaper edition, poorly bound and smelling of pipe tobacco, she saw the gilt apples along the spine of the red morocco volume Michael had held. Clearly written, she remembered him saying; parts quite useful but canceled out by the odd sentences dropped here and there: *If any one thinks that the ether, with all its massiveness and energy, has probably no psychical significance, I find myself unable to agree with him.* He'd pushed the book aside, then, not derisively but with a dismissal final enough to keep her from reading it.

Nor would she now; she pushed it, palm flat as Michael's had been, away. What did she want from this, why did she care? What she'd written was already both too detailed for her book, and not detailed enough for a proper article. Yet that evening, back at her parents' home, she tried again, meaning to convey some sense of Lodge's fame as a teacher and scientist:

Sir Oliver Lodge, long a preeminent physicist, is only slightly less well-known than
Marconi. At an early age he decided that his main business was with what were
then called "the imponderables"—the things that worked secretly and have to be ap-
prehended mentally. So it was that electricity and magnetism became the branch of
physics that most fascinated him. Once, in London, at the height of his fame as a lec-
turer on popular science, policemen had to rearrange the traffic patterns outside the
Royal Institution so that the cabs delivering his eager audience could fit in the street.
Another time, giving a lecture and demonstration on "The Discharge of a Leyden
Jar," he was as astonished as the audience to see the coating on the walls flashing and
sparking in sympathy with the waves being emitted by the oscillations on the lecture
table. From the basement came a man, shaken and pale, to report that the gas and
water pipes were similarly sparking.

She stopped when her mother, walking the house restlessly long after she should have been in bed, leaned over her shoulder and read the last lines.

"I like the sparks," she said, resting her fingers on Phoebe's forehead.

As if the sparks explained how a man could move from the drudgery of his family business—he'd worked for his father, selling clays and chemicals in the potteries north of London—to the heights of science, to an ardent belief in the possibility of communing with the dead. Or how a leading researcher into electromagnetism and the nature of light could end up being the most famous opponent of a radical new theory. If Einstein was right—but he was only *possibly* right; which meant Lodge was possibly not wrong, or at least not wrong about the ether, although utterly wrong about the spirits *in* the ether . . . Phoebe squirmed beneath her mother's hand.

"That's—for your book?" her mother asked.

"Not exactly," Phoebe said. "Maybe. I don't know. I went to hear him . . ."

"I know," her mother said. "Odette mentioned." She traced the outline of Phoebe's forehead with two fingers, as if the friction might extract a clearer sentence. "Let me make you some tea."

Phoebe, pulling away, pushed her mother's hand toward the newspaper, open to yet another of the frequent pieces about Lodge. "Here," she said. "I'm not the only one who's curious about him."

The article, which her mother scanned quickly, offered an impression of Lodge as he'd appeared soon after his arrival in New York. A typical Victorian, the reporter had noted, "of the tradition of Darwin and Huxley, who still reads his Wordsworth and Tennyson, who still appreciates the poet's wonderment in those days at the marvels of science."

Three more columns followed, all meant, Phoebe thought while her mother finished, to drum up interest in Lodge's forthcoming lectures. His next scheduled talk was actually to *be* on "The Ether of Space"—his special area of expertise, and the material she most needed to review. Owen had gone to the meeting in London, to hear the results of the Einstein experiment. Maybe she should go to this in the same spirit and listen to Lodge expound what he really knew, taking from it what she needed. Wasn't science based on weighing evidence for oneself?

Surprising herself, she said, "I should try to hear this next lecture. I think I'll ask Sam to come with me." She imagined his quiet, sturdy presence at her side, his quick intelligence; he'd see things she didn't, and he wouldn't be easily distracted or upset. "He might find it interesting. And I could use the company."

"Since when," her mother asked, moving away, so rich herself in friends and colleagues that she might not have meant her question to pierce Phoebe, "do you want company?"

It was true that she and Sam seldom did things together anymore—he kept to himself, as she did, and he was busy, as she was herself—but to Phoebe's secret delight he said the trip sounded fun; she'd brought him only twice before to New York. Together they took the train and shared the sandwiches Phoebe's mother packed for them; together they rode the subway to the towering Woolworth Building and there took the elevator up and up, braving the last little climb on the spiral stairs for the sake of the view from the observatory. The entire island lay before them, the East River and the ships moving out into the harbor, Brooklyn stretching away to one side and New Jersey on the other. Pigeons wheeled and sank and rose again, seagulls floated on curved wings, radio waves poured invisibly from the windows. Marconi himself, Phoebe told her son, had sent a wireless message from his office across the ocean, announcing the opening of this building.

> **Her hand was writing, words flowing smoothly and rapidly, but her mind had stopped catching hold.**

Sam, who hadn't been there before, leaned against the railing and pointed north, saying, "Look at the park! Look at the rivers! You can see the museum!" When he laughed and tugged his coat from her hands, she realized she'd been clutching it as if he were a toddler about to pitch over the side.

He teased her about that for the rest of the afternoon, as they ducked in and out of bookshops and took the subway back uptown. After a quick bowl of soup, they headed to the theater, where they found seats high in the balcony, and Sam inspected the crowd streaming into the orchestra seats and up the stairs. Around them, coats migrated into seats and hats moved onto laps, until a curtain opened on Lodge's tall, white-haired figure, bowing into the wave of applause and then, as Phoebe studiously readied her steno pad and mechanical pencil, beginning to speak.

Sam brushed her arm with his—an accident? Turning to him, watching him, she missed Lodge's opening lines. Usually, when she reached to straighten Sam's collar or fix his hair, he stood so still it was as if he were willing himself not to flinch. But he bumped her elbow with his again, gently, almost playfully, as he had when he was small. "Thank you for bringing me," he whispered. "This is interesting."

Sam was glad he was there, Sam was interested; she focused her attention on the talk. What had she already missed? The ether, Lodge was saying, far from being beyond all comprehension, was in fact the most substantial thing in the universe. Why then had we taken so long to discern it? Just because it is so universal. If we were fish living at the bottom of the ocean, surrounded by water, so far from the surface that we had no sense of anything *but* water; if we were moving in water, breathing water—what is the last thing we would discover? The water itself. So it had been with the ether of space.

The whole relativity trouble— **that simple phrase made Einstein's theory seem a piece of trickery.**

Now Phoebe listened intently; she could use this. "Hold your hand near a fire," he said, "put your face in the sunshine, and what is it you feel? You are now as directly conscious as you can be of the ethereal medium. True, you cannot apprehend the ether as you can matter, by touching or tasting or even smelling it; but it is something akin to vibrations in the ether that our skin and our eyes feel. The ether does not in any way affect our sense of touch and it does not resist motion in the slightest degree. Not only can our bodies move through it, but much larger bodies, planets and comets, can rush through it at a prodigious speed without showing the least sign of friction. I have myself designed and carried out delicate experiments to see whether whirling discs of iron could to the smallest extent grip the ether and carry it round, with so much as a thousandth part of their own velocity. The answer is no. Why, then, if it is so impalpable, should we assert its existence? May it not be a mere fanciful speculation, to be extruded from physics as soon as possible?"

So far, so good; she was glad to see the whirling discs again, but then . . . her hand was writing, words flowing smoothly and rapidly, but her mind had stopped catching hold. Was it that what he was saying didn't make sense, or that she wasn't concentrating? Action at a distance cannot take place, with the exception of mental action, or telepathy—she looked down at the paper; had he just said that?—and the actions of gravitation, magnetism, and electric force require some intervening medium. The nature of that medium is mysterious, but it is entirely incompressible and might be thought of as a jellylike substance filling all space.

"A body cannot act where its influence is not," her pencil wrote, but her wayward mind pictured a giant jellyfish, pulsing faintly, stretching in all directions. The pictures were *always* wrong; only the mathematics conveyed the truth. "Another and perhaps a better way of putting it is to say that one body can act on another only through a medium of communication. When a horse pulls a cart, it is connected by traces; when the earth pulls the moon, it is connected by the ether; when a magnet pulls a bit of iron, it is connected by its magnetic field, which is also in the ether."

Here he reached below the podium, brought up a candy box striped in yellow and green, and set the box on a table beside him. "Would it be magic," he said, reaching for his cane, "if, by waving this, I caused the box to move?"

Sam was staring raptly at the stage—as indeed, Phoebe saw, was the entire audience. Lodge passed his cane through the air, two feet above the box. The box slid sideways on the table.

"Hey!" Sam said, leaning so far forward that his chin would have brushed the hair of the woman sitting in front of him, had she not herself been leaning over the balcony rail. His own hair was a beautiful color in this light. Lodge raised the cane above his head and the box rose from the table.

After the exclamations from the audience subsided, he smiled modestly and lowered the cane. "When you see action of this kind," he said—the box settled back down—"always look for the thread."

What a showman. The thread was invisible at this distance, but he caught it between the cane and the box and suggested, by a tugging gesture, how it was connected.

"Always look for the medium of communication," he said. "It may be an invisible thread, as in this conjuring trick; it may be the atmosphere, as when you whistle for a dog; or it may be a projectile, as when you shoot an enemy. Or, again, it may be ether ripples, as when you look at a star. You cannot act at a distance without some means of communication; and yet you can certainly act where you are not, as when by a letter or telegram you bring a friend home from the Antipodes. A railway signalman can stop a train or bring about a collision without ever touching a locomotive. A conclave of German politicians could, and did"—his voice rose here, making Phoebe look up from her pad—"operate on innumerable families in England and slaughter their most promising members without the direct action of a finger."

She felt a small tremor, as if that finger had moved, miles away, through the water in which she floated. "No one wants to be deceived," he continued. "All are eager for trustworthy information about both the material and the spiritual worlds, which together constitute the universe. The ether of space is the connecting link. In the material world it is the fundamental substantial reality. In the spiritual world the realities of existence are other and far higher—but still the ether is made use of, in ways which at present we can only surmise."

Her pencil stopped, but he did not. She could feel him gathering up his thoughts, preparing for some final argument.

"Last May," he continued, "when astronomers measured the bending of a ray of light around the sun during an eclipse, they obtained data that when measured made Einstein's theory of gravitation appear to triumph. But what is the *meaning* of this triumph? Is it the death knell of the ether?"

Before Phoebe could frame an answer, Lodge surged on. "Must we now think in terms of four or even five dimensions to explain this warp or curvature of space? In my opinion, we ought clearly to discriminate between things themselves and our mode of measuring them. The whole relativity trouble arises from ignoring absolute motion through the ether, rejecting the ether as our standard of reference and replacing it by the observer."

The whole relativity trouble—that simple phrase made Einstein's theory seem a piece of trickery as foolish as the thread. Caught in the smooth stream of words, Phoebe could question his logic only when she split her attention in two and set one part struggling against the flow. Yet even as she was giving up—he was now discussing the relationship between matter and the ether—he said something that made her write faster.

"Undoubtedly the ether belongs to the material universe, but it is not ordinary matter. It may be the substance of which matter is composed. If you tie a knot in a bit of string, the knot is composed of string, but the string is not composed of knots. The knot differs in no respect from the rest of the string, except in its tied-up structure; it is of the same density as the rest, and yet it is differentiated from the rest. In order to cease to be a knot, it would have to be untied—a process which as yet we have not learned how to apply to an electron."

There—*that* was why she admired him, why she'd come tonight. That was the kind of image she searched for in her own work and found, when she was lucky, with a sense of release that was almost physical. He was not a charlatan; he was a scientist who'd made real discoveries—he, as much as Marconi, had discovered the basic principles of the radio—and he'd drawn many to science through his lectures and his books. He might be old, and distinguished, and British, and a man; capable, as she had not been for years—had she ever really been?—of doing real science: but still they had more in common than just bolting from disagreeable ideas. How strange that what he seemed to care most about now was the possibility of communicating with the dead.

The lecture lightened something in her, or perhaps it was Sam's presence beside her; his arm next to hers, his mind engaged, however briefly, with something that absorbed her. The distance between them had grown, she would have said a week earlier, because he'd developed his own interests, which he didn't talk about much. On the train ride home, though, she considered how little she'd recently shared with him, so busy that she'd lost the habit of explaining her work. But as soon as she exposed him to Lodge he'd responded, which might mean that he'd be interested in the rest of the project; perhaps she could share other sections with him: perhaps the book would be wonderful! With a burst of enthusiasm, she began to draft her chapter on the ether.

> **Waves in the ocean travel through water; light waves must travel through a similar interstellar ocean.**

First a bit of history: a quick glimpse of Descartes and his whirling vortices, and then the newer conceptions answering the need for a subtle medium, universally diffused, that could propagate the undulations of light and electricity while also transmitting the pull of gravity. Waves in the ocean travel through water; light waves must travel through a similar interstellar ocean, which we can neither see nor feel nor weigh. This is the ether, nowhere apparent but everywhere implied. The ether, which, until quite recently, most scientists had assumed *must* exist. How then might we conceive of this omnipresent, impalpable, invisible something?

She touched on Maxwell's ingenious models and the various arrangements by which wheels and rubber bands, gears and pulleys and springs had been set to represent possible mechanisms. Neatly she fit after those pages the sketch she'd made of Lodge's experiments with the whirling machine. Then on to the more recent and less mechanical conception of the ether as the ground from which both matter and energy arise. From Lodge's lecture—she pushed aside the tangle of upsetting digressions and disturbing assumptions—she lifted the image of knots on a string, matter as coiled-up ether: matter may be and likely is a structure in the ether, but certainly ether is not a structure made of matter.

And there the chapter crashed. She meant her tone to be judicious, sketching what had been believed when she was young, and what could fairly be believed now. To write something like *Experiments performed during the recent eclipse suggest that Einstein's theories may be confirmed, in which case we may not need to postulate an ether to explain the transmission of light. However, spirited disagreement continues among scientists as to the meaning of these results, and it seems best, for now, to keep an open mind.*

But even as she wrote that, she knew she didn't believe it herself. No one could find the elusive ether; all the experiments had failed. Lodge and those who disbelieved Einstein wrote as if the ether were real but mysteriously unfindable, the experiments that had failed to detect it somehow defective, and she'd meant to give equal space to that position but—how could she? It wasn't just the lack of evidence; something was wrong with the logic too. How could the ether be composed of knots or vortices *in* the ether? Her brain stuttered, her mind balked. Her eyes burned and ached. The sentences crumbled as she wrote them, and when she thought again about Lodge's lecture, the tangle she'd pushed aside then snared her. The ether was a home for ethereal beings, the medium by which soul spoke to soul; perhaps God lived there: perhaps it was God himself?

> If he's right, then Michael's been within my reach this whole time and I could have been talking to him.

She lay down and pressed a wet washcloth to her eyes. The ether was nothing and it was everything; it was whatever anyone wanted it to be. Writing about the ether was like trying to write about phlogiston. Although she'd explained more complicated models, and outlined concepts in which she believed less, never before had she tried to write something that taunted her with a sense of Michael hovering, just out of sight, in some gaseous form.

———— ◆ ————

Three days of heavy rain trapped her inside. On the fourth day, a front blew through and cleared the air as completely as if a giant hand had sponged it dry. That night, very late, after everyone was asleep, Phoebe went outside and lay down on the flagstones bordering her mother's garden. Late March, the ground alive despite the cold air. There were the stars, circling above. There were the stars. Brilliant, blazing, bright against blackness, as beautiful as when she'd first stared at them so many years ago. White, blue, yellow, red. Once she'd gotten serious about the work to which the stars had drawn her, she hardly ever looked at them. She studied their motions, not them—when did she look at the sky anymore? Months passed when night meant her yard, her street, a few blocks of Philadelphia: everywhere people, everywhere lights. Now the lights were out, there was no one around. With her back pressed against the stones, she smelled dirt and leaves and budding trees. Branches fringed her view of the sky, which was speckled everywhere—and wasn't it remarkable, really, that she should see the stars at all? Inconceivably far away, emitting light that traveled and traveled—how? through what?—and fell upon her optic nerves to form a picture in her brain: stars! She felt herself falling up into them, a feeling she remembered from her childhood. The space between her and the stars was infinite or nothing at all, it was empty or it was completely filled, it was, it was, it was . . .

The next afternoon she went looking for Sam, longing to talk about this. But Sam was gone; he was at a friend's; they were working on a project for school. Disappointed, she sat down and wrote to Owen, describing her struggles and the two lectures she'd attended.

> Strangely, it was listening to Lodge that confused me. I'm not sure why, maybe that—how to say this? Lodge's conception of the ether is one of those models that, like an orrery or a gigantic watch, sets a nearly infinite number of pieces of something into motion, each affecting the other, until the actions are explained. But I don't think we can explain this mechanistically. Listening to him describe the survival of the personality after death as some element held in or made from the ether made me realize how completely attached he is to the ether as an actual physical thing.

Interesting that she'd write that, but not a word about Michael. Not what flared through her mind at night: *Lodge must be wrong, he has to be wrong. If he's right, then Michael's been within my reach this whole time and I could have been talking to him. I could be talking to him now.* Not once had she even tried. She and Michael had held séances and spirit messages in such contempt that even to study the written accounts, never mind visiting a medium, would have felt like a betrayal.

Yet here was Lodge, famous and influential, perhaps even—was it disloyal to think this?—a better scientist than Michael had been, testifying to his beliefs before huge crowds. Either he was a liar, which he didn't seem to be, or she was the worst kind of fool. But Einstein's theories had also generated a similar confusion, especially here, as she wrote to Owen:

> There's a lot of pressure here—far more, I think, than in England—not to accept Einstein's theory. People are so emotional—a prominent astronomer at Columbia

started calling the theory "Bolshevism in science" as soon as the eclipse results were announced, and since then he's written a slew of articles disputing the evidence. Another, in California, repeats him but more shrilly. They have alternate explanations for the advance of the perihelion of Mercury. They object to the interpretation of the eclipse data (you know these arguments, the discarded observations, the large margins of error, etc.) and in the next breath claim that even if the light from the stars was shown to be bent, the cause may well be refraction by the sun's corona, or a spurious displacement resulting from the chemistry of film development. They have plenty of supporters, working astronomers who place a premium on precise observations and think the data from the expedition is nowhere near as solid as claimed.

———————————— ◦ ————————————

The daffodils pushed through the dirt; the trees budded and the forsythia bloomed; the tulips came and went as she struggled with her chapter. Over breakfast one morning, she read about a professor who'd been following Lodge from city to city, contradicting everything he said about the dead and demonstrating some of the fakery employed by mediums; apparently she wasn't the only one disturbed by the mingling of physics and spiritualism. She read the article to Sam, who set aside his toast to listen.

"That seems harsher than he deserves," he said, surprising her. "I liked him, the way he seemed determined to think for himself."

But before she could encourage him to say more, her father passed through the room, humming disconsolately, and Sam rose and followed him, leaving Phoebe alone with her failures. Living under her father's roof, eating at her father's table, when he was getting older and struggling: she *had* to earn more money. She went back to work.

Her mother's obdurate peonies pushed through the dirt and unfolded their leathery leaves as Sam finished school for the year. The peonies budded, the buds bulged. Her mother, wrapped in a green apron, her hands sheathed in canvas gloves, disappeared into the garden, and her father retreated to the attic; Bach wafted down from the windows. She picked up her notebook and wrote: *Sound is a wave that moves through the air, light is a wave in the ether . . .* Then she crossed that out and wrote to Owen again, enclosing a draft of what she had so far. Owen didn't write back, and didn't write back, and then in late July he finally did, complaining about the shortages of food and coal and describing the weekend lectures he'd been giving to gatherings of miners and farmers. Only then did he comment on her draft.

Most of what you have so far seems fine to me, coherent and logical, if too heavily weighted toward the history. Too much context, not enough of the actual theory? That might just be my own perspective. Phoebe, I really am not sure about this— but haven't you fallen into that old trap of trying to make, from the symbols we use to reason about reality, pictures we can view in our minds? You know as well as I do that our ideas about space and time and molecules and matter aren't anything like the "real" universe, although they parallel it in some way; we make models because they help us think, but what we're really talking about here are mathematical statements that describe the relationships of phenomena. It's a mistake to weed out all the mathematics, even when you are trying to explain a theory we already understand to be outmoded. I think you could do this more succinctly. And that you could come down more firmly on the side of what we know now—not what we used to think we knew.

> She had lost Michael, she was at a loss with Sam, her parents were a mystery, she had no home of her own.

Since when did Owen talk to her like that? As if she were his student; as if she were a colleague's undereducated, amateurish wife. Her earlier books had been for young readers, explanations for intelligent twelve-year-olds; she'd been as proud of them as of her newer work for adults, but what Owen was really saying was *You still write like that; this is too simplistic.*

She stared at her draft, unsure how to make it better. Once she'd been able to write, clearly and even powerfully. Once she'd gone to her desk each day with the unthinking expectation that she would pick up her pen and begin, and that from the very movement of pen across paper a train of thought would develop. Concepts would clarify themselves, sentences would flower into paragraphs; in this one small arena, she could do no wrong. She had lost Michael, she was at a loss with Sam, her parents were a mystery, she had no home of her own—yet on the page she could make an object that was shapely, and orderly, and on occasion helpful to others. She'd counted on this for years, without understanding what it would mean if it disappeared. As she'd counted on the sympathetic ear of a man she apparently no longer knew.

"You're so flushed," her mother said, when the heat drove them outside to sit stickily on the chairs they'd pulled into the garden. "Are you feeling all right?"

"I'm fine," Phoebe told her. "Just tired. It's been hard to sleep."

But what kept her from sleeping was not the heat. She tried to squelch the bitter thought that Owen did not, after all, regard her as his equal intellectually.

For all her efforts to keep him from viewing her primarily as a woman—efforts that had cost a great deal in other ways—he still condescended to her.

Quickly, almost mechanically, she wrote over the next few days a magazine article about the implications of the red-shifted spectra Vesto Slipher had observed for a handful of spiral nebulae. Then, with her papers drooping moistly over open books, she returned to her chapter, still unfinished, still not right. She tried this:

> What this was, Sam argued, was evidence of a different sort: evidence of love.

If the ether exists as some sort of rigid jelly, then all of space is filled by it, everything in space is connected to everything else, a ripple here causes effects inconceivably far away—but space, however tied together, is all one thing, and time is something else. In Einstein's vision, etherless, space and time are tied together into one four-dimensional continuum, impossible to visualize but perfectly clearly expressed mathematically. Time is variable in that vision; time expands and contracts depending on the position of the observer, and it seems possible that the past, the present, and the future might all exist at once, so that everything we've ever done and been might be laid out, accessible.

Michael, she thought. The day they met, the moment their hands first touched, the day they were married, the moment when Sam was conceived. She scratched those lines out thoroughly.

———— ◆ ————

September came and Sam returned to school, still without Phoebe having completed what had once seemed like a manageable task. She gave up writing to Owen. She shut herself in her room, still far too warm, and she wrote and wrote, crossed out and wrote more. Then she fell sick for three weeks—the strain of working so hard, her worried mother said—and when she could rise from her bed she was more behind than ever. She'd lost weight, her hair was dry, and her periods had vanished; was it already time for that? Perhaps it was just from being sick. She made an effort to eat the meals with which her mother tempted her, and she put the chapter on the ether out of her mind. An acquaintance who taught astronomy at Bryn Mawr asked if she'd be willing to tutor three struggling students; she took them all. At the request of a high school teacher, she also wrote an article detailing useful experiments, requiring little equipment, for youngsters.

She found herself, as the New Year came and went, in roughly the same place she'd been when Owen's letter about the eclipse expeditions had arrived. Another year older, her hair more gray, still at her desk in her parents' house— except that now she was past the time when she'd promised to send in her book, and her oldest colleague had drifted away, and Einstein was hugely famous everywhere. One by one, essays attempting to explain his theory to the non-mathematically trained reader had been published in *Scientific American*, while across the ocean, *Nature* devoted an entire issue to the explanation and implications of the principle of relativity. In the library, dutifully at first but then with some excitement, Phoebe read through those articles.

She copied out phrases from the well-known physicists who examined different aspects of Einstein's theory but in the end agreed that it was right: all except for Sir Oliver Lodge, who declared stoutly that while the theory might appeal by its beauty and weird ingenuity to mathematicians lacking a sense of physical reality, it so oversimplified the properties of matter as to risk impoverishing the rich fullness of our universe into a mental abstraction.

Now that he and his psychic beliefs were safely in England, his recalcitrance seemed almost admirable. That steadfast insistence on common sense and the reality of a physical world in a physical ether: what did it cost him to maintain that position, now so unpopular? One afternoon, reading with her mother and Sam in front of the fire, she asked what Sam remembered of Lodge from the lecture last spring.

"He remembers it very well," her mother said. "Don't you?"

Sam nodded without looking up from the huge volume open on his lap.

"What are you reading?" Phoebe asked.

"A biology textbook," he said, spreading his fingers over the pages. "My teacher loaned it to me, for an extra project." Which she knew nothing about. When her mother said, "Sam?" he added, "I wrote something about Lodge, for an English class."

"Can I see it?"

He paused, looking down at his book, and then closed it on a pencil and rose. "If you'd like." He left the room and returned with a few sheets of paper, covered in his meticulous small script.

The essay, which he'd called "My Father, at a Distance," started not with a memory of Michael but with a description of Sam's evening at the theater in New York. Here were the rapt women, the box with the thread, the flow of Lodge's talk as she too remembered it—but these things, for Sam, had been only a beginning. Like her, he'd gone to the library and investigated Lodge's writings; but unlike her—she hadn't been able to stand more than a few pages—he'd actually read Lodge's book about his son, Raymond, who after being killed in the Great War had supposedly made efforts to communicate with his family.

I didn't expect to be swayed by it, Sam wrote. *But I was, although perhaps not in the way Lodge meant.* Sam described the letters Raymond had sent from the front, the photographs of him as a boy, the long transcriptions of Lodge's sittings with mediums after Raymond's death, the chapters of theory and exposition meant to help a reader interpret what Lodge presented as evidence for Raymond's continued existence in another form. What this was, Sam argued, was evidence of a different sort: evidence of love. When Lodge wrote, *People often feel a notable difficulty in believing in the reality of continued existence. Very likely it is difficult to believe or to realize existence in what is sometimes called "the next world"; but then, when we come to think of it, it is difficult to believe in existence in this world too; it is difficult to believe in existence at all*, what he meant was *My existence makes no sense without my son.*

From Lodge's longing for his son had come, Sam argued, an entire theory of etheric transmission, which, if it wasn't true—he himself believed it was not—was still a marvelous example of how science was influenced by feeling. About the connection between that feeling and the construction and testing of any scientific hypothesis. Lodge had suggested in his lecture that Einstein's theory had been tested but not completely proven by the eclipse experiments. His book suggested that his experiments after Raymond's death offered a similar level of proof for the theory of survival of personality. Phoebe slowed down and read each word.

My father died when I was four; I miss him all the time. For years I was sure he was up in the air somewhere, among the stars he studied. I listened for him every night; I thought that from someplace deep in space he would try to contact me. When we moved from the house where I was born, I was terrified that if he sent a message it wouldn't reach me. Later, I convinced myself that he could find me anywhere, at any distance, and that the fault was mine; if I couldn't hear him, it was because I didn't know how to listen. If I stretched myself, broadened myself, I'd be like a telescope turned onto a patch of sky that before had seemed blank; suddenly stars would be visible, nothingness would turn into knowledge. Across time and space, my father would reach out to me.

Here was Michael at last: she could see his face as clearly as when they'd first kissed on the riverbank, under the starry sky.

Eventually, I had to give up on this idea, but as I listened to Lodge's lecture I fell back into it, and for a few moments, I wanted so badly to believe him that I did. I understood the ether of space to be exactly as Lodge described it, a universal medium that transmits not only electromagnetic forces but also the thoughts and longings of the dead. Only when I looked around at the audience and saw them all believing the same thing did I realize what was happening.

I don't understand the physics behind Einstein's theory, and I don't believe in the existence of a spirit world, but my introduction to Lodge's work changed the way I think. I don't know, and I don't believe there is sufficient evidence yet to prove, whether the ether is real the way the atmosphere is real, or the way the equator is real. Whether Einstein's theory has been proven, or Lodge's theory of survival of the personality after death, or neither or both. I don't know whether my father exists in some ethereal form or only in my heart. What I do know is that the questions we ask about the world and the experiments we design to answer them are connected to our feelings.

Where had Sam learned to write like that? Upstairs, her father's viola sang, dismantling troubles Phoebe knew nothing about. Across from her, Sam and her mother nestled back in their chairs, each reading with such concentration that when she finished Sam's essay, neither noticed for a moment. Then her mother looked up.

"It's good," she said. "Isn't it?"

"Lovely," Phoebe agreed. Her mother had already read it. Down the stairs, through the empty rooms, triplets rippled in sets of four: the prelude to the sixth Bach cello suite, transcribed for viola, which her father had been playing while she and Sam and her mother read, each of them deep in their own thoughts but sharing a room, the light from the lamps, the sense of piecing together a sequence of thoughts. Then—not a rift, but a discontinuity. How does a person end up like this? For much of her life she'd been listening, sometimes consciously, sometimes not, to her father play those suites. Until just that moment, with the triplets running steadily up and down, she would have told herself that the space between her and her family wasn't empty at all but held light and music, feelings and thoughts, and a bond that could be stretched without breaking. 🔹

Chametla

The last shot fired in the Battle of Chametla hit Private Arnulfo Guerrero in the back of the head. It took out the lower-right quadrant, knocking free a hunk of bone roughly the size and shape of a broken teacup. This shot was fired by a federal trooper, who then shouldered his weapon and walked to a cantina on the outskirts of town, where he ate a fine pork stew with seven corn tortillas and a cup of pulque. The shot was witnessed by Guerrero's best friend, Corporal Angel Garcia, and by Guerrero's dog, Casan. Casan was a floppy-eared Alsatian he'd stolen from a *federales* base the year before.

Luis Alberto Urrea

"Por Dios, Arnulfo," Garcia muttered as he stuffed straw and a long strip of his tunic into the gaping head wound. "What have they done to you?"

Guerrero writhed on the ground, his teeth clenched in a silent rage, froth collecting on his lips.

Garcia stanched the bleeding and wrapped a dirty field dressing around and around his friend's head.

Casan stood to the side, whining and fretting.

Troops were everywhere, and though the Battle of Chametla was over, Garcia didn't know it. So he pulled his comrade onto his shoulders in a straining carry—for Guerrero was at least a foot taller and many pounds heavier—and struggled to a copse of cottonwoods beside a muddy creek. He put his friend down gently on a bed of leaves and cottonwood fluff, and he tied Casan's rope leash to the trunk. Then he snuck down to the creek and filled his hat with water. He tried to wet his friend's lips, but the dying man was already too far gone to drink.

Wasn't this a fine turn of events.

They'd come out of the mining lands of Rosario, Sinaloa, full of revolution and fun. Men were raised to fight and enjoy fighting. None dared admit they were weary of it, weary of fear, and each had learned to dream, and dreamed at all hours—dreamed while sleeping, while awake and marching, while fighting. Only dreaming carried them through the unending battles.

They'd drunk their fill, slept with country girls in every village, ridden trains to battle. Both Guerrero and Garcia were excited by the trains—their first train rides! Then they were sickened by the rocking of the freight cars and choked by the smoke boiling back over the roof, where they fought for space and tried not to be forced off. They coughed black cinders at night.

Casan was just one of their treasures, one of the fruits of their exploits. They'd stolen guitars, rifles, horses. Guerrero had stolen underwear from haciendas, and Garcia himself had stolen a cigar from the pocket of a sleeping federal captain. They'd seen men hang and watched villages burn.

"Don't die now, you bastard," Garcia grunted as he peeked out through the bushes to see if their enemies had fled. "We have so much to do!"

But Guerrero only moaned and kicked his feet.

As night fell, Angel Garcia gathered wood. He was, frankly, surprised that his friend hadn't died yet. He peeled back the sullied bandages to let air and moonlight in. The ugly black cavern blown out of Guerrero's head leaked slow and watery blood. His face was pale. His skin was cold. And still he drew breath and occasionally stirred and mumbled.

Garcia lit a small fire and moved Guerrero nearer to the flames. He tore long strips from his friend's shirt and rewrapped his head. Why waste a swallow of tequila on him? There was a bottle in his bedroll. He lifted it in a silent toast and drank.

He tried to wet his friend's lips, but the dying man was already too far gone to drink.

He must have drifted off to sleep, for it was Casan's whimpering that awoke him. The big dog had worked himself free from the rope, and he stood over the prone body of Guerrero and whined.

"What is it, boy?" Garcia whispered.

Casan tilted his head and stared down at Guerrero. The dog yelped. Then he backed away.

Garcia crawled over to Guerrero and said, "Arnulfo? Are you awake?"

The wounded man didn't stir.

"What the hell is wrong with you?" Garcia chided the dog. "Nothing here."

Then he heard it, too. The faint whistling. He inclined his head. There was a plaintive hooting coming from under Guerrero's bandage. Were poor Guerrero's sinuses blowing air out of his skull? Christ. What next? Garcia pulled open the wrapping and was startled to see a small puff of smoke rising from out of his friend's head. He crossed himself.

"Ah, cabrón!" he said.

The whistle again, then another puff of smoke. Casan barked. Garcia sat beside the dog and stared. Then, was it? It couldn't be! But—a *light*—a small light was coming out of the ragged hole in Guerrero's head.

Garcia bent down, but then had to leap back because a small locomotive rushed out of Guerrero's wound. It fell out of the wound, pulling a coal car and several small cattle cars as if it were falling off a minuscule bridge in some rail disaster. The soft train fell upon the ground and glistened, puffing like a fish. Casan pounced on it and took it in his mouth, shaking it once and gulping it down.

"Bad dog!" said Garcia.

But by then, Guerrero's childhood home had squeezed out of his head. It was quite remarkable. The walls were soft and pink, and the furniture was veiny and tender. Casan ate the back porch. Garcia, starving after the battle, skewered the couch, the bed, and the oven on a wire and roasted them over the fire. They tasted like pork.

Guerrero grunted once and a pile of schoolbooks plopped out.

Soon, Garcia was appalled to see Guerrero's parents and boyhood friends. Their cries were puny and heartrending when Casan ate them. And naked women! Good God! He didn't know Guerrero had mounted so many naked women! He looked carefully—they came out in a parade of breasts and asses, small legs waving. He couldn't bear it. He couldn't bear his own lust and his own hunger, and he couldn't bear Casan's insatiable mouth, and he couldn't bear his own loneliness. If he had tried to make love to them, he would have torn them apart.

All these small beings mewled and quickly expired.

It was the worst night of his life. He found himself praying that Guerrero would die. But he didn't die. And Garcia decided, finally, irrevocably, that he had to leave his friend to his fate. The damage to his own soul would be too great if he sat there any longer watching children, priests, grandmothers, goats, wagons, and toys ooze out of Guerrero's bloody head and die on the ground. So he put the rope through Casan's collar, and he tucked Guerrero's pistol in his own belt, and he put Guerrero's boots on his own feet, and he made his friend as comfortable as possible.

Birds gathered. First, crows. Then magpies and robins. Finally, gulls came from the coast. They seemed to be praying to Guerrero, for they bowed to him repeatedly. They stayed there and fed on his dreams until they were too heavy to fly. 🛡

MIRACLE OF THE BLACK LEG

*—Appearing much later than written versions, pictorial
representations of the myth of the miraculous/transplant
performed by the physicians Cosmas and Damian exist in
several countries and date back to the mid-fourteenth century.*

I.

Always, the dark body hewn asunder; always
    one man is healed, his sick limb replaced,
placed in another man's grave: the white leg
    buried beside the corpse, or attached as if
it were always there. If not for the dark appendage,
    you might miss the story beneath this story—
what remains each time the myth changes: how,
    in one version, the doctors harvest the leg
from a man, four days dead, in his tomb at the church
    of a martyr, or—in another—desecrate a body
fresh in the graveyard   at St. Peter-in-Chains:
    there was buried just today an Ethiopian.
Even now, it stays with us: when we mean to uncover
    the truth, we dig, say: *unearth.*

2.

Emblematic in paint, signifier of the body's lacuna,
    the black leg is at once a grafted narrative,
a redacted line of text, and in this scene: a dark stocking
    pulled above the knee. Here the patient sleeping,
his head at rest in his hand. Beatific, he looks as if
    he'll wake from a dream. On the floor
beside the bed, a dead Moor—hands crossed at the groin,
    the swapped limb pocked and rotting, fused in place.
And in the corner, a question: poised as if to speak
    the syntax of sloughing, a snake's curved form.
It emerges from the mouth of a boy like a tongue—slippery
    and rooted in the body as knowledge. For centuries,
this is how the myth repeats: the miracle—in words
    or wood or paint—is a record of thought.

3.

See how the story changes: in one painting
    the Ethiop is merely a body, featureless in a coffin,
so black he has no face. In another, the patient—
    at the top of the frame—seems to writhe in pain,
the black leg grafted to his thigh. Below him
    a mirror of suffering: the blackamoor—
his body a fragment—arched across the doctor's lap
    as if dying from his wound. If not immanence,

the soul's bright anchor, blood passed from one
    to the other, what knowledge haunts each body—
what history, what phantom ache? One man always
    low, in a grave or on the ground, the other
up high, closer to heaven; one man always diseased,
    the other a body in service, plundered?

4.
Both men are alive in Villoldo's carving.
    In twinned relief, they hold the same posture,
the same pained face, each man reaching to touch
    his right leg. The black man, on the floor,
holds his stump. Above him, the doctor restrains
    the patient's arm as if to prevent him touching
the dark amendment of flesh. How not to see it—
    the men bound one to the other—symbiotic,
one man rendered expendable, the other worthy
    of this sacrifice? In version after version, even
when the Ethiopian isn't there, the leg is a stand in,
    a black modifier against the white body, or
a piece cut off—as in: origin of the word *comma*—
    caesura in a story that's still being written.

THE DARK SIDE

OF DINNER DISHES, LAUNDRY, AND CHILD CARE

Sarah Weinman

Harrowing house tours. Chilling truths.

The history of crime and detective fiction follows two well-delineated schools of thought: the hard-boiled line of Dashiell Hammett and Raymond Chandler and the "cozy" class of Agatha Christie. Pan further back into the genre's many phyla and up springs another genus devoted to espionage fiction (thanks to Eric Ambler and, to a lesser extent, Graham Greene) and still another for noir, where order is transformed into chaos through doomed characters.

But lately I've become more fascinated with a genre that doesn't fit neatly into any of these categories. Instead of the detective novel's classic reliance on nobility themes, those of knights-errant with unshakable moral codes navigating a depraved, irredeemable world around them, or the espionage or international thriller's sky-high stakes where nothing less than global fate will do, the type of suspense that resonates with me more is of a variety much subtler—and in many ways, more dangerous. Rather than the obvious violence of thrillers drenched with the blood of serial killers—a trope that still sells, but whose overuse has become tiresome for me—these novels inspire fear from everyday activities that, with a few tweaks, catalyze extraordinary outcomes.

49

While highly regarded and even thought of as classics individually, these books somehow don't carry the same collective historical weight as the hard-boiled and cozy varieties, despite being written in the same rough time frame, between World War II and the height of the Cold War. They operate on the ground level, peer into marriages whose hairline fractures will crack wide open, turn ordinary household chores into potential for terror, and transform fears about motherhood into horrifying reality. They deal with class and race, sexism and economic disparity, but they have little need to show off that breadth. They aren't off-kilter, like Shirley Jackson's marvelously twisted domestic horror stories, or full-on sociopathic studies, like Patricia Highsmith's books, though Ripley et al. owe a great deal to these earlier works.

Instead, they turn our most deep-seated worries into narrative gold, delving into the dark side of human behavior that threatens to come out with the dinner dishes, the laundry, or taking care of a child. They are about ordinary, everyday life, and that's what makes these so-called domestic suspense novels so frightening. The nerves they hit are really fault lines.

———— •◆• ————

Marie Belloc Lowndes wrote novels at a near-annual pace between 1907 and 1946, which puts her in the same league as most contemporary mystery novelists. A consistent multidecade output guarantees some novels will outshine the rest, even if the reasons for standing out aren't wholly to do with superior quality. In the case of Lowndes, readers return again and again to *The Lodger*, first published in 1914, not just because it's good—indeed, it is, and surprisingly fresh for a nearly century-old novel—but because the premise is so simple and yet so irresistible: a struggling married couple, desperate for money, take in a boarder whom they suspect is a serial killer. That premise has proved a boon to many a filmmaker, starting with Alfred Hitchcock and his debut feature-length silent film in 1926.

The term "serial killer" wasn't coined for at least another half century, but other words—*fanatic, lunatic, multiple murderer,* and, especially, *ripper*—were worthy substitutes on the scare front at the time. Even twenty-five years later, England, and London in particular, remained shaken up by Jack the Ripper's murderous swath through Whitechapel. The crimes of Lowndes's fictionalized Ripper, recast to reflect a latter-day England still hungover from decades of Victorian rule, manage to shock her characters but stay resolutely in the background. Instead, *The Lodger* plays so well because it examines the desperation people feel when they are without money, have subsisted so long without it, and yet must cut back further, discovering just how much they can bear without resorting to despair.

Robert Bunting and his wife, Ellen, are good people: a little on the dull side; suspicious of anything that piques undue curiosity; happy to help anyone, thanks to long years of training as servants for richer classes. But as *The Lodger* opens, this middle-aged couple are at a crossroads—"already they had learnt to go hungry, and they were beginning to learn to go cold"—teetering dangerously toward a worse fate:

They were now very near the soundless depths which divide those who dwell on the safe tableland of security—those, that is, who are sure of making a respectable, if not a happy, living—and the submerged multitude who, through some lack in themselves, or owing to the conditions under which our strange civilisation has become organised, struggled rudderless till they die in workhouse, hospital, or prison.

Had the Buntings been in a class lower than their own, had they belonged to the great company of human beings technically known to so many of us as the poor, there would have been friendly neighbours ready to help them, and the same would have been the case had they belonged to the class of smug, well-meaning, if unimaginative, folk whom they had spent so much of their lives in serving.

This two-paragraph description could have come, with a contemporary rewrite, from today's newspaper and magazine stories and blog posts. The economy is supposed to be in recovery, but the pace is sluggish, and many people in the so-called middle class have underwater mortgages and spiraling credit card and student-loan debts and, despite appearances and technological gizmos, are perilously close to ruin. And they aren't necessarily telling the truth about how much trouble they are in financially.

As a result, the Buntingses' early fate resonates, and their decision to advertise for a lodger makes perfect sense. They clearly need the money to keep the lights on in their rooms, to avoid hawking family heirlooms that would fetch next to nothing, and to keep from admitting that they could use some help, even for a short period of time. So when a "long, lanky figure of a man, clad in an Inverness cape and an old-fashioned top hat" appears, knocks twice at the door, and says, in "a dreamy, absent way," that he's looking for "quiet rooms," there is no answer for Mrs. Bunting to give but yes. With a month's advance paid up front, it's easy to shrug off the lodger's demands that he never be disturbed and that Mr. Bunting never visit his rooms (and Mrs. Bunting keep her visits to a strict minimum, never to touch anything). The money helps the Buntings overlook his habit of reading "aloud to himself passages in the Bible that [are] very uncomplimentary to

They turn our most deep-seated worries into narrative gold, delving into the dark side of human behavior.

[the female] sex," and his aversion to eating meat, and his habit of disappearing in the evenings and returning very late and agitated, even spent, from some mysterious activities.

The pace, which Lowndes keeps deliberately slow, allows the reader to stay well ahead of the Buntings on the deductive reasoning front. But not too far ahead, lest the juxtaposition of the arrival of the lodger—who calls himself Mr. Sleuth, the author's tongue perhaps too firmly in cheek—and the mounting body count attributed to the Ripper-like "Avenger" come off like an anvil dropped on the head. Instead, Lowndes allows both husband and wife to entertain the seemingly ridiculous notion that Mr. Sleuth is up to no good, and to brush off those suspicions in haste. Consider Mrs. Bunting as she cleans her lodger's room and accidentally moves a key piece of furniture:

> A moment later, with sharp dismay, Mr. Sleuth's landlady realised that the fact that she had moved the chiffonier must become known to her lodger, for a thin trickle of some dark-coloured liquid was oozing out through the bottom of the little cupboard door.
>
> She stooped down and touched the stuff. It showed red, bright red, on her finger.

Mrs. Bunting grew chalky white, then recovered herself quickly. In fact the colour rushed into her face, and she grew hot all over.

It was only a bottle of red ink she had upset—that was all! How could she have thought it was anything else?

Their inner lives are filled with emotions whose powder-keg potency needs only the smallest inciting force to create mayhem.

Nor can Mr. Bunting shake the feeling there's something off about Mr. Sleuth, so much so that he checks the morning paper for violent news that isn't there (suppressed by the police until later on in the day, as it turns out) and has trouble sleeping at night from unexpressed worrying. But husband and wife keep mum, on parallel tracks: "So accustomed had [Mrs. Bunting] become to bearing alone the burden of her awful secret, that it would have required far more than a cross word or two, far more than the fact that Bunting looked ill and tired, for her to have come to suspect that her secret was now shared by another, and that other her husband." Even the friendship of Joe Chandler, lead investigator into the murders and an ardent suitor of the Buntingses' niece Daisy, proves a red herring: he can't see what's plainly in front of him, and the Buntings are too timid, too unsure, to tell Chandler or anyone in the police about Mr. Sleuth.

Matters move toward a dramatic conclusion, and the Buntings are more or less saved from penury. But *The Lodger* poses questions of everyday human behavior that remain potent, valid, and disquieting: what, really, would we do in the same situation? Trust instinct, even at tremendous risk, or turn a blind eye because financial stability is more important? Lowndes provides her own answers to these questions, but as society opened up and cast off the repressive societal shackles of the Victorian era, those answers may not necessarily apply in today's times.

———— ·◆· ————

"What would you do?" is the question at the very heart of these domestic suspense novels. The main characters, predominantly women, written by women for women, engage in everyday activity as wives, mothers, homemakers, and friends, their inner lives filled with emotions whose powder-keg potency needs only the smallest inciting force to create mayhem. It doesn't take much imagination to picture oneself in the same situation, if only for the smallest change of fate.

Elisabeth Sanxay Holding (1889–1955) made a specialty of such minor turns when, as the Great Depression hit, the New York–born-and-bred writer switched from poor-earning literary novels to more lucrative detective fiction. Holding's love of travel and her marriage to a diplomat provided some of her books' far-flung settings, like Bermuda, but what distinguishes her as a true suspense queen, and an unjustly neglected one, is her ability to

zero in on what makes a relationship, especially a marriage, fall apart on the inside even as it looks fine to outsiders—the equivalent of a termite-infested building that stays up until one false step destroys the entire edifice.

Holding's first suspense novel, *Miasma* (1929), has many of the off-center qualities that inform her later work, distilled through the idea of "a fog, a miasma of distrust and fear . . . no face seemed familiar and honest; there was no friendly light anywhere." (Interestingly, its plot, with a young doctor invited to stay at a creepy old house, is reminiscent of Sarah Waters's *The Little Stranger*). Her next book, *Dark Power* (1930), mines the "innocent young woman lives with creepy relatives" motif with superior results.

But, to my mind, *The Death Wish* (1934) established her as a major figure and refined her rather loopy sensibility, especially about the relationships between men and women. Shawe Delancey is trapped in a bad marriage, but he is so blind that he's deluded himself into thinking all is well: "He liked to laugh, to be easy and careless and good-humoured, and [his wife,] Josephine, most effectively prevented that. She made his home life a continual uneasiness, with her affectations, her moods, her sudden changes from clinging affection to hostility. Yet he felt no bitterness towards her, no resentment." Even a close friend tells Delancey that he manages "pretty well not to see what you don't want to see." But that friend, Mr. Whitestone, has good reason to impart this information: he's in a bad marriage of his own, in love with a much younger woman, and ready to kill his now-expendable wife. Of course that wife turns up dead.

The setup is reminiscent of Patricia Highsmith's much darker debut novel, *Strangers on a Train*, released sixteen years later, as if Highsmith had read *The Death Wish* and taken the narrative to a greater extreme. In *The Death Wish*, Holding skirts the line between drama and comedy, and the death of Whitestone's wife acts as the necessary rug-puller for Delancey to see what we've long known, planting not-so-conscious ideas in his head about what to do with his own wife, who seems to grow more shrill and vituperative by the day. "What good is she to anyone?" Delancey thinks. "She's not even happy. She makes even herself miserable. If she goes on living, look what happens. I won't be able to do a thing for Robert. Poor Elsie'll be dragged into Lord knows what, a divorce case, perhaps. And the beast Josephine would tell everyone that Elsie was the cause of her leaving me. I've got to do it." But in Holding's universe, resolve does not translate directly into outcome: would-be murderers like Delancey get distracted from their tasks, and real culprits are held up as shining heroes, even legends, for the same reasons of willful blindness that prove such distractions for her protagonists.

Holding's best-regarded book is her 1947 novel, *The Blank Wall*. Its heroine, Lucia, does everything in her power to protect her family from what she views as a terrible fate, even though, tragically, she isn't privy to all the facts. So the reader knows that Lucia's daughter, Bee, does not bear any responsibility for the death of her too old, too unsavory lover, Ted Darby. Darby's death was accidental, the result of a vociferous argument between him and the teenage Bee, but Lucia doesn't know this, and she acts to cover up the supposed crime. Her behavior then becomes a red flag for the police, who investigate what's purported to be a murder. In Lucia's case, acting on instinct is her downfall, but the cruel irony is that any decision she chooses—including the passive choice of doing nothing at all—will rip apart her family and destroy her children's lives. Is it better to be in control and cause terrible things, or to let terrible things happen at others' behest? Such is the dilemma Holding explores brilliantly, and which appeals to modern readers as a result.

Instinct also proves to be the bane of the existence of Mrs. Herriot, the matron who finds herself in quite the web of deception in Holding's wonderfully titled *The Old Battle-Ax* (1943). Mrs. Herriot's long-estranged sister, Madge, has come to visit, and inconveniently dies. For reasons that still confuse her, Mrs. Herriot tells police she has no idea who the woman is. More vexing is that her chauffeur, Silas, and her niece, Carla (who is Madge's daughter), play along with the lie—Carla even goes so far as to pretend to be Madge. But Holding doesn't embellish these arguably outlandish twists, instead presenting them with such sober and terse writing that we're left feeling rather dizzy the whole way. It is a risky way to present a suspenseful narrative, assuming the reader will stay on as twists unfold on their own time, but the payoff is well worth it, not only for the surprises unleashed upon the reader but also for Mrs. Herriot's realization that she never understood the motivations of those closest to her, and that it wasn't a matter of trusting the wrong people, but of trusting anyone at all. Holding takes big risks, but the rewards are even bigger.

———— ·•· ————

Like Holding and Lowndes, Celia Fremlin is far less renowned than she ought to be. Fremlin, who died in 2009 at the age of ninety-four, wrote sixteen novels and three short-story collections in about four decades, but she is destined to be remembered for a single work or two. Still, if one has to be remembered for one's first novel, as Fremlin more or less is, *The Hours Before Dawn* (1958) is the novel to be remembered for, because any woman who has ever given birth to a child—or even thought about having a baby—will feel a horrible chill run up her spine at the book's opening line: "I'd give anything—*anything*—for a night's sleep."

The condition is not named, but Louise, the woman who dreads the thought of voicing the idea that motherhood is not pure joy aloud in a society that insists it is, suffers from anxiety at best and postpartum depression at worst. She loves her baby, but why, oh why, can't he sleep through the night? And why can't her husband understand that all she wants, desperately, is some time to catch up on her sleep? And how can she carry on taking care of her two older children when the new baby sucks up all her time and energy? But no, she must live up to the impossibly high standards of motherhood, slap a cheerful smile on her face at those who would judge her for failing to meet expectations, and try to keep her sanity, though it threatens, increasingly, to disappear.

As she unravels, Louise lets herself entertain ever more upsetting notions: "[She] was conscious of an aching, helpless weariness; and as she glanced at her husband's face, the tired lines more deeply drawn in the lamplight, she felt a tiny stab of fear. For the first time, she wondered: Does it sometimes happen like this? Do men sometimes stand up in the divorce court, tired and bewildered, and say simply 'Yes, I still love my wife; yes, I still love my children; no, there isn't another woman; it's just that I can't go on any longer without sleep.' Do they? And why does it never get into the papers . . ."

Louise's hysterical, hallucinatory state creates the genius of this book. It makes her a perfect foil, susceptible to the increasingly sinister events that befall her. Her baby, in the carriage, disappears, only to turn up a few hours later inside the house.

> These novels lay bare what we fear most, and they do so without mythology or metaphor.

Or she hears strange, creaking noises at odd hours. Or she perceives threats, whether through not-so-innocuous letters or telephone calls from unnamed voices. These oddities can't have anything to do with the arrival of her new lodger, Vera Brandon, can they? And surely she must be imagining these strange events, because sinister doings just don't happen in her neighborhood, let alone her house.

That the reader is left guessing as to whether Louise's fears are real or whether she's making it all up is a testament to Fremlin's understanding of the female mind, and especially what that mind hopes will never happen. Other Fremlin novels, like *Seven Lean Years* and *Appointment with Yesterday*, also expertly mine psychological territory, but none quite match the tour-de-force quality of her first, and best, examination of suspense in a domestic setting.

These authors, a handful among many, ought to be more highly regarded. Such psychological suspense greats as Highsmith, Ruth Rendell, Minette Walters, and, more recently, Val McDermid and Tana French, owe a significant debt to the likes of Lowndes, Holding, and Fremlin, even if such debts aren't conscious. These women peered into the never-discussed abyss of family and home life and lifted rocks that revealed a pit of crawling worms. They didn't have to rely on outside monstrous forces like serial killers or cataclysmic events to create dread, for the inner psyche—and slight perforations in the form of doubt, guilt, and shame—provide all the inciting force these authors needed. These novels lay bare what we fear most, and they do so without mythology or metaphor, without overdramatization or oversimplification. Readers end up more frightened of the dangers in their own homes than what's outside them. 🜏

YELLOWJACKETS

The first sting is fragrant with war. Our skin
incites a thousand alarms, furious to find us.
We retreat, scatter tools and wild ginger,
clutch our punctured arms. Accidental

incursion was mine: a rake across the vespiary
mouth, the breach unleafed. Below, a hollow
where droves of rabbits slept is swollen
with spreading cells. The killing frost is not far,

he says, proposing to wait. We take sides.
I tell him: the queen will survive, overwinter,
wake in spring, build a new home, birth
a new colony. I tell him: farther south,

a nest fills a Chevy stalled out in a barn.
The experts decide there are many queens,
with armies of workers keeping domains
apart. But he still wants us to wait.

Once, a strongman found hiving bees
inside a carcass, enough to fill his hands
with honey for wedding gifts, but this ground
is not a lion's body, there is no sweetness here.

Fractures spread from small intrusions, enemies
are papered in sibilant secrets. To become
foundress, the queen must be unseated.
My new reign begins with massacre. At dusk,

for three nights, I empty cans of poison
into the rift. A chrysanthemum of paralysis
sealed with stones. Home requires vigilance,
as someone macerates, waiting to overthrow.

FEAR

There are five instances in which the weak cast fear over the strong.

—TALMUD

I. Invisible Thing & Lion

The traps are set, cannons aimed, patient
for you, the chosen target. It wants a trophy

of your glorious head. You have made doctrine
of this war, your belief explains the long winter,

the blight, and names you, its only martyr.
Nothing is there, but you will never believe that.

II. Mosquito & Elephant

Your delicate wires sizzled, dismantled,
it cannot take you whole and lets go.

Left for salvage, you are put back
with solder and epoxy, still alive

but numb in places, your knees twitch,
a buzz remains; you will always taste of lead.

III. Spider & Scorpion

It takes many forms—loosened brick,
a rampant virus, the smashed atom—

and arrives without music. You will try
to seal yourself off with Kevlar, duct tape

and prayer, but your body is so much
soft flesh, between each rib, an open door.

IV. Swallow & Eagle

For altitude, you forsake the low trees,
the easy prey and branches flush with fruit.

The thin air barely sustains you. Sink down
and you could glide as effortless as those

beneath you. From the ground, everyone
is smudged and range cannot be measured.

V. Minnow & Leviathan

Your skyscrapers rival mountains, steel peaks
spread and rise upward, the monoliths of cities

calcify. With all your brilliance and strength,
you advance toward the end, lumbering.

You will lose the kingdom, and your successor,
your miniature, will survive you in supple swarms.

YOU HAVE NOTHING TO FEAR
BUT FEAR HIMSELF

Benjamin Percy

A Conversation with Peter Straub

Peter Straub—novelist, essayist, poet, short-story writer, editor, critic, soap-opera star, music connoisseur, eater of bone marrow—is a national treasure. If you have not read him (and you must), you have not experienced the terrible pleasure that comes from encountering an author who explores the dark caverns of the mind with lamps lit by blood.

Though I have known Peter most of my life through his books, we didn't meet until 2007, when he approached me after a reading, grabbed me by the shoulders, drew me close, and said, "You have another Ben inside you. He has a buzz cut. He wears white T-shirts, black jeans, combat boots. He keeps a bowie knife duct-taped to his chest because he likes the feel of metal against his skin. Don't ever let him die." Which is probably the coolest thing

anybody has ever said to me. We've been friends since.

He has won the Bram Stoker and World Fantasy awards. He has penned shelves' worth of best sellers, including *Ghost Story*; *Lost Boy, Lost Girl*; and *A Dark Matter*. He is more than one of our country's great writers—he is a fascinating, brilliant man, as you will gather from the shadow-soaked conversation that follows.

BENJAMIN PERCY: Scare me.

PETER STRAUB: So you think it's that easy, do you? *Scare me*, right, like I'm going to put on a pig mask and jump out of the bushes when you walk down the street at night. Of course, that might be pretty scary, but not, I think, for any of the obvious reasons.

What would be frightening about me jumping out of the bush wearing a pig mask is not the sudden surprise, but that the ordinary world had split open.

BP: Do your worst.

PS: Okay, let's try this:

Suppose you find yourself, without any preamble or explanation, in a horse-drawn carriage with three other passengers. *Oh, you wonder, how did I get here?* But you suppose, not unreasonably, that, very likely, you are dreaming. If not, everything is still all right, as you feel no sense of alarm, merely a mild curiosity as to your destination. Seated beside you is a tall, strikingly good-looking older man with longish white hair, a gleaming white shirt, a dark suit, a floppy black bow tie. There may be buckles on his black shoes or boots. The two women on the opposite bench may well be mother and daughter: separated in age by perhaps twenty-five to thirty years, both bearing artificial-looking "beauty marks" on the left side of their upper lips, and dressed alike in strangely dated, if not period, costumes with frills at their necks, long sleeves, dresses that come down past the tops of their buttoned boots. They, too, are quite attractive, good cheekbones, good eyes, and abundant dark hair, the details of which are lost in the general gloom of the carriage. Both women have high foreheads, the mother's lightly scored with creases.

Oh, you think, this is a family, how nice.

You glance sideways at the husband and father. He smiles at you, as if he knows what you are thinking. The younger woman says, "Is it now? Is it now? Is it now?" Her voice sounds oddly mechanical.

Her mother shakes her head and smiles at you, as if asking for your tolerance.

"I want it to be now," the daughter says, and her mother shushes her.

"Oh," the daughter says, sounding sulky, and looks you straight in the eye—*wham*—straightforward, undisguised sexual interest, a look that says *I want you.*

Then she looks away, and the moment is gone, but you are left with an overwhelming sense of the younger woman's body beneath her strange period clothing. To distract yourself, you look out of your window, and can see only a leaden gray. Then you realize that for the past five or ten minutes, you have heard nothing, not birdsong, not the creaking of the traces, not even the sound of the horses' hooves. You cannot even be sure the carriage is moving forward.

I get it, you tell yourself, *I'm in a movie, only I don't know my lines, and I'm going to screw everything up.* You turn to the man beside you, intending to tell him that you need more time, and find that he is smiling at you again, but differently, more genuinely.

"I need it to be now," the daughter says, and you see her father's hand flap up and down about an inch and a half.

You look back at the daughter, and something strange seems to be happening up in her hairline, a slow, funny widening-out like that of a splitting seam. Whatever this is, you absolutely know, it's going to take a long time.

Or this:

You are six years old and alone in the living room of your boyhood house. You are not supposed to be left alone for long, but here you are, not quite sure of what is happening. From somewhere distant in the house comes what could be either a low, quiet human moan or the sound of some electrical appliance. This sound, whatever it is, rather alarms you . . . it does not quite sound human; in fact, it sounds completely and in some sense terribly inhuman.

On a little table at one end of your living room sofa stands a little wooden table on which sit a lamp, an ashtray, and a telephone. When the inhuman sound cuts out, you know it came from nowhere distant but instead from one of these three objects on the little table. Much worse than that, it stopped because you had abruptly become aware of it. When you focus on the lamp, the ashtray gives a spectral shiver like that of something waking up. All of a sudden, really afraid, you look at the telephone, which appears to look back at you, full of some intention you have no way of decoding.

What would be frightening about me jumping out of the bush wearing a pig mask is not the sudden surprise, not me, and not the pig mask, but that the ordinary world had split open for a moment to reveal some possibility never previously considered.

BP: I'm officially creeped. Thank you.

And isn't that a curious thing? My hunger and gratefulness for a scare? I remember very clearly the moment in elementary school when I withdrew from a library shelf the Universal book of monsters and cracked it open and found the Wolfman staring back at me, with his hoggish nose and shag-carpet fur and underbite of a snarl. I spent most of that night awake and calling for my parents. But the next day I visited the library and again pulled the book from the shelf.

When I was a kid, I spent a lot of time cowering in bed, the sheets wrapped around me like armor, a little breathing hole available for my mouth. I remember staying up most of one night, certain a shadow in the corner of my room might come alive at any moment and come rushing toward me.

I know I'm not alone, when I go to a horror movie and hear the screams and laughter all around me, when I walk the streets of Salem on Halloween with thousands of people dressed as vampires and ghouls, and even when my son says to me, "Pretend to be a monster," and I savage my expression and make my hands into claws and he runs from me, squealing.

Why do I—why do people—dare the nightmare?

PS: I have been asked this question over and over for maybe thirty years, and by now it lacks a certain, shall we say, freshness. The most conventional answer is that the Wolfman and Dracula, et al., serve to render into once-removed, almost trivialized form the constant and difficult horrors of everyday life, from getting beaten by bullies in grade school to having someone very close to you be diagnosed with a stage-four cancer. You could say that these formalized representations of real-world terror contain a certain built-in social relevance, too: they are conversions into fictive form of racial or sexual anxieties; they express concerns like poverty and war and systemic failure, often changing focus decade by decade.

BP: You often see horror stories playing off cultural unease. From the Industrial Revolution comes *Frankenstein*. From the Red Scare comes *Invasion of the Body Snatchers*. From Guantanamo Bay and Abu Ghraib come torture porn films like *Hostel* and *Saw*.

PS: Exactly. I would say, however, that human beings almost always require an education in loss, grief, fear, and pain, because at some point in their lives, almost everyone is going to experience each of these conditions. Without these conditions and experiences, one hardly has a life at all. We construct our souls very gradually, being deepened by loss and death and heartbreak. In general, everything is broken, and nothing's going to be all right—whoops, I just quoted Mose Allison. In a world where everything is (or is soon going to be) broken, and nothing (or almost nothing) is really going to be all

right, we human beings need practice in dealing with the conditions actually at hand, which, of course, differ vastly from the version of the near-at-hand offered up by most popular movies and novels.

Haven't you, from time to time, seen a parent pushing an empty stroller alongside a two- or three-year old child pushing a toy stroller, also empty? This always strikes me as funny. By insisting on doing what the big people do, the child turns the parent's helpfulness into an empty gesture. There they go down the street, parent and child, playing charades. Yet the child must learn to cope with the world by observant modeling, and the weary, unhappy parent consents to enact the charade. Late that night, perhaps, the parent will tip over the edge, lose control, and shake the screaming child into concussion. That big stroller's going to be empty, all right, in the territory just created by the use of the word *perhaps*.

BP: Let's talk about your own empty stroller. Childhood provides a lifetime of stories, gives rise to our sensibilities as writers. Tell us about the accident you were in as a child and how you think it contributed to your hard wiring.

PS: Oh, dear. It's true, my childhood was, in a way, wildly colorful, though in another, more superficial way, it was utterly conventional. The accident you're talking about was a catastrophic event shoveled under the carpet as soon as possible; in other words, when I had relearned how to walk and was able to rejoin my second-grade class at

I could almost say, as a small child I was raped and murdered, because that statement is true, except that the two acts were not directly consecutive.

Webster State Elementary School. I had been half-killed, grievously broken in many crucial places, undergone a terrifying and ecstatic near-death experience; then endured what seemed an epoch of hospitals and operations and unrelenting, accumulating, increasing pain; gone through body casts, then a foot-to-hip leg cast, wheelchairs, crutches, absence of balance . . . and the advice offered me by the adult world was *It's all over, just forget about it.*

These adults somehow failed to understand that the boy bearing my name was a different, infinitely more angry, disturbed, and troubled person than the boy known by that name in the past. Trouble was, they wanted that boy back, the seven-year-old continuation of the six-year-old, and they couldn't get what they wanted. That six-year-old was dead; he had been run over by an old car, and he would never again be seen. Which is to say that the seven-year-old was no longer a child, his childhood lay in the same grave as his six-year-old self, and other children from that point on seemed like creatures of another species: baffling, boring, incredibly attractive, utterly without thought.

Yet that was not all. Two years before, in another neighborhood, the five-year-old boy with my name was undergoing completely typical, textbook-case sexual abuse at the hands of a neighbor, the father of two little girls. Having heard from my father that I liked to take off by myself—a five-year-old boy!—and go to the movies at the little theater around the corner and two streets down, this fellow offered to solve the problem and ensure my safety by accompanying me to the theater. Into the theater he took me, and to the last few rows, the rows where no one else ever sat, he led me, and when the lights went down and the music started up he put his hands on me and got me to do exactly what he wanted. How long this wretched business went on, I have no idea, but after a while, maybe a month or two, I refused to go to the movies anymore, and that was that. Then, I forced myself to forget everything that had happened in the last rows of the theater. I don't now know exactly how it worked, but by an act of black, psychic, self-destructive magic I pushed every bit of that sordid, terrifying, deeply humiliating material into a little box, where it seethed, and pushed the box far down into unseen darkness.

Go on, Pete, my parents would have counseled, *forget about it,* so that was what I did.

> For a long time I had to hide that material, and I hid it from myself very successfully, but like everything that you do that with, it bubbles up another way.

By means of a magical act I could never replicate now.

I could almost say, as a small child I was raped and murdered, because that statement is true, except that the two acts were not directly consecutive.

Whatever entered my mind had first to pass through these two smoky, evil-smelling conditions before it could be considered and classified.

BP: Jesus Christ.

PS: You should know that I've never said any of this stuff—about the child abuse—really anywhere. I put it in the fiction, and, the truth is, I still cannot directly remember, but I know damn well that's what happened—I can remember making myself forget, is what I can remember. And I can remember it feeling like black magic, and that if I did it, I'd never be the same again. I remember knowing that at the age of five or six or whatever it was. That I would do permanent damage to myself if I forgot it, but I couldn't bear it so I had to forget it.

BP: This is terrifying to hear, and you should know that if right up to the last min-

ute you want to carve out this portion of our conversation, you need only let me know.

PS: Thank you for saying that. The reason I probably won't is that the impulse has come over me, which has come over me from time to time. In the *Locus* interview I did I spoke of the matter very elusively and less directly than I have to you, but the impulse is really driven not to hide, to let people—I guess, I mean, my readers—let them see who I really am, the kind of history I really have, and that this kind of stuff formed me. It isn't exactly confessional, but it has to do with sharing and with a desire for knowledge, and so I don't have the feeling I'm hiding anything.

Because for a long time I had to hide that material—really, really, really hide it, and I hid it from myself very successfully, but like everything that you do that with, it bubbles up another way.

BP: As it bubbles up now, it feels so relevant because it's foundational: it's shaped so much of your work.

PS: Yeah, that's right. I wrote this story "The Juniper Tree" one summer because

I'd an irresistible impulse. I couldn't not do it. The idea came to me when I was reading Marguerite Duras's little novel *The Lover*, which is about a love affair between a teenage French girl and an older Chinese businessman in Vietnam, and the girl essentially has the power, and I thought, *Oh, I could do something really dark and smelly with this stuff*, and I came home—I was living alone in my house 'cause my wife and kids were living in Westport while carpenters were working on the house here—and I worked all day on that, and I revised it over and over; I was writing it by hand, and when I was done with it, I looked at it and I closed the bound journal I'd written in, and I just put it on a shelf and I didn't look at it for at least a year. It just seemed too much, you know, like a loaded gun. And then later, I was asked to write a story for an anthology—and I thought, *That's a place to put the story; it's the wrong place, but we'll see what happens. It's not a horror story per se at all, but it sure is horrible.* So, I typed it up, I revised it, I revised it again, revised it and revised it, and I sent it off, and there it was. And years later, I was riding down Columbus Avenue in a taxicab with Gary Wolfe, and Gary turned to me and said, "Peter, did that thing in the movie theater actually happen?" and I said, "No." The fact is it was too awful to bring up to the light at that moment.

And I feel as though it's not going to damage me if people know this about me now. You know, it happened a long time ago—and I've certainly recovered from it. And I have made the most of it, besides that. You know, it was the engine for a lot of work that to me seems very, very powerful.

BP: All of this makes me think about what you said earlier—about the ordinary world splitting open . . .

PS: Yeah.

BP: This strikes me as your aesthetic. You put a crack in the mirror, and we're terrified and thrilled by the broken image, the ordinary made extraordinary.

PS: When I speak of a crack in the world, I mean a fissure from which unease can leak, because all of a sudden, things aren't operating the way they're supposed to operate, and when you see that in your own world, you can't count on anything anymore, nothing works. It'd be exactly the same as if you were standing in the middle of your street, and you saw the houses begin to flare up and down and the buildings fall down. And you'd say, "Uh-oh, that—what is that? It's an earthquake! Oh my God! [laughs] The world isn't behaving the way it's supposed to!" And you'd feel panic, dread, tension, fear.

Other times, when I speak of the world splitting open, I'm talking about an experience of very great joy, a kind of bliss that comes from a sense of being able, for a moment, to perceive the actual condition of the world, the actual nature of reality, which is seen in those moments as astonishingly blessed and radiant with intelligence and consciousness, so all of a sudden everything really is alive, it all thinks, it's unimaginably gorgeous, and it's so beautiful that it's also very, very painful. That's why I can never stay in that state. It doesn't come to me very often. It used to come to me more when I was a kid, and all during my young manhood it'd visit me every five years, then every ten, but it hasn't for a long time now. However, I remember it very, very precisely, and it's . . . one is always grateful and one never thinks, *Oh, this is a delusion.* Instead, you think the rest of life is a delusion and this is reality.

BP: Sounds like the same heightened kind of knowing that can come when all guns are blazing at the keyboard, when you're in a kind of trance, swept away by another world. I'm thinking about this division between the imaginative world and reality—and I'm thinking about the divisions, too, between the many Peter

PS: S.

PS: [laughs]

BP: You're a man with several doppelgängers. What draws you to the double?

PS: I always liked the idea, and I think it's rooted in what we were talking about before, the sense—whether or not I understood it consciously—that I always had something to hide . . . I packed my pockets with secrets, and the point of having a secret is that you look as though you don't, you know? [laughs]

It's rooted in that sense of knowing something's out of whack, being unable to identify it, and not wanting it to exist, so you pretend. I pretended rigorously with everything I had as though nothing was wrong, as though everything was fine. The fact that I talked to myself, the fact that I had crazy mood swings, that I occasionally did antisocial things, that I stuttered. I was one step away from lighting fires, you know. The fact that I gave signs of early disturbance. I didn't want to interfere with the actual picture of me because I didn't want to see myself as that at all. I wanted to be like all the other kids on the block. I didn't do a great job of impersonating, and it wasn't impersonation, but I did have friends all through my childhood. Sometimes I wondered just how good these friends were, since you could never talk to them, you know. [laughs] Children never really want to talk about anything, so I talked to their parents when I was child. I had a very good time talking to my friends' parents, and they were surprised, but they didn't mind, you know. It was like having a little old man in the room, I suppose.

Anyhow, that speaks of a kind of a split in the self that's both conscious and not.

BP: Sure. And later, this split carried over into your work.

PS: For my reading, Nabokov was like swallowing a kind of poison pill, because I loved it so much, especially *Pale Fire*. There's this man who gets everything wrong and lies about everything in his life—this, for some reason, led me to invent Putney Tyson Ridge, a critic that I used to make fun of the people who made fun of me. It

I had crazy mood swings, I occasionally did antisocial things, I stuttered. I was one step away from lighting fires.

was tremendous fun. I could write in that guy's voice; I had made up a whole bunch of stuff about popular culture that made me very happy, and I began to use him as a reviewer's name, just to amuse myself.

And Timothy Underhill appeared, of course, because of *Koko*. He was so admirable, and I hadn't planned for this to happen, but during the writing of *Koko*, Timothy Underhill enacted some of the progress I was making myself as a writer, some of the effort and results I was getting, in the same way I was getting them. The more he wrote, the better he got, and the better he felt, the more territory he could encompass. So then, that automatically made him a kind of doppelgänger of mine, and eventually, I felt that he had more to do and he had more to say to me, so there he is all over *The Throat*, where he's very useful, and he does things I could never dream of doing.

Occasionally, I had him do specific deeds that a man of my own age had done. This guy Tom Nolan had done three tours of Vietnam and he'd been injured very gravely, again and again, and when he came back from Vietnam, he was a little hard to deal with. He was a difficult character but a tremendously honest man who knew how to be as violent as a typhoon but never wanted to do so. I got two specific things from Tom Nolan. He

once said to me, "I still have trouble walking across a field." Oh my God. Whoa. And the other thing he told me was, some kid on Ninth Avenue came toward him and held out a knife and said, "You old fuck, give me all your money," and Tom remembered what they used to do in training, and he grabbed the kid's wrist with his right arm and grabbed his upper arm with his left arm, and broke the kid's arm over his leg.

BP: You have these doppelgängers who give you entry to other worlds, other lives, and then you have these metafictional devices that call attention to the story being told, that play around with the idea of stories within stories, stories borrowing from other stories. You're drawing from fairy tales in *Shadowland*. You're mimicking the style of H. P. Lovecraft in *Mr. X*. I've seen firsthand your expansive library, and I'm amazed at how you've seemingly read everything—you're citing John Ashbery one minute, Henry James the next. You're the editor of so many anthologies. Does this move toward metafiction have anything to do with your awareness of your part in this larger conversation of storytellers?

PS: I hope so. It seemed inevitable that after a long time—after decades of doing

If you buy a Yum Yum or whatever, the pussycat detective novels, you know exactly what you're going to get and when you get it you purr.

what I call narrative heavy lifting, having one big slab of narrative slide up very neatly against another—that I would begin to think about why it was necessary to do that all the time and why it was so often assumed to have absolute authority.

Once I started to think that way, then I couldn't help myself. I of course did keep putting stories into stories, but I also sometimes undermined the larger stories. The greatest example of that is *Lost Boy, Lost Girl*, which is a completely subversive book, in a way. There's scarcely a true word in it. It's all wish, it's all compensation, it's all desire. And I felt that I did it very beautifully. A lot of people didn't get it, but a lot of people liked the book.

BP: When joining this larger conversation of storytelling, you're often tipping your hat to Lovecraft.

PS: Well, Lovecraft and Henry James for sure, and with *Mr. X* in particular, there are many references to Lovecraft, but the real guiding genius, if I can be this pretentious, is Henry James's story "The Jolly Corner," because there are, like, three different versions of "The Jolly Corner" in that book. Of course, I love "The Jolly Corner." I think it's amazingly profound, and it's about a man meeting his other self at night in a mansion, and his other self is not appealing, his other self is scary, and really rich, too.

And Stephen King, of course, is part of the conversation in general. Very often, I was indelibly marked and inspired when I was much, much younger by *The Shining* and *'Salem's Lot*. I thought they were just amazingly powerful and finished books, great works of narrative art. When people started to criticize him, wag him as just being a populist, I objected. I said, "Okay, you be a populist like that, buddy. Let's see if you can pull it off." [laughs]

BP: And your admiration turned to friendship and to collaboration. I hear that the next installment of the *Talisman* series is about to get underway.

PS: It isn't about to get underway, but it is ahead. We agreed to work on it about two years ago, and I haven't even made a significant dent in the novel that I wanted to have done by now. I'm still making notes and trying to find the parts that are still underground. I gotta dig it up, or find it, anyhow.

So, it'll take a while, and I want it to be very ambitious, a very powerful book with a lot of inner gears, and that's not easy to do.

BP: You're sharpening your knife against those who call Stephen King a populist. So much time is spent splitting hairs over what it means to be a genre writer versus what it means to be a literary writer. You're a poet, you're a short-story writer, you're a novelist, you're an essayist, you've written crime novels, you've written horror novels, fairy tales, nonsupernatural stories about war, crime, troubled marriages. It seems like no matter what your medium and no matter what your subject, you have characters who are psychologically complex, you have sentences that are rich and lyrical, you have intricately structured plots—and I'm wondering how you feel about all this squabbling, if you find it tiresome, ridiculous, offensive, what?

PS: [laughs] Well, you put that kind of question in the most positive possible way for me, and I must say I love the way you've been reading my work. That's the ideal way I wish it to be seen. A lot of people don't see it that way, and they have a right to whatever they think. Probably they like a lot of stuff I would dislike. It's a really complex issue, though, at base. I used to think that if you wrote a novel about supernatural events and made it suspenseful and tense with high stakes, and if you wrote it as though it were pure realistic Updikian, Rothian, Flaubertian fiction, that you would be able to prove that everything is the same, that a novel could be both horror and art.

Very few people agreed with me at this point—I'm talking about the early eighties. I spent a lot of time trying to make the point that the distinction between what people on my side of the fence call "mainstream," which is a bit derogatory, really, and what people on the other side of the fence call "crime" or "horror," that the distinction was meaningless, that everything must be judged case by case. If you read *The Long Goodbye* and don't understand it as a world-class American novel, you have missed the boat. [laughs] I still think that.

But by now, I've been beaten down quite a bit, and I understand that one can never change people's minds. Basically, the vast majority of readers are going to say, "Okay, well, I like *The Corrections* because that's a real novel, and I got a kind of a kick out of . . ." (let's say something of mine) ". . . *The Throat*, but you know, it was pretty lightweight." Or, "It was very good for a book like that." People will never make that final erasure.

Well, I myself have been working pretty doggedly toward exactly that erasure. I keep talking about it in these anthologies I've been doing. In the introductions to them, I try to make my weary little point over and over, and the world itself seems to be chiming in—I mean you and Kelly Link and . . .

BP: Dan Chaon . . .

PS: Dan Chaon for sure . . . People like Dan and yourself act as though there is no real boundary between stories of different kinds. In the nineteenth century, when

Hawthorne was writing one kind of story, did he stop and say to himself, "Well, of course, this is a little cheaper and more degraded than my ordinary work, but I'll rush through it anyhow"? I really sort of doubt it. The matter is confused by those people—and they are numerous and extremely worthwhile—who want to do nothing but write genre fiction.

They want to write the sort of books they've enjoyed all their lives. They want to write novels like Rex Stout, novels like Chandler. They want to do Lovecraft-like stories. And they very happily go out and do those things one after another; the books repeat the same effects, they have the same kind of structures, the same consolations and satisfactions, and people buy them for that reason.

If you buy a Yum Yum or whatever, the pussycat detective novels, I'm pretty sure you know exactly what you're going to get and when you get it you purr. That's what you want. You like the flavor. I like the flavor of Rex Stout and I've had times where I've read three or four in a row. I did the same thing with Ed McBain a little later in my life. I read a whole bunch of those 87th Precinct novels because I really like them. They're wonderfully written, in an understated way, and they just gave you the satisfaction that comes from repeating gestures in a reliable and not-too-clichéd form. So, if that's what people want to do, God bless 'em, and they'll sell a lot of books. I think there's certainly another way to go.

BP: Among the writers you admire most, those who are kicking down doors and not acknowledging boundaries, if you could make a demand, not a suggestion, if you could strap everybody into a chair and staple open their eyelids, what books would you make sure they'd read, what writers?

PS: [long laugh] I would say, begin by reading Kelly Link's first two books, for sure *Magic for Beginners*. Be sure to read Brian Evenson's *The Open Curtain*—

BP: Definitely *The Open Curtain*. I don't think I've ever said, "What the fuck?" so many times when reading a book.

PS: Oh boy, oh boy, what a great book. And I didn't mention Dan Chaon yet. *Await Your Reply* is a really stunning book, but even more so, or perhaps equally, his collection of stories *Among the Missing*. That's a collection of stories I would very cheerfully call horror stories, and Chaon himself was always a breath away from doing that.

BP: Sometimes approaching horror more as an emotion than as a genre. He definitely occupies that black territory.

PS: Which is a very rich territory indeed. 🝔

PROMISING LEADS

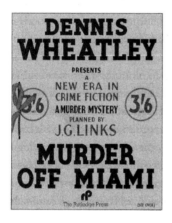

ON DENNIS WHEATLEY
AND J.G. LINKS'S
Murder Off Miami

PAUL COLLINS

The Western Union cablegram is an aged one today, its paper browned by the passage of nearly eighty years. It is the first document in a battered folder of mug shots, evidence exhibits, and typed police reports, all barely held together now by a single length of faded red ribbon, and all detailing the overboard disappearance of Mr. Blane from a yachting party.

None of it ever happened.

"A New Era in Crime Fiction," announces the cover of *Murder Off Miami*, one of the strangest experiments in fiction of the thirties and certainly the oddest from the prolific crime writer Dennis Wheatley. For their three shillings and sixpence, what readers got in 1936 was an utterly novel sort of novel. Instead of a traditional narrative, it's a dossier of evidence on the apparent suicide of soap tycoon Bolitho Blane. He's vanished from a yachting party,

75

leaving little behind other than a torn scrap of stock market figures and the hasty annotation *So the game is up*. What the Miami PD discovers is a disguised murder, and an onboard rogue's gallery of whodunit characters: Lady Welter, Count Luigi Posodini, even a disgraced bishop. And all of them, of course, turn out to have a motive.

"This is a very distressing affair," the bishop stutters. "Very distressing."

Rather than simply reproducing this distressing affair on the page, Wheatley and designer Joseph "J. G." Links opted for a raggedly bound collection of documents and physical evidence, right down to a pasted-in burned match and a blood-stained fabric swatch from the crime scene. Even the mystery's solution is kept carefully in character: it is sealed in the back as a typewritten jailhouse confession.

It was indeed a new era in crime fiction, though perhaps not in quite the way Wheatley or anyone else imagined.

———— • ————

"Not more than one secret passage or room is allowable."

Sensible advice for any home, you'd think—but the line comes from crime writer Ronald Knox's jocular 1928 list of ten "rules" for detective fiction. By then, scores of writers like Agatha Christie and the two men known as Ellery Queen were wreaking havoc on country mansions and locked drawing rooms—daggering millionaires, garroting servants, giving nosy old ladies rat poison in their scones. And

while Knox's rule number 5 ("No Chinaman must figure in the story") sounds odd today, other rules—that the perp be introduced in the beginning chapters of the book (rule number 1), that vital clues cannot be withheld from the reader (rule number 8)—remain strikingly recognizable in these "Golden Age" detective novels as whodunit fair play.

And it *was* play. A craze for "murder parties" had already led, in 1928, to a hugely successful series of "Baffle Books" that were, as *Vanity Fair* put it, "sweeping the country like a new broom." *The Baffle Book* was a series of mystery scenarios (rural stranglings, high-society blackmail, art theft) to be used in "Baffle Parties," where, armed with two copies of *The Baffle Book*, opposing teams would try sifting through a summary of clues to be the first to finger the culprit.

Mystery writers could hardly help but take notice. The conceit of presenting readers with actual documents had been around since the first detective novel, *The Notting Hill Mystery*, appeared in 1862 in *Once a Week* magazine as a nearly unnarrated series of depositions. With enough time and martinis to really get the idea going again, by 1930 Dorothy Sayers's *The Documents in the Case* was purporting to give the notes on the demise of an unfortunate mushroom collector. Even the eccentric writer Harry Stephen Keeler—who *did* use Chinamen, secret passages, and villains introduced on the last page—released a "documented novel" in 1935 featuring the Flying Strangler Baby, a disguised dwarf who garrotes victims from a helicopter. After that, perhaps the only line left to cross was between transcribing evidence and presenting an actual physical simulation of it.

When *Murder Off Miami* arrived in stores one year later, it sold a staggering two hundred thousand copies. Three more sequels followed, though with dwindling success: after all, with the listing of rules the evolution of detective literature from an implicit formula to an explicitly rule-governed game was already becoming complete. Why bother with a book at all? By the time Wheatley's last dossier novel came out in 1939, he was already releasing an outright board game whose name reflected the more pressing concerns of that year: *Invasion*.

Knox's list and *The Baffle Book* were all in good fun, but they were also a fatal foreshadowing: the subtle clue that someone in the drawing room was about to drop dead. That someone was the classic detective novel itself. No genre with such a devastatingly accurate list of rules could last as the state of the art. Instead of tidy, locked-room mysteries, the postwar era would belong to existential noir and police procedurals.

What the rules of old-fashioned detective fiction fossilized into, though, is all the more fascinating: namely, an actual game. I am referring, of course, to Clue. Created in 1944 by British patent clerk Anthony Pratt, Clue was a mighty monument to the classic whodunit. Forever embodied on the game board is the country manor, the suspiciously wooly-minded Professor Plum, the femme fatale Miss Scarlet, the blustering Colonel Mustard, the discarded pistol: the gang's all here. And, like any good murder mystery, a second and darker crime lurks behind the first one: a dastardly theft. Clue pretty much lifted its idea from an earlier game called Mr. Ree! Advertised in 1937 as the "Fireside Detective Game," Mr. Ree! features a board with a floor plan of the murder scene, characters like Aunt Cora and Higgins the Butler, and everything from a dagger to a bottle of poison—every weapon needed, in short, but a subpoena on the makers of Clue.

Both are games of deductive elimination: at heart, it's the logical minimalism of the color-coded pegs of Mastermind, but dressed as permutations of suspects, rooms, and weapons. But while Mr. Ree! tippled its last bottle of poison long ago, Clue's extraordinary hold on the childhood imagination has lasted over sixty years now. Along with innumerable spin-offs—a movie, a TV series, a Simpsons edition—it's migrated into every computer format from a 1984 Commodore 64 game to a new iPhone app. By the time Clue's inventor died, in 1994, the humble board version had already sold nearly 150 million copies worldwide; many children imbibe the rules and deathless archetypes of Clue before they've ever tackled their first full-length novel. If you want to know where Wheatley and his dossier-novel genre went—or, for that matter, Hercule

Poirot and all his colleagues—you need look no further than the game shelf in your summer cabin.

Even so: the yellowing telegrams and scowling mug shots of *Murder Off Miami* retain a peculiar charm. I confess that when I reached the end of Wheatley's dossier, I hadn't figured out who killed Bolitho Blane. But as for who killed *Murder Off Miami*, I'm pretty sure I know the culprit: it was Colonel Mustard, in the library, with the candlestick.

ON G.K. CHESTERTON'S
Father Brown stories

JUSTIN TAYLOR

Gilbert Keith Chesterton—whose nicknames include both "The Apostle of Common Sense" and "The Prince of Paradox"—may have never sounded so much like Walt Whitman as in his 1901 essay "In Defence of Detective Fiction," wherein he commends the genre for being "the earliest and only form of popular literature in which is expressed some sense of the poetry of modern life." The sentiment is a charming one, but more than passing strange, coming from a man whose polemics on behalf of Christianity, Empire, and tradition led his contemporaries to accuse him of a nostalgia for the Middle Ages.

Chesterton trained as a painter at the prestigious Slade School in London, yet he would make his name and his living not as an artist but as a man of letters. All the letters. During his lifetime, Chesterton produced volumes of light verse, essays, biographies, satires, an autobiography, theological tracts, his own magazine (*G. K.'s Weekly*), books of literary criticism, a half dozen novels (including *The Man Who Was Thursday*), and fifty-odd short mystery stories featuring a Catholic priest with a flair for what Edgar Allan Poe called "the art of ratiocination."

Father Brown debuted in 1910, and for many years was the most famous fictional detective after Sherlock Holmes (who debuted in 1887, when Chesterton was thirteen years old). Brown was modeled on a really existing (though not actually mystery-solving) friend of Chesterton's, Father Joseph O'Connor, but I prefer to think of Brown as a kind of funhouse-mirror image of his author. Chesterton stood six foot four and tipped the scales at just under three hundred pounds. He kept a bushy mustache and often strolled about in a cape, with a cigar in his mouth and a cane—if not a swordstick—in his hand. Few photographs of him contain all of him; he probably never slipped into (or out of) a room unnoticed in his life. This is all in starkest contrast to the diminutive Brown, "round and dull as a Norfolk dumpling" in his rumpled vestments, with "eyes as empty as the North Sea." His manner is unassuming to the verge of blandness, and he often comes off like a miscast extra in his own stories—at least, that is, until he opens his mouth and solves the mystery of the hour. Most authors are mice who write in order to see themselves as elephants, but here we have something much more interesting and rare—an elephant who dreamed of being a mouse.

Father Brown is a keen observer and listener, but his real specialty is a kind of inductive moral logic informed by a deep understanding of evil gained during countless hours served in its close proximity—as a hearer of confessions, as a comforter to those who have been dealt life's harshest blows. Brown is typically called in to work cases that seem to have a supernatural dimension, but he refuses categorically to entertain any explanation that involves the occult, black magic, superstitions, ancient curses, evil ghosts, or anything else to which a good Christian ought not give credence. As he explains to a bemused onlooker in "The Curse of the Golden Cross": "It really is more natural to believe a preternatural story, that deals with things we don't understand, than a natural story that contradicts things we do understand." What he means is that reason and faith are not mutually exclusive categories, but reinforce and amplify each other. It also doesn't hurt that, as one character remarks in "The Arrow of Heaven," "Somehow you're the sort of man to whom one wants to tell the truth."

Because he's a priest, all the other characters in a given story will tend to make two assumptions about him—first, that even if nobody called him, he has a basic right to hang around and do as he likes; second, that he is some kind of walking anachronism with no understanding of worldly things or the exigencies of modern life. Father Brown always takes full advantage of the first assumption, and he always upsets the second. This is necessarily to the chagrin of the assorted academics, Bolshevists, Darwinists, journalists, Nietzscheans, spiritualists, dandies, poets, policemen, cult leaders, anarchists, atheists, industrialists, swindlers, murderers, Americans, and crooks Brown encounters—all of whom Chesterton relished hoisting by the petards of their own presumptions, hypocrisies, predilections, and newfangled ideas.

The "original" Father Brown stories are collected twelve apiece in *The Innocence of Father Brown* (1911) and *The Wisdom of Father Brown* (1914). The next book, *The Incredulity of Father Brown*, did not appear until 1926, followed by *The Secret of Father Brown* in 1927 and *The Scandal of Father Brown* in 1935. Like Sir Arthur Conan Doyle before him, Chesterton had become the slave of his own success. Doyle threw Holmes over Reichenbach Falls in the hopes of being rid of him, but eventually—succumbing to popular pressure and the need for a sure cash fix—contrived to bring him back. Chesterton, who would have seen Holmes die and return before publishing his first Brown story, never made such a mistake. Several introductions to collected or selected Father Brown anthologies relate that whenever his wife told him money was running low Chesterton would reply, "That means Father Brown again." David Stuart Davies, introducer of the *Wordsworth Classics Complete Father Brown Stories*—the best and the cheapest edition I have come across, if not the most handsome or durable—adds the colorful detail that this utterance was accompanied by a sigh.

A general consensus exists that the first twenty-four stories are superior to what came later. Most Selected Father Brown editions that I've seen draw sparingly from the latter three volumes. Some simply reproduce *Innocence* and *Wisdom* in their entireties, and leave it at that. The main critique of the later Brown tales is that they wax didactic and feature flimsier mysteries, because the author is palpably less interested in the stories than in their morals. (In the twelve years between *Wisdom* and *Incredulity* Chesterton officially converted from Anglicanism to Roman Catholicism.) This is a fair complaint, to be sure, but as a full and final judgment it is insufficient. In an essay called "The Labyrinths of the Detective Story and Chesterton," Jorge Luis Borges—who knew a thing or two about paradoxes, and who revered Chesterton's work—gently chides *The Scandal of Father Brown* for its lack of "felicity" to the detective form, but he is quick to assert that two entries in *Scandal*—"The Blast of the Book" and "The Insoluble Problem"—are "stories I would not want excluded from a Brownian anthology or canon." (Appallingly, neither story is contained in any Selected that I've seen.) But the biggest problem with the wholesale dismissal of the latter three books is the implicit suggestion that the first two are above critique.

Chesterton's work is peppered with stunning moments of racism and anti-Semitism, only some of which can be excused (if still not forgiven) on account of the time and place in which he lived. For two of the most egregious examples, one need look no further than "The Wrong Shape" from the first book and "The God of the Gongs" from the second. But since that unfortunate aspect of the work is more or less evenly distributed throughout the Brown catalog, let me return to my original point, which is that the late work contains much to admire and enjoy. The stories are stellar pieces of literature, theology, and rhetoric, if not always precisely of detective fiction. *Incredulity* is an especially strong collection— "The Arrow of Heaven," "The Miracle of Moon Crescent," "The Ghost of Gideon Wise," and "The Oracle of the Dog" are all first-rate mystery tales. The same cannot be said of "The Dagger with Wings" or "The Doom of the Darnaways," two of my personal favorite examples of the kind of Brown story that so understandably irks the mystery purists. The premises are precarious, the only action takes place offstage, the real endings come in the middle, and no pretense whatsoever is made of pursuing— much less capturing—the killers. They're unbalanced, to say the least, but all the more arresting and valuable for their peculiarities, which is not necessarily to say flaws.

In the Borges essay mentioned above, he suggests the six major rules for working in the mystery genre. The last one he gives is this: "A solution that is both necessary and marvelous." In addition to being a supremely good rule for all fiction, not just detective stories, this is notable for being an uncannily Chestertonian description of Christianity. So if you go into a Brown story looking for a mystery and can't seem to find one, it doesn't mean that one isn't there. All the small mysteries of this world are solved, sooner or later, or else cease to matter. It is only the large one that abides above our heads, emphatically pressing and perennially insoluble; an investigation that can—and should—never be closed.

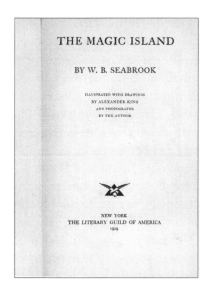

THE MAGIC ISLAND

BY W. B. SEABROOK

ILLUSTRATED WITH DRAWINGS
BY ALEXANDER KING
AND PHOTOGRAPHS
BY THE AUTHOR

NEW YORK
THE LITERARY GUILD OF AMERICA
1929

ON WILLIAM BUEHLER
SEABROOK'S
The Magic Island

HUGH RYAN

I'm a sucker for a good monster-origin story. What's Cujo without the rabies, Godzilla without the bomb?

So how about this: Imagine a man born at the end of the nineteenth century, the all-American son of a traveling preacher. He drives a French ambulance in World War I, gets gassed, and receives the Croix de Guerre. He becomes a reporter for William Randolph Hearst, but something is wrong. He can't sit still. He travels—Arabia, West Africa, England, Timbuktu. He becomes obsessed with the supernatural and befriends Satanist Aleister Crowley. He moves to France and cavorts with ex-pats. Gertrude Stein writes about him. His sex life is the stuff of morbid pulp novels: bondage, sadism, wife swapping. He samples human flesh, which he categorizes as "like good, fully developed veal, not young, but not yet beef." His drinking spirals out of control, and for eight months he has himself institutionalized. When that doesn't work, he plunges his arms into a vat of boiling water, hoping that by immobilizing them, he will stop himself from drinking. Eventually, at sixty-one, after writing nearly a dozen books, he kills himself, destroying the monsters in his mind.

All but one.

That man was William Buehler Seabrook, and though he's forgotten now, his book *The Magic Island* midwifed into existence a monster that lives on in undead fecundity, reaching out from beyond the grave to top the *New York Times* best-seller list, meddle with Jane Austen, and routinely scare the crap out of me: the zombie.

"From the palm-fringed shore a great mass of mountains rose, fantastic and mysterious. Dark jungle covered their near slopes, but high beyond the jungle, blue-black, bare ranges piled up, towering."

This is Port-Au-Prince, 1927, as described in the foreword to *The Magic Island*. Divided into two parts, each chapter describing a different ceremony he saw or story he was told, the book recounts Seabrook's forays into the mysterious worlds of Haitian religion and politics—the former infinitely more interesting than the latter. Seabrook traveled to Haiti with the express purpose of learning voodoo and writing a sensational follow-up to his wildly successful travelogue, *Adventures in Arabia*. It was a gamble. As Seabrook recounts in his autobiography, *No Hiding Place*, his editor warned him: "No white man can write a book that's any good about voodoo." But this was Seabrook's shtick. Travel somewhere exotic, "go native," and write about it. It had worked well among the Druze in Syria, and would work later among the Guere in Nigeria. In Haiti, however, he had his biggest success, and he wrote the book that changed the nightmares of the world forever, although he never quite realized it.

Maman Célie, the matriarch of a large family that included one of Seabrook's Haitian servants, was his entrance into and guide through the world of syncretic Afro-Catholic-Caribbean spirituality. Seabrook wrote of Célie: "It was as if we had known each other always, had been at some past time united by the mystical equivalent of an umbilical cord; as if I had suckled in infancy at her dark breasts, had wandered far, and was now returning home."

As in many good monster stories, from *Beowulf*'s Grendel to *Psycho*'s Norman Bates, Seabrook's life was dominated by mommy issues. He divided his birth mother's life into two periods. There was the beautiful willow girl who was the epitome of what a woman should be; in his earliest fantasies (which may have been aided by doses of laudanum from his Spiritualist grandmother), Seabrook dreamed of taking women like that and tying their hands behind their backs, dangling them by ropes from the ceiling, and chaining them to pillars—fantasies he would carry out, publicly and privately, as an adult. When she grew older and less attractive, Seabrook came to despise his mother. He described the mother-son relationship as a "silver cord [that] strangled more struggling males than all the knotted nooses of hangmen and assassins." His second wife, writer Marjorie Worthington, believed that every woman he brought into his life (and there were many: wives, guides, prostitutes, teachers, mistresses, lovers) was an attempt to work out his Oedipal issues. His entwined fear and desire were a large part of what motivated his peripatetic search for mystical salvation. He looked for women he could control sexually, and for ones who could save him.

Célie was one of the latter, and she became his Haitian mother, the woman who brought him into the community of priests and ceremonies, *loas* and *oduns*. With her he watched white oxen ceremonially butchered, and learned to make fetishes and other religious objects. But it was a roadside encounter with an unnaturally leaden work crew that brought him to zombies, his major contribution to Western culture. Here are the first words ever published in English about the zombie: "I recalled one creature I had been hearing about in Haiti, which sounded exclusively local—the *zombie* . . . a soulless human corpse, still dead, but taken from the grave and endowed by sorcery with a mechanical semblance of life . . . it is a dead body which is made to walk and act and move as if it were alive."

These zombies were a far cry from the ravening horde of today's Hollywood blockbusters. They were dumb brutes, mournful and confused over being pulled from their eternal resting places. They had forgotten even their own names. Seabrook (and soon, all of America) didn't fear the zombie itself—he feared becoming one. Being turned into a zombie was literally a fate worse than death. It was the perfect monster for a country terrified of racial ambiguity and miscegenation. The zombie caught the American zeitgeist for the same reason Seabrook himself did: both flirted with becoming "the other." It was the Roaring Twenties and the Harlem Renaissance, a time of blurring racial lines. Nella Larsen's seminal novel *Passing*, published the same year as *The Magic Island*, told what was for some bigoted Americans the ultimate horror story: that of a mixed-race woman who successfully "passed" as white and married a white man.

When *The Magic Island* was published, the American press (and Seabrook's birth mother) were repulsed by the things he had done, and the thing he had symbolically become through his relationship with Maman Célie: black. In its review, *Time* magazine stated in dread fascination that Seabrook "himself, a white, an American, shared in the rites" of voodoo. The book quickly led to a boom in American zombie stories. Movies got in on the action with 1932's *White Zombie*, in which a young white woman about to get married is transformed by a lecherous Haitian priest. Its tagline evoked the era's fear of white slavery: "She was not alive . . . Nor dead . . . Just a White Zombie performing his every desire."

Seabrook was only dimly aware of the seismic shift he had brought about in American horror. When he died in 1945, the zombie as he knew it had become a familiar, if staid, part of the cultural landscape. New horror stories were more concerned with Nazi experiments and radioactive mutants. It would be nine years before Roger Matheson would re-create the zombie (in his 1954 book *I Am Legend*) as the modern, world-annihilating plague that audiences now love to fear.

Shortly before he killed himself, Seabrook wrote of *The Magic Island*, "I'm not building up to assert—to persuade myself or anybody else at this late day—that it was a good book. I'd give my life to write one good book, as I suppose any author would, but doubt that I ever have, or will."

What Seabrook wanted was what he had already unknowingly achieved: life after death. His name may be forgotten, but we owe him a huge debt. Perhaps another writer was waiting in the wings. Perhaps the zombie would have crawled here, with or without Seabrook, to spread its contagion upon American shores. But perhaps not. The zombie was the right monster for the right moment, and Seabrook, with his unique dichotomies (a white man who saw nothing wrong with saying he wanted to "be Negro," a dedicated reporter not above exoticizing or exaggerating whole cultures for a story, a man many described as noble even though they disapproved of his sexual peccadilloes), may have been the only one who could have brought them here when he did. His travelogues may never be republished, his name may be erased from history, but his undead legacy shambles on.

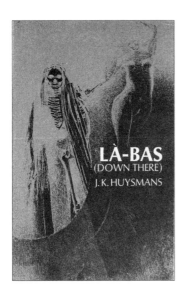

ON J.K. HUYSMANS'S

Là-Bas

COLIN FLEMING

When you're a fourteen-year-old boy, you tend to have a bent for a particular branch of the macabre. I'm not talking movie nights with Messrs. Lugosi and Karloff, or a spin through Stephen King's back catalog. What I mean is something more subversive, something that offers the tantalizing, heady sense of the illicit.

I was no different. Only, I had the good fortune—to my soul's impending peril, as some pious critics would attest—to discover a little-known 1891 novel called *Là-Bas*, just as I was settling into my first year of high school. Not that any teacher would have assigned the thing to me. Written by J. K. Huysmans, a put-upon French civil servant, *Là-Bas* translates to "Down There." As in, you know, the boiling pit of the earth, where the devil rules his minions! Huysmans was what was known at the time, somewhat quaintly, as a "decadent." One inglorious riposte even claimed him to be a "sodomitical" writer, no light charge in late-nineteenth-century France.

Huysmans writes in dense, impeccably controlled word clusters, with commas offered up as brief resting places before a reader can make his descent into the next supplementary clause. That's the stylistic hallmark of *Là-Bas*, the story of Durtal, a Huysmans stand-in lamenting the death of culture. Everything he encounters is vapid, disposable. Were there computers in fin-de-siècle Paris, Durtal would not have been a blogger. So he makes like a good übermalcontent and buries himself in writing a biography of Gilles de Rais, a child murderer who enjoyed a hearty black mass—and may or may not have been the inspiration for Bluebeard—as well as masturbating onto the stomachs of young children before he beheaded them.

Durtal pals around with des Hermies, another writer, who is also a classic tempter, one of those guys with a knack for getting you to go further in any shady matter than you ever should. He's also something of a gossiping fishwife, but with an understated "ah, easy come, easy go" speaking style, so it's not uncommon for him to describe some witnessed debauchery with the same nonchalance of a man recounting what he ate for lunch.

At fourteen, I'd read Horatio Hornblower, some Jack London, and a bit of

Booth Tarkington—boys' fare—but *Là-Bas* was another proposition altogether. Even if I'd known I might have liked this kind of writing, I wouldn't have had a clue where to find it; when you're a kid, there are just some books you think the library couldn't possibly own. But there was this older guy on my street named Clifton. No one knew if that was his first or last name. He absolutely wrangled girls. There were always three or four hanging around, and he'd tell us there was an English teacher the juniors had named Clitoris, and we'd think we were neighbors with James Dean, a true badass.

Turns out her name was Cloris, which is rather different, but I've decided to let this slide in my memory, because it was Clifton who gave me a copy of *Là-Bas*. His father was this out-of-place, shambling hippie kind of guy, and I like to imagine he had a penchant for the subversive himself, which he then passed on to his son. One night, we were horsing around behind the hockey rink across the street from school. Clifton was groping some girl. I was watching him grope away. He told me to take a hike and flipped the book at me from out of his back pocket. And so away I went, into the rink and up into the bleachers, and straight to the Paris underground of 1891.

The big, splashy moment of *Là-Bas* is its ending, a florid description of a black mass that wouldn't have been out of place in one of those old Hammer Films devil-worship flicks. But what really appealed to me then—and what appeals even more to me now—is how conversational the novel is. Durtal and des Hermies spend most of the book in a church, with a bell ringer named Carhaix and his wife. There, they have dinner parties and discuss a number of subjects, from des Hermies's preferred netherworld pursuits to the Coltrane-worthy tone of Carhaix's bells. Both Durtal and des Hermies are staggered by his artistry, even if des Hermies puts his normal ghastly twist on matters. "Carhaix is good for a few more years yet," he remarks to Durtal, who has expressed admiration for Carhaix's youthful spirit, despite his advanced age. "After that, it'll be time enough for him to die. The Church, which has begun by installing gas in the chapels, will end up replacing bells with powerful electronic chimes."

Personally, I like des Hermies a lot, for the same reason I like the Pogues' front man Shane MacGowan—a vulgarian with one knee on the floor—a lot. With des Hermies, you often get the sacred and profane served up at once, in the same sentence. Or the same clause. There's the sense that something entirely sacred would horrify him. But you also realize that something that's entirely profane would be just as unwelcome. The sty and the altar—they go together more than a lot of people think, and especially more than a lot of writers today seem to think. To me, that's the big instructional element of *Là-Bas*. Sure, it was naughty paper-bag lit during its heyday, but it blends Romanticism and Naturalism in a manner that mirrors life. Realism, at all costs, was then the vogue of Parisian letters. The story wasn't so much the thing, but rather the rendering of day-in, day-out existence, with all minutiae intact. Screw narrative, in other words. Des Hermies, however, begs to differ:

> "The problem," des Hermies claimed, "is that there was always a fundamental intellectual difference between you [Durtal] and the other realists, and no truce could be cobbled together which was ever likely to last long. You execrate the age in which you live while they adore it. That is the truth of the matter. Sooner or later, you were bound to flee this Americanization of art in order to seek more airy and mountainous regions."

That's not a passage that you might expect from a horror novel. *Là-Bas* is weird and slippery, but it strikes me as ironic that there was a time when I thought it was a monster-gonna-get-you kind of book. I prefer it as I now see it each time I return to its pages: a work still capable of a good jolt or two, but one that's better defined by its juxtapositions and contrasts. Funny how much more sinister horror becomes when it's buttressed by the quotidian.

ON SYLVIA BROWNE'S

Adventures of a Psychic

TONAYA THOMPSON

I discovered Sylvia Browne in the early nineties, after dropping out of my first try at community college. When not enduring epic county-transit bus rides from northern Washington to temp agencies in Seattle, I could usually be found in front of the television in my largely absent mother's split-level house. My brother and I wasted entire nights trying to level in Ninja Gaiden, but daytimes were for talk shows: Jerry Springer, Jenny Jones, Sally Jessy Raphael, and, of course, sensitive, soulful Montel Williams. That's when, listlessly flipping from channel to channel, fantasizing about my yet-to-exist life, I saw her.

With a voice like Froggy from *Our Gang*, glossy blond hair, and long, flashy acrylic nails, Browne frequented *The Montel Williams Show*, eventually becoming a weekly installation. She'd make political, economic, and weather predictions about the world that were generally as positive as they would later prove to be incorrect. Then there'd be a Q&A with the audience: Browne assures a woman that the double rainbow she saw when leaving the hospital was "absolutely" her daughter's boyfriend, who passed away there. Browne describes the rainbow: "It was one right . . . on top of the other." Emphatic nodding, exit music, cut to commercial.

I found Browne incredibly magnetic. It wasn't just my insatiable need to know what the future held—a need I religiously supplemented with horoscope scrolls from the Safeway checkout line—it was that voice, that hair, those nails, those dark eyes that seemed fixed on some dimension no one else could see. She was every Pall-Mall-smoking, *National-Enquirer*-reading, kitchen-table-sitting woman I had ever known and loved. In a different life, she could have been my grandmother. Maybe if I asked her, she'd say she was.

Twenty years later, having long since pulled out of that motivational slump—and several others—I came across Browne's *Adventures of a Psychic*. I was nostalgic for some supermarket reading, and thought this would fit the bill. It's an autobiography of sorts, coauthored by Antoinette May and rendered in the third person. In the preface, Browne states two reasons she wanted this book written: first, "to give people an understanding of what a psychic is truly all about," and second, to tell a "story about a woman . . . who is perhaps (is this a crime?) too giving, too naive, too understanding, and too selfless."

The book opens in the present tense, at a talk show: "The capacity audience is restless, eager. This isn't just any TV show . . . they want answers." Browne then astounds everyone with her incredibly specific details about audience members. They all *ooh* and *ah*. Someone asks her what's in store for herself. She shakes her head and gives her trademark answer: she's not allowed to see her own future, her own "blueprint."

We then get the story of Sylvia né Shoemaker's birth, childhood, and adolescence. Although born with "a gift" she claims she inherited from her maternal grandmother, Browne discovered her real magic through a "spirit guide" named Iena, an "Aztec/Inca" born in northern Colombia in 1500 who began appearing to Browne when she was a child. Browne calls her "Francine." Francine has information about the future, which she delivers to Browne sometimes through the ether and sometimes by entering Browne's body. As a young adult, Browne marries a local cop, Gary Dufresne. They live a very unhappy life in a home built on top of an Indian burial ground. Browne works as a schoolteacher, and Dufresne takes all her money. She has two sons; one almost dies. Then *she* almost dies from hepatitis—though how she contracted it isn't mentioned. Finally, at thirty-five, she walks away from the marriage. As she frequently points out in the book, this is all a surprise to her, since she's not "allowed" to see her own future.

Cut to chapter 7. Browne has married Dal Brown and is giving a class on the paranormal in their apartment. During the class, she channels Francine, who gives a lengthy presentation—at times highly generalized, at times absurdly specific—about the "Other Side." According to Francine, the Other Side is "another dimension. It's paradise, it's heaven, it's the ultimate reality of existence. It's the living world; yours is moribund by comparison. The puny lifespan of 100 years is a tiny drop in a great sea of eternity."

From here the book heads in more of a technical, how-to direction, with testimonials throughout. On ghost hunting: "NO ALCOHOL OR DRUGS BEFORE OR DURING TRANCE." On "life themes": forty-four incongruously termed categories, including Activator, Aesthetic Pursuits, Controller, Emotionality, Humanitarian, Infallibility. If you are ill, surely there's a psychic reason for it: "Dizzy spells? What's keeping you off-balance? Back problems? Who's on your back? Bleeding ulcer? Who can't you stomach? The possibilities for healing are endless." All you have to do is find the appropriate pun, and you're cured. If that doesn't work, you can use the "Laboratory Technique," a self-hypnosis in which you imagine yourself in a room with a blue, purple, gold, and green stained-glass window. Eventually, "spiritual helpers" will appear to heal whatever you've asked them to. It goes on. And on.

The final chapter describes Browne's betrayal at the hands of Dal Brown, from whom she has distanced herself by adding an e to the end of her name, and her founding of the Novus Spiritus church, which holds to this singularly convenient tenet: "Take what you like and leave the rest behind."

Outside the pages of Browne's book, however, there's a dark side. While Browne and her supporters point to her frequently incorrect predictions as honest human error (without once addressing the very suprahuman nature of "Francine"), some say that Sylvia Browne is an outright fraud. There's even a Web site called StopSylvia.com, whose logo is a fake-nailed hand in a stop sign.

In 2003, on Williams's show, Browne swiftly dealt the parents of the missing Shawn Hornbeck a "no" when they tearfully asked if he was "still with us." The perpetrator, Browne said, was "uh, dark-skinned, although he wasn't black, he was more Hispanic . . . looking. Um, had real long, dark hair . . . and . . . strange enough Hispanic, but he had dreadlocks." She later offered to continue to help them search for their son at her "normal rate"—about $700 an hour. Hornbeck was discovered four years later, held hostage by the Caucasian and short-haired Michael Devlin.

So is that warm, gravel-voiced grandma a fraud? Without a doubt. I had approached Browne's autobiography with genuine interest and mild bemusement, but by its end had to confront an obvious hack and my own misguided hunger for cheap knowledge. Still, the desire to know what the future holds is irresistible, even if it's ultimately impossible. To have an answer for everything like Sylvia Browne does: what a dream!

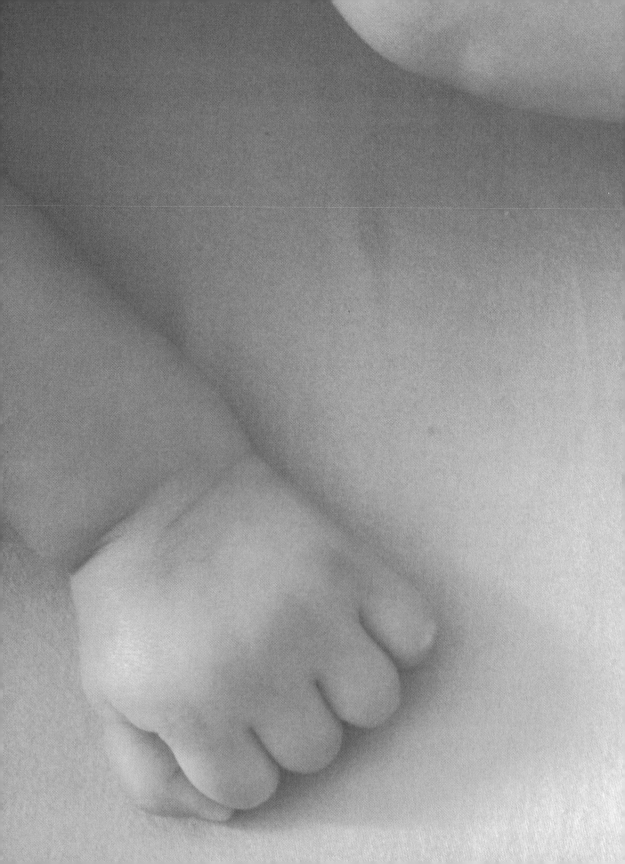

FICTION

Then

Kenneth Calhoun

THEN Jorie was standing in the doorway holding the baby, bouncing him lightly on her shoulder, trying to get him to sleep. She was wearing her fuzzy pink robe and athletic socks, and her hair burst forth in every direction like Lady Liberty's crown. The old floor creaked under her feet. Adam was watching from the nursing chair by the window. The baby was murmuring into his wife's terry-cloth-covered shoulder. He heard the baby say, Don't answer that. It's undoubtedly those telemarketers again. This struck Adam as a very odd thing to say, since the phone wasn't ringing.

T H E N Jorie was in bed next to Adam, causing a commotion. Adam had his back to her. He must have had microsleep. That's the term they had learned on the radio. Experts said it would happen. He was a filmmaker and knew it was indeed occurring because the flow of reality now had jump cuts. Jorie was pushing and kneeing at his back. Was she trying to change the sheets without asking him to leave the bed? He felt he would never leave the bed. It was difficult to even imagine standing, walking about. The bed was now their white place of perpetual torment, a starchy pressure at their backs.

Baby, he said calmly, you'll never get to sleep going at it that way. She hadn't slept for five days. When she didn't respond, only whimpered, he sat up to find her frantically searching the blankets. He assumed that she had lost her wedding ring. He said, Do you remember when it was our thinking that we had lost it up at that rest stop in the redwoods, and we drove back down the map half a day's distance to dig through the trash with our hands and no gloves on them? We gave up and went on in our car up and up into the north, and then it dropped in your lap from the map when you unfolded it to see what was that lake.

The baby, she said, turning on him savagely. I can't find the baby that is ours!

T H E N Adam was on the couch, with the baby like a dense beanbag on his chest. There was pale light coming in through the window. His hand rested lightly on the baby's warm back, patting lightly on the little drum of tiny human torso. He was ashamed to find himself praying now, after all those years of silence. It's not like I'm asking to have anything done for me, he insisted to no one.

T H E N she was pregnant with the baby again. She knew that he was sitting right in the booster seat of her belly. How odd to know his face and fingers and toes, his tiny little fleshy hinges of wrists and ankles, and the feel of his hot little mouth pulling at her breast. All this before he is born again. She could not see over the mountain of her belly to where Adam was holding the baby in the nursing chair. She could not move with the baby like a boulder in her middle. She felt confused and grounded at the same time. That was why, she recognized. Because everything is happening now *at the same time*. The mechanism that puts one minute after another has broken so that, now, it's just forever in all directions at once.

T H E N Jorie found the baby on the floor, between the sofa and the armchair, alive with battery-operated movement and a clear plastic mask on its face.

T H E N she went into the nursery to check on the baby. The night light projected an aquatic light over the walls. She peered into the crib, careful not to wake her sleeping son. She did not know if other newborns could sleep at this point, nor would she let it be known that their baby was still doing it several times a day. The insomnia epidemic had made people hungry for sleep and, in their starved state, capable of anything. They were always standing in the corner of her eye, until she looked at them directly and they vanished. She believed they would consume any vessel in which sleep was found, hoping to absorb the ability. Yes, she believed they would eat her baby.

The baby heard her think this and started to cry.

T H E N Adam came out of the bathroom empty-handed, with the toilet gurgling behind him. She asked him, Is the baby something you have? He went back in and came out with the baby wriggling and squawking in his hands. Oh my God, Adam, she shouted. That you cannot be doing!

He wept and said, Forgive this from me because I have not slept now for over a week plus forever.

T H E N sometimes she had the baby or knew where the baby was and sometimes he had the baby or knew where the baby was. Then the baby was sometimes perched on them, driving them like oxen, using a hard yoke of emotion. Then, sometimes, more and more often, neither of them had the baby or knew where the baby was.

T H E N the baby turned up in Adam's sock drawer. It had learned how to meow.

T H E N Jorie wanted to know what the officers had brought that would turn off their heads for a while, knock them out and let the aching in their bones move one way or another off an unreachable place.

The police couple was sorry but they had brought nothing. That's because there is nothing, they said.

Adam stood up, the chair falling back behind him, and snapped into a rage. He fell to the ground and bit at the table legs. You have sleeping in you, the way you talk, and your eyes are telling me so fucking obviously so!

T H E N the baby told Adam a bedtime story into his chest. The words went through the sieve of skin and bone, leaving behind a pool of drool. The baby said, Even though you had heard reports of the giant sparrow, you brought me to a certain park in the carriage. You and Mother were having a picnic when the bird came down from the black trees and landed on the handlebar of the stroller. Its weight—because it was the size of a dodo—caused the stroller to spill forward, and I flew into the bird's beak. I was wailing into the sparrow's dry tongue, which smelled like fresh mud. The beak locked down on me, solid as furniture, and in a tumble and roll, with flapping like an umbrella opening again and again, we were aloft. Your shouts and Mother's screams were muffled and growing distant but not gone. The sparrow took me up into the trees, where it perched and tipped back its head, working me into the tight suitcase of its gullet. It was like being born into darkness. You and Mother hunted for us in the trees with your eyes, but the bird had roosted in the girding under a bridge, tucking its head under its wing. I was inside, refusing to be digested. I knew what to do, since the bird, on the inside, was not unlike Mother. I introduced a maddening nursery rhyme into the bird's tiny brain, preventing it from sleeping. Deprived of food and sleep, the bird became very susceptible to suggestion and it was then that I began a campaign of unreasonable suggestions. When the bird was weakened and the belts and tethers of its dark interior had gone slack, I assumed the role of pilot and puppeteer. I pulled sinews from the weave of the fleshy fabric and, using nubs of bone from digested animals as spools, built an array of pulleys that controlled the bird's every move, even after it had died. At the time, you knew nothing of this. The police couple that came to investigate were outraged by your claims. You were alternately persons of interest and suspects. They separated you and lied about what the other had said. But you and Mother held firm, when not quaking with grief. You were with the police and their cadaver dogs in the park when the bird appeared above you, flying with the jerky movement of a marionette. I landed it in the grass with a tumble. The skin, which was now as dry as paper, tore upon impact and I tumbled out, little fists curled around the bone handles and levers I had devised. Mother scooped me up and attacked the remains of the bird with her boots, until I made it clear to her that the animal had died a long time ago.

Then the baby turned up in Adam's sock drawer. It had learned how to meow.

T H E N the police came to the door. It had been four days since Jorie and Adam had reported the baby missing. The police that came were a couple. They knocked at the back door with a flashlight, and Jorie thought they were shadow people. She looked at them directly, through the window in the door, and they did not disappear. She went right up to the glass and stared at them for a long time. They stared back, a man and woman in uniform, holding light in their hands. Open the door, the man was saying. We're here about a missing baby.

T H E N Jorie cleared dishes out of the sink with the intention of giving the baby a bath and was startled to see the drain at the bottom of the basin. Of course it made sense that it would be there, but she found its existence oddly surprising and novel. She recalled a time when she and her brother, only four and five years of age, would wander around their home and point out things that were always there—light switches, door stoppers, vents in the floor—saying, Remember this? Remember this? It was as though they had already lived a thousand years and had forgotten the basic, utilitarian details of their surroundings after initially learning their purposes, marveling at them, and then moving on to other discoveries.

> Then he was so tired that he vomited. There were things in it that he didn't remember eating.

Now, sick with exhaustion, Jorie felt the same sense of rediscovery, looking into the drain. And, like she had as a child, she marveled at the practical details. Who could have ever thought of it all and how did human living get so cluttered with detail? For a lucid moment, she believed she understood that the epidemic was somehow connected to this accumulation of practical—not ornamental—details. A threshold had been reached.

T H E N Adam wondered out loud, his words slurred and weirdly ordered, looping and logically wavering, why he could never make a kite that actually flew. Maybe it's time to try to make love to each other, he said to Jorie. He didn't care if there were people sometimes standing in the corners of the room. In the corners of the world, Adam thought. *Shadow people* was what they were calling them on the radio. Just figments of the sleep-deprived mind.

T H E N he was so tired that he vomited. There were things in it that he didn't remember eating.

T H E N they had to start taking averages of their perceptions. If they saw the baby on the left side of the couch three times and on the right side three times, they would conclude that the baby was in the middle of the couch. If it was two times on the left and three times on the right, then their guess was that the baby was slightly to the right of the middle of the couch. If the baby said, This can't go on, but the baby also said nothing, then what they heard was more like Go on or Can't go or This can't.

Give a gift! ONLY $24.95

I want to give a gift subscription to *Tin House* at the incredibly low rate of just $24.95 for one full year (four issues). I save $26.85 or 50% off the newsstand price!

○ Bill me later ○ Enclosed find my check payable to *Tin House* for $24.95

My Name _____ (Please Print)

Address _____

City/State/Zip _____

Email Address _____ Phone number _____

Gift subscription for _____ (Please Print)

Address _____

City/State/Zip _____

B0047B

Order online at www.TINHOUSE.com or call toll free 1 (800) 786-3424.
Canadian orders add $15.00. All other international orders add $30.00 and send prepaid in U.S. funds.
Please allow 6-8 weeks for delivery of your first issue.

Only $24.95

Newsstand Price $51.80 ~ Subscribe and Save 50%

Enter my subscription to *Tin House* at the incredibly low rate of $24.95 for one full year (four issues). I save $26.85 or 50% off the newsstand price!

○ Bill me later ○ Enclosed find my check payable to *Tin House* for $24.95

My Name _____ (Please Print)

Address _____

_____

City/State/Zip _____

Email Address _____ Phone number _____

B0047A

BUSINESS REPLY MAIL

FIRST-CLASS MAIL   PERMIT NO. 99027   ESCONDIDO CA

POSTAGE WILL BE PAID BY ADDRESSEE

Tin House

PO BOX 469049
ESCONDIDO CA 92046-9552

www.TinHouse.com

BUSINESS REPLY MAIL

FIRST-CLASS MAIL   PERMIT NO. 99027   ESCONDIDO CA

POSTAGE WILL BE PAID BY ADDRESSEE

Tin House

PO BOX 469049
ESCONDIDO CA 92046-9552

T H E N the baby was gone. They tore the house apart looking for him. Adam searched the garage, took apart the car, while Jorie checked every can, carton, and box in the pantry and squeezed out every tube of medicinal pastes. In the yard, there was a pile of leaves that they gently combed through. They did not blame each other. The search, in some ways, brought them together. They made love for the first time since the baby was born. It was safe to do so.

T H E N Adam insisted that the officers tell them what the news was, regarding the epidemic. What would be good to be knowing, he said, is how we're finding the things we need to end this never sleeping at all.

The policeman and policewoman said that things were tough, explaining that it took them four days to respond because the entire city was being served by fewer than a dozen police officers. There were rumors about help from the government, but also rumors that the government had collapsed. The only thing they could do was their jobs, which is what they had come here to do. Let's just tackle one problem at a time and find your baby, the policewoman said.

T H E N the baby told Jorie a story, while flopped over her shoulder for a burping. I became fixated on the notion that I was going to hurt you, the baby told her. I knew that as I grew I would encroach on that which was you. If things continued and I was never to emerge from you, I would take from you beyond what your body was prepared to give. Life would slowly transfer from you to me and I would eventually shed you like a snake sheds its skin. All this resulted in a great deal of worry, made all the more excruciating by the fact that I could not willfully refuse nourishment in an attempt to end the escalation of presence. I loved you even before I was led to you. It broke my tiny heart to know I could not stay within you, since that would mean your demise, nor could I leave you without causing damage and pain. If you recall, being birthed is much like being drawn slowly toward a gaping drain. You feel the pull very subtly at first. Before long, it has taken you like a riptide, and it's in everyone's best interest not to resist its demands. I had to recognize that the moment of surrender had arrived and all I could do was keep my head down and my shoulders hunched, and hope I didn't cause a tear in making my exit. And it worked, or so it seems. I was so relieved to learn that a cut at the opening was not necessary. I can only hope that this was in some way a result of my efforts, since I love your flesh as though it were my own. More so, actually, since it continues to provide nourishment, and mine already strains toward decay and dust.

T H E N the police couple walked into the living room, looking at the mess Adam and Jorie had made in their searches for the baby. The couch was overturned and the shelves emptied of books. The TV was in pieces on the floor. CDs and DVDs were scattered about like fallen leaves. The policewoman looked at the policeman and then both looked at Adam and Jorie. When and where did you last see the baby? the policeman asked.

Adam pointed to a place on the floor, which was approximately the middle point between the two places where he believed he last saw the baby, but Jorie patted her shoulder. The police officers exchanged looks again and ordered them to stay in the kitchen while they searched the rest of the ransacked house. They came back into the kitchen and Adam shouted at the officers and fell on the floor, thrashing and biting like a sick animal. We smell that you have sleeping in you! When they tried to handcuff him to the table leg, Jorie screamed and threw herself on the back of the policeman. The policewoman grabbed her by the throat and slammed her to the floor. They were both left facedown on the floor, hands cuffed behind them.

The police couple went outside and began searching the yard, shed, and garage. Adam could see their flashlight beams cutting at the air. The officers must have split up, searching different areas of the house, because they could hear the policewoman call to her partner, saying she'd found something.

Oh, Jesus, they heard her say.

T H E N they were staring at each other with the same idea burning behind their eyes. 🜛

TRUE ENOUGH

Cheston Knapp

Look! Up in the sky! It's a . . . wait, what is that?

"Why do my eyes behold the sky and not my feet? It is because my eyes are more like the sky than my feet."
—SAINT BERNARD

On June 24, 1947, pilot Kenneth Arnold was flying alone from Chehalis, Washington, to Yakima. The wide, bright sky was sharp-edged and vast as a hallucination. Arnold decided to spend some time searching for a marine transport plane that had gone down, lost in the mountains west-southwest of Mount Rainier. After an hour of circling, empty-eyed of any jetsam, he nosed his plane back to Yakima. He hadn't flown this homeward course but a minute or two when a tremendous pulse of light enfolded his plane. Before he could count his thoughts and scan the sky, another thunderless bolt of lightning

lit his cockpit. But this time the corner of his eye caught where it was coming from. East. Toward the mountains. He focused his gaze, and against Rainier's stark-white snowfield there appeared a chain of nine peculiar aircraft careening southbound over the ridged, rocky vertebrae of the Cascade Range.

He'd never seen anything fly like these things flew. They were semicircular and arranged in a geese's V and seemed linked together. They darted through the valleys in between the smaller mountain peaks. Every so often, individual crafts would flip and flash against the snow and sky, and while dark in profile, when the sun reflected off their highly polished surfaces, his cockpit glowed blindingly, like a revelation. When seen on edge, they were blade-thin, nearly

invisible. But perhaps most astonishing was their speed. Arnold later figured they were flying at about 1,700 miles per hour, almost three times faster than any manned craft had gone in 1947.[1] Asked later to describe their flight, Arnold said they looked like speedboats racing over rough water. But he captured the public's imagination and forever embedded a bogey into its consciousness when he added, "They flew like a saucer would if you skipped it across the water."

⊷ — ⊶

"The UFO phenomenon comes in waves," Keith Rowell said, while we sat on his back deck in West Linn, Oregon, a suburb of Portland. "There's always a background of stuff going on, but there are peak times of activity."

With wispy white hair cropped close to his head and a well-kept, matching mustache, Keith could double for a late-career Richard Dreyfuss. During longer pauses, when he'd compose answers to my questions, I half expected, and more than half hoped, he'd start quoting *Close Encounters of the Third Kind*. His little dachshund-beagle mutt lay mutely curled in his lap. Rocks were randomly arranged on a glass table, and Keith never offered to explain them. He's sixty-three years old, a retired technical writer, and has been studying UFOs since 1974. Now, he serves as assistant state director of the Oregon chapter of MUFON, the Mutual UFO Network—an international organization whose mission is "the scientific study of UFOs for

the benefit of humanity." He has created, and maintains, an exceedingly informative Web site under the auspices of the group. In the way I badly want Ohio to be a palindrome, I'm teased, tortured by how close Keith Rowell's name comes to being a perfect "aptronym." Like Ms. Booker, the librarian, or Dr. Fingers, the gynecologist, he is one letter short of being Mr. Roswell, the UFOlogist.

"The Roswell crash," Keith continued, "came more or less at the beginning of the 1947 wave."[2] Between June 14 and July 14 alone that year, there were more than 830 reported sightings. Some headlines from the time read: "FLYING DISCS ARE SIGHTED BY HUNDREDS"; " 'SKY DEVIL-SHIP' SCARES PILOTS; AIR CHIEF WISHES HE HAD ONE"; "FLYING SAUCER MYSTERY GROWS"; "FLYING SAUCERS EVERYWHERE; NEW TALES CONVERT SKEPTICS"; "FLYING SAUCERS TO BE HUNTED DOWN"; "RAAF CAPTURES FLYING SAUCER ON RANCH IN ROSWELL REGION"; "ARMY SAYS HAS DISC."

To this day, according to Keith, we know very little for certain about the events at Roswell, and much of its appeal and intrigue lie in the persistence of the mystery that surrounds even the most basic facts about them. "There were one, possibly two crash sites within a fifty-to-seventy-mile radius of town," Keith said. "And we still

---

1 Chuck Yeager would not officially break the sound barrier until October of that year, at a speed of roughly half what Arnold estimated for the craft he saw.

2 The modern era of the UFO really began during WWII, but Arnold's was the first sighting to make national and even international news.

don't know the exact date of the crash." I'm convinced that, as a smoker develops a rasp, the nasally, muted, nerdy quality of his voice is the consequence of hours and hours of UFO research. That puzzling process has occurred between him and his dog whereby people come to look like their animals. "If you decided to grind through all the books about Roswell—and it'd take you about a year—you'd find that people report it as happening sometime between July 2 and July 5." And all roads lead, very quickly, to the government's involvement in maintaining this mystery.

The story's beginning, by now, is well known. A rancher named Mac Brazel found some debris from a crash on his farm. He came to town a day later and told the sheriff, who in turn told military personnel—the only atomic bomb unit in America at the time was stationed in Roswell. Lesser known, perhaps, are the events that followed. News traveled through the chain of command that too many civilians had caught wind. Questions needed answering. General Roger Ramey approved a press release written by Walter Haut, the public information officer, so the story goes.[3] Keith dispensed these names and the sequence of events with the careful, studied ease of a history professor. "The press release is short," Keith said. "It's just around a hundred words or so, and goes something like, 'A flying disc was captured today outside of Roswell and it was sent to higher headquarters.'[4] This is big. It's the only time in history that any U.S. government agency—the air

force, CIA, NSA, DIA, whatever—has ever issued an official document that acts as if the flying-saucer stuff is real."

— — —

The first person to define "delusion" for psychiatry was Karl Jaspers. He outlined three main criteria for doctors to look for when diagnosing one. First, the patient believes with utmost certainty. Jaspers went so far as to reject the idea that a delusion consists simply of a patient's false beliefs about his situation. Rather, delusions are a particular kind of knowledge. Second, the patient is incorrigible, unfazed by any compelling argument. The third and final criterion is the belief's impossibility, bizarreness, or flat-out falsity. Many movies and stories toy with this fine-line distinction—the paranoid, persecuted person is cast as an eccentric loon early on until it's revealed via dramatic peripeteia that in fact he *is* being

3 Reading about these events, and about UFOs in general, is like finding yourself in a narrow, smoke-filled, he-said–she-said hall of mirrors so mind-bendingly anfractuous that it feels like it must debouch into a nuthouse somewhere. It's a melodrama with all the trappings and trimmings—posthumous affidavits, sworn denials, supposed character assassinations— wherein factual truth hinges on whom your gut tells you to trust. In whom can you place your faith?

4 The press release begins: "The many rumors regarding the flying disc became a reality yesterday when the intelligence officer of the 509th Bomb Group of the Eighth Air Force, Roswell Army Air Field, was fortunate enough to gain possession of a disc." Even cursory research into Roswell like this gets you thinking twice about the government's explanation that the crash was nothing more than a downed weather balloon.

watched. *Terminator*, *Conspiracy Theory*, countless episodes of *The Twilight Zone* (e.g., Shatner and his gremlin in "Nightmare at 20,000 Feet"), and on and on. But, furthermore, "impossibility" and "bizarreness" introduce an element of doubt. Questions are begged. "Bizarre" to whom? What about religion? Spirituality? What about the entire spectrum of suprascientific phenomena? At what point and along what lines can faith be considered delusional?

> "I think I would be remiss if I didn't remind you that UFOs are thin ice material. Don't fall in."

— ◦ — — ◦ — — ◦ —

In our early e-mail correspondence, after learning of my intention to write an essay on MUFON and, more particularly, his involvement with it, Keith cautioned: "I think I would be remiss if I didn't remind you that UFOs are thin-ice material. Don't fall in. To maintain your reputation in establishment circles, standard practice says you should maintain a studied distance from the subject. The reality aspects are to be avoided or at most treated in a very circumspect way. Writing about what the culture of UFO 'believers' is like is just fine. 'Looky, here! This is what the freaks are like. How amusing!' That tone is just fine, but not the tone and style of a person who takes the subject seriously as if it should be treated by academia as a normal part of human experience and the world. Just be careful. A Pulitzer-Prize-winning

Harvard professor of psychiatry (John Mack) almost lost his tenure while in his sixties for treating UFOs seriously."

— ◦ — — ◦ — — ◦ —

The Oregon chapter of MUFON meets on the second Tuesday of every month. They rent a conference room, Muir Hall, from Mount Tabor Presbyterian Church, in southeast Portland. To help pay for the room and other group needs, MUFON asks for a three-dollar donation to attend its meetings. But twenty-one dollars buys you a full membership and includes a subscription to the organization's monthly journal.

Keith sat behind a table at the front of the room, beside our leader, State Director Tom. On the night's agenda was a MUFON-produced movie presentation. But the schedule first allowed for an open round-table discussion. People talked among themselves, though often loud enough for all fifteen of us to hear, as though casting out a line to see who might bite.

"I can feel it," said the boisterous Italian man in a baseball hat. "The world is uniting under the banner of antidebunkerism."

The man wearing a camouflage Hawaiian shirt said, "We can't destroy consciousness. Not even in chickens." He said he could prove chickens have souls: Take a chicken, any chicken. Cut off its head. If you point it to the south, he said, it would flap about wildly. But if you point it north, it'd go calmly about its headless business. Try it.

"Are you farsighted?"

"Of course."

"Suppose humanity has an expiration date?" a man in sweatpants said, and, when no one answered, "I think it's time for the bees to take over. The honeybees."

"I'm trying to secure ten thousand debunker-buster bombs from the Pentagon! Who's with me?"

Chicken Guy said that when we die, our bodies become lighter, that something measurable escapes us. "It's not just like a fart, either."

Someone exclaimed excitedly: "Do you know the role of bismuth in antigravity?"

The woman next to me called to a man across the room, "But you might not have any conscious memory of being abducted." He replied, "True enough." And they both appeared to ruminate on that epistemological chestnut.

Tom called the meeting to attention. Before starting the movie presentation, he encouraged people to watch the premiere of a television show called *The Event* on NBC. A flutter of excited assent rippled through the room. He reminded everyone, though, how often the media had burned them in the past. Did anyone recall the hatchet job Peter Jennings did back in '05? Yes. Almost everyone did.

> "I'm trying to secure ten thousand debunker-buster bombs from the Pentagon! Who's with me?"

The lights were then shut off, the movie begun. What followed was a two-hour documentary lecture that recounted the eerie goings-on of late December 1980, at RAF Bentwaters, the air force base in England's Rendlesham Forest. Tom had described this as England's Roswell, maybe even bigger. The documentary's purpose was to debunk the debunkers' "explanations" for the strange, mysterious lights that appeared in the sky and the top-secret cover-up that immediately ensued.

The movie was based on such exacting investigation, such thoroughgoing attention to detail—to minutiae, really—that for many of the MUFONites there in the dark of Muir Hall the affect was largely soporific. About thirty minutes in, I looked across the room and could make out the Italian anti-debunker with his arms crossed, his chin in his chest, eyes closed. Two others at the end of his table had their heads down. There was deep mouth breathing coming from someone on my side of the room. At just over an hour, we lost radio contact with our leader, Tom. Through it all, Keith was a wide-eyed hoot owl.

The movie ended and the credits rolled. A handful of people clapped. Someone flipped the lights on and there was a nervous, startled rustle of stretching and eye rubbing and seat adjusting.

"So," Tom said as he stood, "any questions?"

The room erupted in gleeful laughter.

The first people to speak up asked about plot details, as though trying to piece together a thriller's twists and turns. "What happened to the camera?" "Did he ever get to see the pictures he took?" "How long was he unconscious?"

Deeper speculation began when someone brought up the topic of time travel. The events in Rendlesham Forest, as well as those at Roswell, present a knotty nexus of past, present, and future. The spacecrafts must have the ability to tap into whatever it is we understand as time and manipulate it, or themselves within it. The knot-of-time analogy provoked questions about memory retrieval and hypnosis. A number of people wanted badly and very earnestly to know whether memory blocks could be implanted in us, preventing us from accessing certain parts of our own histories. Every question seemed to present an equation that had one too many variables to solve.

"No one knows how it's done," Keith said. "But it is."

Someone opined, "This is strange beyond the limits of imagination."

A Russian lady in back who'd come in late said, with a heavy accent, "They decide what's real for us."

Keith agreed that the intelligence and security around these events are airtight and strictly need-to-know. He said the government ran "deep black projects," about which we'll likely never know the full story.

The man in sweatpants sadly said, "Man, we'll never know what's real. It's just gonna be a headbanger's ball until the end of eternity."

"This goes deep," Keith said to end the meeting. "So deep that it's really about consciousness and the nonrational world. It's not irrational but there are no so-called 'answers.'"

—◆——◆——◆—

"We have left the land and have embarked. We have burned our bridges behind us—indeed, we have gone farther and destroyed the land behind us ... Woe, when you feel homesick for the land as if it had offered more *freedom*—and there is no longer any 'land.'"

—NIETZSCHE, *The Gay Science*

—◆——◆——◆—

"He was sorry I had not properly appreciated the true source of religious sentiments. This, he says, consists in a peculiar feeling ... which he would like to call a sensation of 'eternity,' a feeling as of something limitless, unbounded—as it were, 'oceanic.'"

—FREUD, *Civilization and Its Discontents*

—◆——◆——◆—

In the shell of a Rendlesham Forest or a Roswell rest the two parts of what, for Keith, make up the nut of the UFO phenomenon: paranormal activity and government involvement. And of these two, the paranormal fascinates him more. "The more the UFO is studied, the more it seems to lead to the world of the paranormal," Keith writes on the MUFON Web site.

"Practically no contemporary UFOlogists think that UFOs and the apparent intelligence that guides them are completely limited to 'physical reality' as that is defined and understood by modern science."

In 1974, Keith was twenty-seven and, having recently finished a degree in library science, was working as a library clerk for the Portland public school system, when a couple of books about UFOs came across his desk. "It turns out that 1973 was a huge year. Lots of activity," he said. "So in '74 the publishers were responding to the public's interest." Growing up, he had a natural aptitude for science, and strange and weird factoids always intrigued him—he relished *Ripley's Believe It or Not.* He took the books home and started reading.

But UFOs acted as a gateway drug of sorts. "Unfortunately for me," Keith said, "I kept reading." We met at his home, in part, so he could give me a tour of his library, which he wanted to save for last, after we finished on the deck, like a dramatic unveiling. He had told me in our correspondence about the shelves that line his entire basement as though part of an elaborate fortification, on which sit over fifteen hundred books. The lion's share are about UFOs, and almost all of them cover one of many topics that fall under the umbrella of the paranormal, like telepathy, ghosts, out-of-body experiences, clairvoyance, et cetera. I couldn't wait to see them all. He guessed fewer than thirty people in the world had the same collection.

"Transpersonal World Phenomena," he said. "That's the big overarching concept. You'll never really understand UFOs without a serious study of that."

Keith asked me to imagine myself as a boat on an inconceivably vast ocean, a body of water that nowhere touches a shore. It's empty as far as the eye can see. The color of the water suggests a depth beyond reckoning. Every once in a while, the boat will spring a leak. Water will trickle or rush in, depending on how large the hole. He said the boat is our incarnated body and everything that attends having a body—pain, memories, love, appetites, and so on. And the ocean is the transpersonal realm just beyond us. The boat's job is to hold the water out. But sometimes it fails. We experience a breach. And in those moments, we taste some part of our true potential as perceiving beings.

When I asked whether a person, as a boat, could take on too much water and therefore surely sink, Keith said, "There are levels and layers of the other world. Multidimensions or however you want to say it." Metaphors mix and must all fail somewhere. And I couldn't help but realize, as he took me on this guided visualization, that the bottom really drops out of the UFO phenomenon at an alarming rate.

Scuba divers sometimes talk about going so far down that their water world is all the same dark color, or of finding themselves caught up in a kelp bed and surrounded by weedy green, and that in such moments they can become so disoriented as to no longer be able to discern up from down. The mind in such moments of crescendo-like panic must grasp after anything to settle its nauseating vertigo. This calls to memory the first time I read, with true terror, the section of *Moby Dick* called "The Castaway," in which Pip, tender-hearted deck hand, falls overboard. Melville writes, "The intense concentration of self in the middle of such a heartless immensity, my God! who can tell it?" And he goes on to describe how Pip responds, after his rescue, in a flight of lyricism that has haunted me for years and strikes me as incredibly apt and therefore worth quoting at length:

The sea had jeeringly
kept his finite body up,
but drowned the infinite of his soul.
Not drowned entirely, though. Rather
carried down alive to wondrous depths,
where strange shapes of the unwarped
primal world glided to and fro before
his passive eyes; and the miser-mer-
man, Wisdom, revealed his hoarded
heaps; and among the joyous, heart-
less, ever-juvenile eternities, Pip saw
the multitudinous, God-omnipresent,
coral insects, that out of the firmament
of waters heaved the colossal orbs. He
saw God's foot upon the treadle of the
loom, and spoke it; and therefore his
shipmates called him mad. So man's in-
sanity is heaven's sense; and wandering
from all mortal reason, man comes at
last to that celestial thought, which, to
reason, is absurd and frantic; and weal
or woe, feels then uncompromised,
indifferent as his God.

I couldn't help but realize that the bottom really drops out of the UFO phenomenon at an alarming rate.

On Keith's deck, in the fading light of the setting sun, a slight chill had whipped up. Wind chimes tinkled their irrational music. Keith's dog readjusted itself in his lap. We'd head inside soon, for the tour, and, feeling I might have let the conversation stray too far afield, I asked about the intelligence that must guide UFOs.

"The UFO phenomenon can't be completely explained in simple terms as 'space people' from outer space, very much like us, coming to visit earth," he said, more or less quoting his Web site. "It's much more than that, and maybe not even that at all."

"I guess I'd like to try to ground this in some concrete thing," I said.

Keith laughed a laugh that was more like a scoff and said, "Good luck!"

— — —

"There are higher and lower limits of possibility set to each personal life. If a flood but goes above one's head, its absolute elevation becomes a matter of small importance; and when we touch our own upper limit and live in our own highest center of energy, we may call ourselves saved, no matter how much higher some one else's center may be."
—WILLIAM JAMES,
The Varieties of Religious Experience

— — —

If you want to study UFOs and the paranormal systematically, as Keith has done for the better part of his life, you must first fight through a system of defense made up of and reinforced by at least three different parts.

The first hurdle is found in the fact that the knowledge out in the world about UFOs is a mixed bag of accurate information, misinformation, and what's called *dis*information, which is false information spread by the government deliberately to mislead. Complicating matters further is the fact that, in order to be more readily believed, disinformation is spun out of partially true and patently false information. Cutting through the blubber-like buildup of these illusions, unraveling the truth from all the lies, can take years and years of intense, solitary investigation. As Keith laid this out for me, I kept thinking of that classic one-liner: "I'm paranoid. But am I paranoid enough?"

The second apparent obstacle can be thought of as a corollary to disinformation, and that is the refusal by mainstream science and academia to consider and study seriously the UFO phenomenon and the paranormal. It's this difficulty that seems to cut closest to Keith's heart. "They've shipped us to the intellectual ghetto," he

> No fight is complete without a worthy opponent, and the great and sworn enemy of the seeker after the truth of UFOs is the debunker.

said. Anything that might be categorized as paranormal falls under "abnormal psychology," which only serves to magnify the already prevalent stigma against such an experience of the world. "UFOs have *not* been proved beyond a reasonable *scientific* doubt to exist," he writes on his Web site. "The scientific establishment must engage in serious, long-term study of UFOs to prove this one way or the other. Sadly, the scientific establishment has decided to be intellectually dishonest and avoid this study." And there's a rich history of such scientific disregard. In 1995, New York Review Books released *The Hidden Histories of Science*, which has essays by Stephen Jay Gould, Oliver Sacks, and other popular scientists, each of which describes discoveries or breakthroughs that, when first presented, were overlooked by the scientific community of their time, and remained so in some cases for as long as a century.

Now, no fight is complete without a worthy opponent, and the great and sworn enemy of the seeker after the truth of UFOs is the debunker. The debunker stands on the shifting sands of his strident skepticism and discounts entirely the world of the paranormal. Western rationality reigns over him. He trumpets the triumphs of what he calls "reason." "His extreme skepticism," Keith said, "is used as a protective mechanism so that certain subjects are never looked into." This tack, though, is reinforced by pretty much all the major advancements of our time. "Look around," Keith said. "This world we live in was built by applying practical science to our environment. It's powerful stuff." But this power comes at the expense of a broad field of vision regarding humans' true potential for experience. And it's under the sway of such power that we have been brought up and encouraged by science to question to the point of delirious nonsense the whole notion of truth and what that might mean. We are discouraged from asking: If such severe doubt shatters the ground we stand on without replacing it with anything, does that doubt necessarily enlighten us? Is it not possible that it, in fact, corrupts some forms of knowledge?

Keith explained society's tendency to cast the UFO believer as delusional, or out of touch with reality, or a loon, as being the result of an alliance between systematic disinformation and hard-core debunkerism.[5] The government's various intelligence agencies have infiltrated all manner of media outlets, Hollywood in particular, and are devoted to clouding the public's knowledge about these phenomena, diluting their power. Take, for example, *Men in Black*, which has its roots in the real reported appearances of such mysterious men. *The Event*, the show the MUFONites were stoked about, uses disinformation ("What do we tell the public?") from the get-go as one of its many narrative rocket boosters.[6] Keith said it was common knowledge among UFOlogists that certain debunkers have even been

on government payroll, like Carl Sagan, for instance, who, in a Faustian turn, defected to the dark side in order to obtain insider knowledge that continues to be withheld from the public. He could know, but couldn't tell anyone what he knew. The idea here is that as long as the public associates these stories with fiction, *make-believe*—what overtones, that phrase—there's no danger to them, no chance of them being taken seriously. But the situation is then primed for a rhetorical do-si-do, the old syllogistic two-step: if disinformation is part of our world, and if a delusion can be derived from deception, as it's commonly classified, then UFOlogists have just as much right to call society delusional for its strict, stubborn adherence to the idea that UFOs *don't* exist.

The last line of defense against understanding the UFO phenomenon is the one that's closest to you and therefore hard-

---

5 A 1953 study commissioned by the CIA, the Robertson Panel, concluded that a public relations campaign should be undertaken to "debunk" UFOs in order to reduce public interest in them.

6 This show is so impressively bad it's borderline offensive. The main characters are everywhere demanding to know "the truth," but the show sacrifices any notion of seeking in favor of overblown and unbelievable one-note emotions. So, in addition to peddling factual falsities, I'd have to ask Keith if such blatant badness counts as a subcategory of disinformation, i.e., whether emotional dishonesty and silly melodrama of this sort can be suspected of compromising the seriousness of such an impassioned search, in the public's subconscious, of course. Contra *The Event* stands David Lynch's unflinching *Twin Peaks*, which, as it dove deeper and deeper into the paranormal through its second season, alienated and lost much of the audience that had made it a national hit. What does *that* tell you?

est to combat: your own mind's makeup. "Paranormal or occult phenomena of the type I'm talking about are most like religious phenomena," Keith said. "They're mostly ephemeral, hard to conceptualize. They're in the perceptual world. And the problem is they don't happen every day, so therefore don't have a close connection with ordinary human experience." Keith summed this up well with his boat analogy. Hearing him explain his ideas brought to mind Henri Bergson, the late-nineteenth–early-twentieth-century philosopher, who helped turn classical models of perception on their head when he argued that, rather than being productive, the brain's function, with respect to the nervous system and sensory organs, is largely eliminative. In illustration, Bergson also argued against the idea that film depicts a perfectly reliable picture of reality. He questioned what happened in the moments *between* each film still, the whole process that created the illusion of movement. The metaphoric leap isn't hard to make: a person's mind is a projector's light, his perceptions the individual film stills. What escapes him as his brain creates the world?

As boats, our incarnated bodies must keep water out. And so there are shades of meaning, in other words, when people say they're "open-minded" to things like UFOs and the paranormal.

— — —

"Reason must acknowledge that its world is also unfinished and should not pretend to have overcome that which it has managed simply to conceal."

—MERLEAU-PONTY,
The World of Perception

— — —

"It is a curious enigma that so great a mind would question the most obvious realities and object even to things scientifically demonstrated . . . while believing absolutely in his own fantastic explanations of the same phenomena."

—FLANN O'BRIEN, *The Third Policeman*

— — —

"See, the key to me is that it's all up here, intellectually," Keith said. We had moved to his basement. Just as I had imagined, there were books everywhere. Most were neatly arranged on floor-to-ceiling shelves that might have been load-bearing. They were arranged by subject, alphabetized by author—Keith does hold a degree in library science, after all. There were two stacks of more than one hundred duplicates that he did not count toward his total collection. As he took me through the tour, I picked a book at random off the shelf nearest me: *Sex and the Paranormal*. I put it back, now even more confused about something I'd thought I was beginning to understand. "I'm not an experiencer type person," he continued. "I want to figure it all out from a rational point of view. That's probably why I was attracted to science."

Keith admitted that maybe as high as 95 percent of UFO sightings could be explained by simple scientific means. But the cases that intrigue him, of course, are the 5 percent that, after rigorous investigation, cannot be explained; the truly mysterious ones, those that mainstream science persistently overlooks. I had sat down in a recliner, he on the couch. Keith looked at the chair a few times in a way that might be described as longingly, but when I offered it to him, he said, no, no, it wasn't his chair, but did I know it could lean back?

There have been official scientific studies, of course, most famously one commissioned by the air force that came to be called Project Blue Book.[7] But they have all ended badly, Keith explained. None worse than Blue Book, which in over twenty years rolled through director after director, each of who brought a varying degree of commitment to the intellectual rigor of investigation. The government closed it down in 1969, after the results came back from a panel the air force commissioned, headed by physicist Edward Condon. The report ran more than 1,400 pages in hardcover, and concluded, once and for all: "Nothing has come from the study of UFOs in the past 21 years that has added to scientific knowledge . . . Further extensive study of UFOs probably cannot be justified in the expectation that science will be advanced thereby."

But the investigation is shrouded in controversy. That equivocating "probably"

> The parallel struck me that, like Keith, UFOlogy has been driven down into the basement.

screams out to Keith & co. The study's methodology begs many questions. The shadow of the Robertson Panel, its emphasis on debunkerism, looms. "If you read the Condon Report closely," Keith said, "you discover that it contradicts many of Project Blue Book's own findings, set out in special report number 14." UFOlogists point to these things as the writing on the wall; the Condon Report has been weighed and found wanting. But regardless, its pronouncement sounded a death knell for official involvement, not to mention the fact that it shattered UFOlogists' hope for any sort of mainstream scientific acceptance. And since then, all serious study of UFOs has been driven underground and is pursued only by maverick scientists, who in doing so risk societal stigma and even their careers. The parallel struck me that, like Keith, UFOlogy has been driven down into the basement.

As a kind of proof, Keith asked me, "Do you believe in pink elephants? Do you believe in unicorns? Do you believe in Superman?" No, of course not. No reasonable person would answer yes to any of these questions. Yet, he said, he could

---

7 Keith had never seen *Twin Peaks*, two of whose characters, Major Briggs and Windom Earle, worked for Project Blue Book. I told him I bet he'd approve of its depiction of the paranormal, that he wouldn't consider it disinformation, and felt, however briefly, I had contributed.

ask twenty random people on the street whether they'd ever had an experience with the paranormal—had they seen a ghost? A UFO? Ever had an out-of-body experience?—and at least two of those twenty would say yes, they had. In my own experience, I've been amazed by how readily people will say they believe there's life on other planets, as even Stephen Hawking said in early 2010, and yet still their eyes will roll and they'll scoff when you ask them about UFOs. Why is that?

All this presented an unavoidable question to me, there in Keith's basement: how might the process scientists use to distill truth and knowledge from their perceptions be distinct from, and better than, the ways we arrive at truth in other human endeavors? And how is it that discoveries can come to be overlooked, even ignored?

In 1796, the British Royal Astronomer Nevil Maskelyne fired his assistant, Kinnebrook, for persistently recording the passage of stars more than half a second later than he, his boss. But Kinnebrook insisted he'd done nothing wrong, had been unjustly relieved of his post. Through protests that followed this dismissal, scientists developed the idea of the "personal equation" to account for such minor perceptual discrepancies that occur between people. This notion bewitched nineteenth-century scientists working to standardize systems of measurement, and later greatly influenced the work of many early- to mid-twentieth-century philosophers and scientists. One such thinker, Karl Popper, believed that statements of direct experience, as such, could be infinitely questioned. The logical end of this was that "the basic statements . . . which we decide to accept as satisfactory, and as sufficiently tested, have admittedly the character of dogmas." So if not exactly faith-based, science does appear to assume this religious aspect.

And, arguing the limits of artificial intelligence, Michael Polanyi cited a photo finish from a horse race. The photo shows one horse's head just a fraction of an inch in front of the other's. But, he said, the verdict still could not be clearly established, because from the flappygummed, bucktoothed mouth of the other horse swung a six-inch rope of spit. Well ahead of the finish line. The rules didn't account for such a situation, and the final decision had to be referred to a jury of Jockey Club members.

Though improvements may be made to methodology, or to the technology involved, the personal, interpretational dimension of science can never be removed. Even the most seemingly objective methods of observation can result in vagueness and ambiguity. Rather than being able to rely on objectivity—especially after the physics of relativity—science at its best can attain

> Even the most seemingly objective methods of observation can result in vagueness and ambiguity.

only the strong intersubjectivity of the scientific method. Scientific knowledge may advance only when the twin wheels of trust and consensus spin together. We are always already caught up in the world, and come to know it and ourselves by the very fact that we cannot abstract away from either. Robinson Crusoe could not arrive at scientific knowledge, strictly speaking. (What if he were color-blind?) His findings would have to be agreed upon and accepted by a community of scientists. And such a community could choose to ignore his findings, no matter how true they might prove to be in the future. There's a kind of existential truism at the heart of all this: everyone is alone and yet nobody can do without other people. And we, as individuals, can only hope to see not too subjectively, and strive to account for the personal equation by better knowing our peculiar selves.

When I asked Keith what he hoped for with respect to science's involvement with the UFO, he said, "I don't think rationality is ultimately up to the task of giving us a full understanding of the UFO or paranormal phenomena. But we're very far from knowing that." He stood from the couch. It was time to end our interview. "I can tell you what, though," he said. "It's amazing what you won't know if you don't ask. I think the UFO phenomenon is the biggest open secret of them all."

─◆─ ─◆─ ─◆─

The skywatch run by Keith's friend Randy was scheduled to meet at 4:00 P.M. in Nan-sen Summit Park, which is nothing more than the small, flattened top of a dormant shield volcano in Lake Oswego, Oregon. It's less a park than a scenic viewpoint. I'd heard and read enough by then not to be surprised by much of anything relating to UFOs, including the fact that we were to meet during the day.

I was the first to get there. The park had one bench. I stood on it and turned slowly around and could see almost all of Portland, out to the Cascade and Coastal mountain ranges in either direction. The sky felt high up and was quite blue and seemed to go on forever. Only a little haze hung out around the mountains. Keith had told me it'd be prudent to bring a camera, so I had my Sony point-and-shoot with me.

Going in, I didn't know what to expect from the skywatch. There'd been a flurry of news stories about UFOs. A book had recently been published called *UFOs: Generals, Pilots, and Government Officials Go on the Record*, which consists of exactly what its title suggests. I watched the author's appearance on *The Colbert Report* and was impressed by how Colbert didn't dismissively demolish her like I've seen him do to other author guests. The rumors flying around the Internet about the United Nations' plans to appoint an ambassador of alien affairs were still more intriguing. People I'd had conversations with about UFOs started e-mailing me all sorts of articles. Did I see what Stephen Hawking said? What about these generals? What did I make of *The Event*? All this was kicking around in the back of my mind. Did I expect to see something?

Would I believe it if I did? And if not, why? I couldn't say. "Some persons," William James writes, "never are, and possibly never under any circumstances could be, converted."

I sat back down on the bench. I scanned the sky and, sure enough, I saw something hovering out to the west, toward the Coastal Mountains. I literally sat on the edge of my seat. I squinted to try to see through the faint haze. A bubble rose in my chest. I could feel my heart beating. A here-we-go sensation of anxious excitement washed over me like a crashing wave. The bubble grew. I got my camera out. I made small adjustments to my position in attempts to bring the object into sharper relief. The object grew larger in the sky, drew closer. But the thrill of the moment passed. I burped. It was just a helicopter.

Keith arrived with his camera hung around his neck, his hand out to support its two-foot telephoto lens. He had a camera bag slung from his shoulder. He wore a vest and sun hat and looked ready for a safari of sorts. When he got to the top, he asked, "You the only one here?"

I looked around and, seeing no one, said, "Yeah." I sheepishly slipped my camera back in my bag.

"A couple months ago there were almost thirty of us." He talked about how Randy had a psychic connection to UFOs. They seemed to materialize when he was around, even to follow him. It was only a matter of time before people figured that out.

"Here he comes," Keith said. He fiddled with his camera's settings.

Randy walked up, wearing a black T-shirt on which appeared an artsy representation of the Eiffel Tower done in silver and faint glitter. Keith made introductions. Randy's camera, too, had a massive lens. In my chest I felt a pang of lens envy.

"Where is everyone?" Randy asked.

"I don't know," Keith said. "Looks like it'll just be the three of us."

I told them about my experience with the helicopter. They both laughed. "Don't worry," Randy said. "We got blimped out here last time."

Randy had a Southern accent, was from Tennessee, and we bonded over our common heritage. Keith reminded us exactly what that heritage was by making Civil War jokes. Randy said UFOs were a recent fascination of his, that he'd only become interested in them a few years ago. He talked about something called a kundalini experience and a fire snake at the bottom of his spine and the opening of his third eye—all well predating his study of UFOs. He said he'd seen auras since he was young. "I saw a red aura around my nephew," he said. But he broke off midthought and pointed his colossal lens to the sky and, according to an unknowable logic, fired off about twenty shots at the sky. Keith followed suit and hoisted his camera and shot the same area. Their cameras' shutters clicked away like very small automatic weapons. I looked around excitedly. What was happening? I tried to follow where they were shooting. Was this my moment? What did they see? But they both stopped before I could zero in on what they were shooting. Randy resumed his thought as though nothing had happened, "He turned out to be a pretty famous artist."

"Wait a second," I said. "Just what was that all about?"

Randy explained that he doesn't actually see many of the UFOs he captures on film. They're either too small to see with the naked eye or too fast. He practices a deeper kind of vision in order to see them. His methodology involves this "banging away at the sky with his camera" and then checking out later what he's caught. And the two of them continued to do this while our conversation developed. I learned not to get excited when they abruptly broke off and took upward aim.

"We're gonna ask to see a UFO here today," Randy said, more than once. He sounded like a Baptist preacher.

"I'm sick of the round ones," Keith said. "I want to see a triangle."

I asked them what their families thought of UFOs, of the skywatches and MUFON meetings.

"Mine just thinks I'm delusional," Randy said.

"Just a weirdo thing Dad's into," Keith said.

After an hour and a half without seeing anything promising, Randy suggested we go back to his place to check out some recent photos, ones that even Keith hadn't seen yet. His house was only a

Through the series, he had captured the unbelievable movement of these circles.

five-minute drive away. When we got there, Randy had us take off our shoes before we headed to his office upstairs. The house smelled strongly of potpourri. Keith and I sat on the small couch in the office and watched, in the dark, as Randy scrolled through thousands and thousands of pictures of the sky. As thumbnails, they looked like pieces of a jigsaw puzzle from hell. Resized to fit the screen, though, you could see little flaws in each image. Randy then used a magnifying feature to make the flaw larger and larger on the screen. In some you could make out a semicircular shape surrounded by explosions of color or light. Others were nothing more than smudges of color. Some had distinctly nipple-like excrescences about their centers. Randy said he wanted to show me a series of pictures of what he called "the armada." But it was on another flash drive. He had four in a plastic bag. When he finally found the right one, he pulled up a picture of eleven black circles in front of a wall of clouds. Through the series, he had captured the unbelievable movement of these circles. And for the next twenty minutes, Randy showed us strange picture after strange picture. At one point, I looked over at Keith, and he said, simply, "Out of this world."

When I left Randy's house, trying to put everything in perspective, I thought that, like Pip, I had felt the bottom give way from under me. I had felt the first inklings of limitlessness that attends inquiry into that which has no bounds. I had lain awake in fear of such uncertainty, such utter and open possibility. In those moments I longed for land. I had woken up with my jaw sore from grinding my teeth. I had been set supine in a dentist's chair with four latex-gloved hands in my mouth, held open well past what was comfortable, my ears ringing with the drill's high squeal and the pneumatic whoosh and gurgle of the nubby-tipped suction tube, and I guessed then that this must be how abductees feel. I had thought: if Keith is not in it for the experiences, as many New Agers and occultists are, and if he believes reason and rationality are not ultimately up to the task of explaining these phenomena, then what's the point? To what end, all this study, all these photos? I had been haunted by the ideas of science and faith and by the parallel histories those twin giants have spun for us on the loom of time. And in the face of both, I returned over and again to the idea that Kierkegaard pitied his professors, whether of science or philosophy or theology, sad men who together bewitched the world with their cleverness, their proficiency, but who never got to experience that critical point in themselves where everything flipped on its head, after which one can only grow to appreciate more fully that there will always be something that one can never understand. My God! Who can tell it? 🜨

Raphael Allison

NEW VOICE

A COMMON MISUNDERSTANDING

The song poured over thorns and I took my time.
She was just a girl in the place of Ein Gedi.
She was a daughter, a rising cedar near the river
in Heshbon. I gave her gold rods and beryl,
warming balms and a singing cricket. And there was
this song. The men pull back. You've been away
too long, they say, in shanties, where it's news
to survive. This love is too early and too much.
We are roasting sardines over a fire of driftwood
and seaweed. Their eyes are buttons, I say, pointing.
These fish were unbuttoned from the sea
and just like this, she unbuttoned me. She was roughness
water washed from the rocks. I gave her cinnamon
and spikenard and she folded her veil above them.
She was torn from the wild springs and given
to Jordan. I could only provide her what I had
and the having there takes time. There were lilies
and perfect blossoms, wild grapes and beads
on oxtail cords. I found ointments for her skin
and clusters of henna in stone pitchers. There was
little else. I gave her a milking calf, and this song.
She was not good for this, the men say, eating now.
They strip the flesh straight from bone or swallow
the sardines whole by the head. The talk turns
to fishing and the abundance of fish to fish.

OUROBOROS

Eternity has no feet, I begin. It doesn't move.
No, that's not right: it contains all movement.
Eternity does cartwheels in its brine
but you'd have to be in a different eternity
to watch them. To us, sunk in eternity's gut
like intractable sesame seeds, it doesn't move.

Roy says when we die we all enter eternity.
Roy says he's read Saint Augustine. Roy says life
is expulsion, death a return. He says, eternity
is the center of a perfect cube with round edges.
If you ask some people about paradoxes, they
remain silent for a moment before answering.

Eternity is a snake, I continue. It's Ouroboros.
Eternity has plugged time with its rattle—no,
its tail. It needs no rattle because to rattle is to warn
and to warn implies sequence, cause and effect.
Upon eternity's tongue is a tongue of smooth tail,
striped gold and yellow, black and every color.

There's no coming and going, life and death.
It's everything all at once, like Wal-Mart or
a Robert Altman film. We don't come and go
in a house, we're not outside and then in.
We're picking oakum from your couch cushion
and talking. This is as eternity as it gets.

Roy doesn't buy it. We decide to go out. It's fall
and leaves are falling. Don't you think, he begins,
something else is out there? Not Rudy's? I ask.
No, no, something really else. How many stars
do you see in a lifetime? he tries, getting poetical.
Then we're silent until the first round of beers.

METAPHYSICS OF THE CAR

You move the car
and it moves you
parked in its gut
like the pit in a plum.
You make it turn
and stop short, back
up, French curve and
swivel. Sometimes
on wet roads at night
it whispers about
what happens when
a girl leaves a boy
or a man can't go on
without some other
and your ears listen
vaguely, your head atilt
as you drift eight inches
above this darkness
it lights in the nick of time.

As close to *caritas* as *cart*,
sometimes this hard body
for your soul lets a high
hill do all the work. Then,
you close your sleepy eyes
and hear a great rushing,
the enormous secret
you sit solemn and
still to unlearn.

NOIR
FOR A NEW CENTURY

Eddie Muller

One man's campaign for a redefinition of terms

Noir and Nostalgia:
A Back-Alley Meeting

Noir, that black tide of exquisite existential despair that washed over fiction and film in the post–World War II years, has reached its high-water mark of mainstream recognition. A measure of its resurgent popularity clearly stems from a younger audience discovering the superiority of mid-twentieth-century style in clothes, cars, furniture, architecture—almost everything. These days, however, noir's cloak of sexy sophistication is not only draped over any old crime or mystery movie, it's also used as a marketing term—albeit a vaguely defined one—in publishing, criticism, fashion, interior design, cocktail culture, you name it.

A period drama such as *Mad Men* is often tagged "noir," because the cast wears snazzy hats, drinks early and often, and smokes more than six Bogarts combined.

This acceptance is fine, inasmuch as it maintains the popularity of the original noir films, allowing a new generation to experience the efficient craftsmanship and artistic innovation that earlier storytellers such as Billy Wilder, Anthony Mann, and Joseph H. Lewis brought to well-scripted, modestly sized crime stories. It took Wilder a budget of less than one million dollars, after all, to change the course of movie history with *Double Indemnity*. The greatest B-film of all time, *Gun Crazy*, was

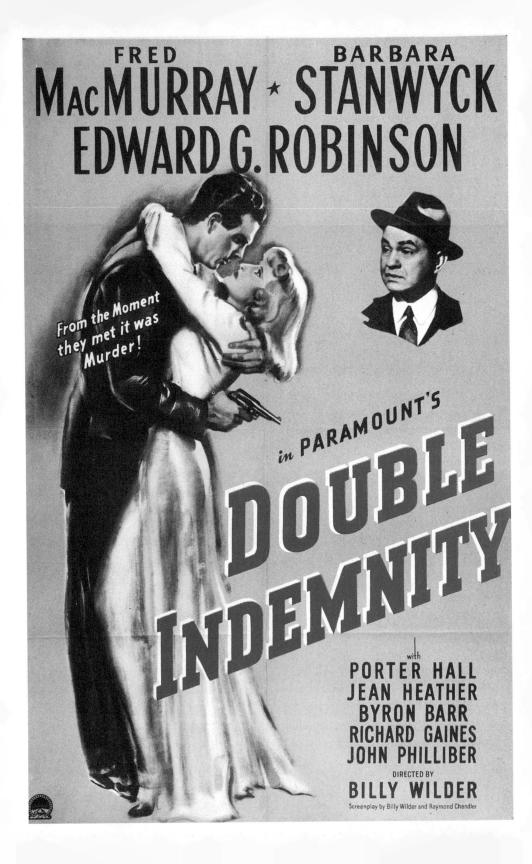

made by Lewis in fewer than thirty days, on a $400,000 budget.

The renewed appreciation for noir should not, however, regress into nostalgia; it would be antithetical to what made the noir movement exceptional in the first place. Films of the original era were (for the most part) contemporary tales, drawing dark power from the escalating sense of desperation, alienation, and anger many people felt as they tried to cope with a callous and chaotic modern society. The sinister allure of the cinematography—a surge of black-and-white splendor before the onslaught of color—lent itself perfectly to the crime genre, where fear and desire lurked in every shadow. It also represented, for Hollywood artists, a sneaky freedom from the constraints of the pubescent Production Code; film noir abandoned the sexless myth of happily-ever-after in favor of the dangerous delights and dreadful lessons found in a bitter, merciless world.

Film noir is where American pop culture lost its innocence and started growing up.

When contemporary filmmakers return to that era, they often miss the sanguine spirit of the original films because they focus—lovingly, obsessively—on surface details. During the past thirty-five years, only two American films have successfully re-created the classic noir era without wallowing in toothless nostalgia: *Chinatown*

(1974) and *L.A. Confidential* (1997). Both are about far more than style, exposing the modern American city's core of corruption. For the most part, though, making a forties-era noir now smacks of a longing for style over substance. Recent attempts at "period" noir, such as *The Good German, Lonely Hearts,* and *The Killer Inside Me,* have failed—sometimes artistically, always commercially. *The Black Dahlia* (2006) was the most disappointing. Adapted from James Ellroy's epic novel, the film starts as a hopelessly muddled crime drama and devolves into campy farce. Director Brian De Palma wasted a huge budget trying to get the window dressing right, while completely missing Ellroy's obsessive passion and genuine noir vision. Movies like these are a cowardly retreat from taking a hard-edged look at the darkness of our *contemporary* world. Time to hang up the fedora and move on.

New Paths to Dark Places

In its halcyon days, film noir was an entirely organic artistic movement. Writers and directors inspired each other with something new, an approach to storytelling more adult and dark and daring. Although they were often imitating each other, the writers, directors, cinematographers, and actors were also pushing the boundaries of what was possible. My favorite films of that era—*Sunset Blvd.* (1950), *In a Lonely Place* (1950), *Criss Cross* (1949), *Nightmare Alley* (1947), *Night and the City* (1950), *The Asphalt Jungle* (1950), *The Killing* (1956), *Force of Evil* (1948), *The Prowler* (1951)—pulled movies ahead and challenged the audience's complacent expectations, both narratively and stylistically. If noir is to retain its credibility, today's storytellers must be courageous enough to look for new ways of ushering people into their dark places.

The most successful example of this, to me, is David Lynch's mesmerizing *Mulholland Drive* (2001), which uses many of the tropes of traditional noir in an utterly fresh, spellbinding fashion. All of the genre's main thematic elements are present—uncontrolled passion, lost innocence, deceit, betrayal, clandestine conspiracies, hidden identities, a self-destructive protagonist—but it's all reconfigured by Lynch's unique dream logic, which leads viewers on a spiraling descent into the scariest and saddest parts of the human psyche.

Most people, to be honest, don't want to go there. It's the worst part of *Our Town*. While standard dramas weave in and out of that bad part of town, noir *lives* there, all day, every day. You go to that side of the tracks to explore how bad it can get for some people. That's why noir will always be marginal. Contemporary writers should realize that even as noir's iconography is homogenized and absorbed into the cultural bloodstream, noir itself will always be confined to the margins of the market. Efforts to make it palatable for wider consumption by focusing on its retro style rather than its timeless substance miss the point entirely, and undermine what is powerful and essential about this type of story.

Too many young writers turn out callow, churlish, adolescently violent books and films thinking they've caught noir's dark spirit. Noir has nothing to do with the level of ugliness and violence to which its creator will descend. A steeper body count or crueler and more cavalier behavior doesn't make a book or movie more *noir*. What characterizes genuine noir is not the depth of depravity depicted but the depth of empathy shown to characters who, through cruel fate or their own destructive natures, face dire life-and-death decisions.

Consider: A pair of adulterers who meet regularly for illicit sex hatch a plot to murder their spouses. If the teller of this tale makes the readers or viewers empathize (despite their better judgment) with these ill-fated lovers—*that's* noir. It doesn't need to be in black and white. You don't need Venetian-blind shadows on the wall. It doesn't matter if the woman's brassiere is vintage lace. You are empathizing with characters who have crossed into the darkness.

Noir does not call for ironic detachment—an attitude that affixed itself like a leech to most works labeled "neo-noir." Rather, it calls for the ultimate commitment: a willingness to go to the darkest places and remain compassionate in the face of hopelessness. It requires artists to be willing to walk in the steps of the doomed.

I propose, from here on out, that this should be the basis for labeling something

"noir," be it a book or a film. To that end, once and for all, let's separate the term *noir* from its progenitor, *film noir*. Let's concede that whenever people refer to film noir, they are thinking of a specific visual style from a specific historical era. Noir, however, continues to evolve. Like the best of the classic films and novels, it takes risks, pushes boundaries, and addresses our present moral predicaments.

A major theme of noir has always been identity—loss of identity, the danger of adopting a new identity, fear of the true face behind the mask—and this theme is being played out on a massive scale in America right now. Are we still the good guys? Will our moral certitude and righteousness be the very things that eventually destroy us? People are deeply afraid, on all ends of the social and political spectrums. Rather than trying to recycle the 1940s into escapist fantasy after escapist fantasy, perhaps the noir of our time should be addressing this very real fear. 🔱

BITTER
SWEETS

Edward Gauvin

An Introduction to Maurice Pons

We travel to France for well-kept secrets—this unknown wine, that local specialty—and certainly Maurice Pons is one of them. This retiring writer, known for the economy and discretion of his style, has been saluted by his peers as "one of the most quietly disturbing authors of the twentieth century," and inspired comparisons to Samuel Beckett, Malcolm Lowry, and Julien Gracq.

In 1955, his first collection, *Virginales* (Virginalia), drew the Catholic wrath of François Mauriac for the delicacy and subversion with which its stories limned the almost-unconscious awakening of childhood to sensual adolescence. The collection's final story, "Les Mistons," became the basis for François Truffaut's 1957 short film of the same name. Elegance, melancholy, and occasional wickedness became hallmarks of his prose.

His novels are altogether less reticent, more audacious affairs, featuring flagrantly supernatural conceits and interventions that might, in retrospect, be termed magic-realist. His best-known novel remains *Les Saisons* (Julliard, 1965); the American translation, *Seasons of the Ram*, was published by St. Martin's Press in 1977. The chronicle of a town beset by rain and ice for forty months at a time, it is animated by a powerful grotesquerie, and noted for its brutal, sublime atmosphere of marvelous unease. Nominated for that year's Prix Renaudot, it lost to Georges Perec's *Things*.

Pons has, since the seventies, the era of his profligacy, become something of a cult figure in French letters, his rare collections cause for delectation among a select readership. These tales, for which he is justly renowned, belong to what might be termed the "gentle impossible"; while most fantasy opens up a rift in reality, Pons is content to point out discreetly a crack in its seemly veneer. Often, he allows this crack the last word, and as W. H. Auden reminds us, "a crack in the teacup opens a lane to the land of the dead." From Pons, the teacup of our common sense emerges intact—the glaze of doubt suffices to hold it together—but the damage is irreparable; henceforth, having been shown how brittle it truly is, we are careful to set it down lightly. Pons has said that "literary creation . . . consists of distorting reality, cheating the real and the lived."

Death, that abrupt guest, enters all the stories in *Douce-Amère* (Bitter Sweets), from which "The Baker's Son" is taken. Uniformly in the first person, the stories often turn on some macabre or mystical coincidence, sometimes not disclosed

until the final line or paragraph, when both reader and narrator are faced with the blunt fact of it, impossible to dismiss. Nor is Pons above indulging, with a Roald Dahl cackle, judicious use of the twist ending, a narrative tactic still respected in France, if out of fashion in the States. And yet the best stories in the collection push past these twists to some rueful, yet unspoken, accommodation on the narrator's part with impossibility.

Since 1957, Pons has lived near the Moulin d'Andé in Normandy, a center for writers, musicians, and filmmakers where Truffaut shot the end of *Jules and Jim* and Perec finished writing *La Disparition*. His novels and collections have been reprinted multiple times by various publishers, and adapted for theater, dance, and film.

FICTION

THE
Baker's
Son

Maurice Pons

translated by Edward Gauvin

My father was a baker and the son of a baker. I was a boy when he took over, in turn, the only bakery in Saint-Gratien, in the Creuse. I can recall with great detail our move to this new village, this new house, this new shop. The Creuse is a land of harsh winters and gloomy summers. I went to the only school in town and was particularly studious. The schoolmistress often saw in my eyes my desire to work, learn, do well, and maybe someday succeed her as teacher in this very school. But I also knew that my father had decided to take me on as an apprentice as early as possible, to teach me himself the art and style of the bread trade, so that I could succeed him honorably before the oven and behind the counter. In his mind, my fate was certain, my path already laid out.

From what they say, my father was a good and honest man, a relentless worker. But as far as I can recall, he was taciturn and withdrawn. I think now that, all his life long, he hid some terrible secret.

The bakery in Saint-Gratien was a prosperous affair. It was well situated in the center of town and drew a regular clientele. On Sundays, my mother and her salesgirl moved a considerable number of pastries and tarts.

My father had soon noticed that at lunchtime young female factory workers flocked to the bakery instead of going to the cafeteria, to buy croissants and *pains aux chocolat*, which they devoured on the benches by the square when it was nice out, and at the café-newsstand when it was cold or raining. He decided to hire an assistant and began making meat pasties, ham-and-cheese *croque-monsieurs*, even pizzas, in addition to bread and pastries. This initiative, rare at the time, met with considerable success all over Saint-Gratien.

My father baked at night, of course, so the bread would be ready before dawn. Once his batch was ready, bread and baguettes in rows on metal shelves, his assistant showed up to relieve him. My mother would go down and open up shop. My father had picked up the habit of heading over to the café-newsstand, which opened at the same hour; he brought an armful of baguettes and a basket of croissants; he sat down at a table to have his coffee, read the local paper, and smoke a few Gauloises; then he came home around the time I left for school, and went to sleep till early afternoon.

This ceremonial, this schedule, seemed immutable to me, but over the years, I came to notice that my father's morning stop at the café-newsstand grew longer and longer.

I'd see him through the window almost daily on my way to school, sitting at his regular table at the back of the room, heavyset, silent, alone, absorbed in reading his paper or lost in thought. What would he do there for such a long time? Why was he always putting off, longer and longer, the moment when he'd come back home?

> A man of forty-odd years doesn't vanish just like that, between the local newsstand and the bakery across the street!

Sometimes he'd spot me on the sidewalk and wave for me to come in. I'd kiss him quickly; he wouldn't keep me.

"Run along now," he'd say. "Don't be late."

***

The day of my fourteenth birthday, a snowy, fogbound January 4, my father didn't come home. I'd seen him through the window that morning, silent, heavyset, alone at the back of the room, his sheepskin jacket thrown across his shoulders over his baker's outfit.

If ten times then a hundred, first to my mother, then to the gendarmes and the judges, I had to repeat all the details of my account, which was confirmed and further clarified by the café owner, Madame Vacher. She'd seen my father leave her café around eight thirty, as he did every day, after paying for his paper and his Gauloises.

A man of forty-odd years doesn't vanish just like that, between the local newsstand and the bakery across the street! And yet, that was where my father faded away one morning of snow and fog. No one ever saw him again after he stepped out of Madame Vacher's café-newsstand in Saint-Gratien, in the Creuse.

At home, the reigning feeling was at first astonishment and annoyance.

"Have you seen your father?" my mother asked, as soon as I got home from school.

Yes, I'd seen him that morning through the window of Madame Vacher's café.

"Where on earth has that fool gone?" she added, with a lack of affability that struck me.

We remained convinced that he couldn't have gone far, for the car was still in the garage. The most pressing problem at the moment was that night's batch, for we at home all knew that the first rule of running a bakery was never to be out of bread. "Don't be short so much as one baguette any day you're open," my father often said. That first night, the freezer saw to our needs, but just in case, my mother asked Frédéric, our assistant, to come and see to the morning's batch. A good thing, too, for my father didn't come home that night, or the next day at dawn.

> At home, we refused to entertain the thought that my father was dead.

Surprise and annoyance were followed by sincere or feigned worry. On the evening of the third day, my mother called the gendarmes to notify them of her husband's inexplicable disappearance. They made a note of it, but seemed less moved than she was. They assured her, at any rate, that they had no record in the last forty-eight hours of any auto accidents or drownings in the Petite Creuse or the ponds of the Sorgue.

To them, it was nothing more than another common case of a married man running off, which would end as quickly as it had begun.

"He hasn't had any affairs that you know of in the area?" they asked my mother with great tact.

Offended and blushing, she swore that in the seven years we'd lived in Saint-Gratien, my father had never been away from the bakery for a single night. Even Sunday nights, he stayed home and watched television.

The following Monday, everyone in town began to gossip, and my mother asked that his description be circulated. To this end, the gendarmes came to the house for the first time. They inspected, in detail, the bedroom, the closets, the drawers, and my father's bake house. They questioned me at length. They gathered clues and statements. They came to the conclusion that my father had indeed left without papers, bags, even money, dressed only in his baker's garb and sheepskin jacket, wearing leather slippers. But even in this rather eccentric outfit, he hadn't caught the eye of a single resident of Saint-Gratien, or Boussac, or Bonnat; no railroad worker had seen him catch a train in Gueret or Montluçon; his picture, run in the local paper, tacked up in stations and on the notice boards of public buildings, gave rise to no eyewitness accounts of any sort.

———— ·—· ————

Frédéric Noche, our assistant, who'd saved the bakery by filling in for my father at the oven, wasn't long in filling in for him around the house. At the dinner table, I mean, and in my mother's bed.

He was around my mother's age; a cheery, charming man, he was as open and outgoing as my father had been withdrawn. I got along well with him, and he treated me more like a younger brother than a son.

He had convinced my mom to buy a new car and a trailer; for the first time, we went on vacation, and traveled. We saw the sea at Grau-du-Roi, near Nîmes.

I owe it to him that I was able to pursue my studies. After the general certificate, which I passed with flying colors, he insisted that I attend the lycée in Guéret as a boarder. I came home every Saturday; during the holidays, I helped Frédéric and my mother at the bakery.

The people in the village and my friends at school took a more or less kindly view of the situation. "That Noche really pulled it off," we'd sometimes hear people say. Several years after my father disappeared, some still uttered the saying heavy with innuendo: "Can't hurt if nobody knows, eh?"

At home, we refused to entertain the thought that my father was dead, much less that anyone could have made an attempt on his life. It was unthinkable. We clung resolutely to what my mom had decreed once and for all: "He left! He left!" We no longer sought to know where, or how, and, all told, I must admit we felt more resentment than sorrow.

The night of my fifteenth birthday, which fell on a Sunday that year, and which we'd celebrated at home, Frédéric had driven me, as he did every Sunday, to the bus that would take me to Guéret. As usual, there were few other passengers at this hour and this time of year, and I had taken a seat at the front of the bus, in the first row on the right side, by the driver. Monsieur Martiaux had driven the route for years, and I knew him well.

Night had fallen, and we were going slow; the headlights shone on a narrow road, empty and fogbound. At the Ladapeyre stop (request only), in the middle of nowhere, I saw from a distance, beneath the streetlight, a man waving down the driver. Martiaux slowed, stopped the bus, and opened the doors. The man was about to step in. I'd swear he already had a foot on the platform when he changed his mind and set off on foot along the road, heading the other way.

Martiaux shrugged, shut the doors again, and drove on. The whole scene had lasted no more than a minute, and I'd barely glimpsed the man's face. But I was suddenly plagued by an incredible premonition.

I rose from my seat and approached the driver.

"That man," I said, "who wanted to get on . . . You're not going to believe me, but I think it was my father."

Monsieur Martiaux reacted sharply.

"What are you, not right in the head?" he said. "Your dad's been gone for how long now, and you think he's still hanging around here?"

I went and sat back down, but Martiaux hadn't completely settled my doubts. I knew that, busy driving as he was, he couldn't have seen from his spot behind the wheel the solitary traveler any better than I had. While the bus rolled on through the night toward Guéret, I remained racked by the same torment, the same uncertainty. Martiaux only deepened my doubts when, at our arrival, he thought it best to take me aside and tell me, in secretive tones: "Main thing is, don't tell your mom about this, OK? You'll get her all worked up for nothing."

I kept this terrible secret to myself, but every Sunday after that, as I headed back to Guéret, I couldn't help keeping an apprehensive eye out at the Ladapeyre stop (request only). The traveler I'd glimpsed that night never showed up again.

I was on the soccer team at school, where I played right wing. That year, with a new coach who'd once played professionally for Red Star, we'd had a very good season, and one Thursday afternoon we found ourselves in the finals of a junior tournament at Montluçon. It was a big day for us, and even more so for me, as the game fell on my birthday, the fourth of January. I was confident and determined to outdo myself. The week before, I'd been instrumental to the goal that sealed our victory over Aubusson; I hoped to score one myself.

Right from the start of the game, I shot forward like a cannonball to receive, at full speed, a forward pass from Amoudruze. I smacked right into a defender from the other team, who'd rushed for the ball just like me.

I came to wrapped up in a blanket, on a stretcher. A man dressed as a referee was leaning over me and patting my cheeks. It seemed like my father. I lost consciousness. I was taken to the hospital in town, where they kept me under observation for a night.

Our coach came to get me the next morning and took me back to Saint-Gratien. Our team had won 2–1. He didn't know the referee, or the judges on the sideline.

———————— ◆ ————————

The next year we went on a ski trip. For the first time, I discovered the Alps, a real resort town, and the joys of skiing on trails of packed snow. I turned out to be fairly adept for a beginner.

On the morning of January 4, the ski instructor had us climb into a cable car that passed over the resort and took us up to the top of La Croix-des-Perches. I stood pressed against the window at the back of the cabin,

> I felt such a violent emotion that my legs went weak, and I clung with both hands to the railing.

watching the town's buildings dwindle as we mounted higher and higher. I played a little game, picking out the bar and café, the terrace of La Clémence, the sporting goods store where we'd rented our skis, the supermarket, the dry cleaners, the grocery-deli . . . and I spotted, heading down to the deli, a man in baker's garb and a sheepskin jacket, a large leather suitcase in his hand. Heavyset, dogged, he took small, awkward steps in the snow, something fierce in the way he walked.

Through the fogged-up windows of the cabin now drawing swiftly away, I could only see him walk into the shop and close the door behind him. At that moment, I felt such a violent emotion that my legs went weak, and I clung with both hands to the railing that went around the windows. I must have looked pale and distraught, for one of my friends thought it wise to ask, "Hey, are you all right? What's the matter?"

"Nothing . . . nothing," was all I said.

When we reached the top of la Croix, I stepped quickly into my skis, but instead of joining the rest of the group, which was to descend into the neighboring valley under the instructor's supervision, I set off straightaway, warning no one and flouting every rule of caution, down the Green Circle trail that led back to town.

I arrived right in front of the deli and walked into the shop, which was deserted. A woman appeared behind a curtain of wooden pearls. She had the pleasing face of a Savoy native, well-fed, with a rosy glow, deep-blue eyes, and a healthy set of teeth. She wore a tiny blue apron over a thick sweater and woolen pants.

"Excuse me, ma'am," I said, "I'm looking for my father. I saw him come in here earlier."

She assured me there was no one else there but a young man who helped out in the kitchen, and that she hadn't seen any man around age forty that morning come into the shop in baker's garb and a sheepskin jacket, carrying a big leather suitcase.

> These unusual encounters deeply affected me even more than my father's sudden disappearance.

That woman couldn't have told a lie or been hiding a thing. I went back to see her several times while I was there, and, oddly enough, put at ease, found myself confiding my uncertainties and torments to her. Today, I have no choice but to acknowledge that, with the exception of myself, no one at that resort town saw my father that morning or any other.

These unusual encounters deeply affected my adolescence even more than my father's sudden disappearance, particularly as they always took place inevitably on the same day: my birthday. January 4 had become, for me, the anniversary of my father's disappearance.

At that age, an uncertain mind tends easily to superstition. Toward the end of every year, no sooner had December started than I began dreading vacation and the holidays, at once fearing and expecting the advent of that fateful day when I might cross my father's path.

When the chance for a trip or an outing came up around that time of year, I couldn't keep from getting a vague, unconscious premonition of our next encounter. I was attentive to the slightest sign of anything strange. I couldn't stop myself from thinking that, one way or another, my father, in his other life, kept himself informed of my acts and deeds, my movements, that he still loved me in his way, and that, on his end, he planned his fleeting appearances.

As a kind of contest of wills between my father and me, one January 4—a Sunday—I resolved to stay at home all day without setting foot outside.

Mom and Frédéric had offered to take me out to dinner in a new hotel that had opened near Chambon. But, using homework as an excuse, I opted to stay home alone, with a terrine de pâté in front of the TV.

I held out well until the Sunday-night movie, doing my best to keep my mind far from the doubts that assailed me. But during the nightly news on Channel 1, they ran a few minutes' footage for a local story on a terrible traffic accident: near Moulins, on Route 7, a bus full of children had crashed into the back of a truck that had broken down. And among the firemen who'd rushed to the victims' aid, beneath a golden helmet and a jacket of black leather, for a few seconds, I glimpsed my father.

Another year, filled with the same apprehension, I'd gotten permission to spend the holidays in Paris with my friend Bertrand, whose uncle had offered to put us up. We weren't actually in Paris, but in the nearby suburb of Gagny, where Mr. Gagnière owned a house. All day long, we hung out on the streets of Paris, changing neighborhoods daily, seeing museums, monuments, cinemas, shows—as many as we had the money for. And at night, we "got back to Gagny," worn out but thrilled and happy, on the last train from the Gare de l'Est.

On the night of January 3, since vacation was almost over and we had a fair amount of money left, we decided to treat ourselves to a really nice sauerkraut and sausage in one of the brasseries by the station while waiting for the train. We'd even drunk an entire bottle of Alsatian wine, which had left us euphoric.

As we were leaving the brasserie, we were approached by two women—very pretty, very merry, and utterly shameless. Out of the blue, they suggested we take them dancing, "as friends," to a club they "adored," which was "totally rockin'," but which they didn't dare go to alone, for fear they'd be taken for hookers.

Right away, Bertrand brought up the last train to Gagny, which was leaving in five minutes.

"Don't worry, we've got a car!" the girls assured us.

Bertrand took off running, but I couldn't resist this terrific temptation and soon found myself at a table in a cabaret between the two young things, before a bucket of champagne, which had appeared as if by magic.

I took turns dancing with one girl, then the other, then began flirting a bit first with one, then the other. They joined right in, laughing at my little game. It didn't take me long to notice that each time I got back to our table, some mysterious hand had filled the empty glasses and, more often than not, brought a new bottle of champagne. Once I even glimpsed one of the girls emptying the glasses into the bucket of ice while I was dancing with the other . . . Naive as I was, I caught on to the con, but in my champagne-induced euphoria, resolved to take the high road: I myself ordered new bottles of Mumm and downed glass after glass. So many, and so well, that I wound up collapsing on the table, my head between my crossed arms, plunged into a sudden, deep sleep.

At dawn that January 4, a man leaned over me from the other side of the table; with a large, strong hand, he gave my shoulder a firm but gentle shake.

"Time to pay up and leave, kid," he said.

I raised my head and, as if in a thick fog, suddenly saw his face above me, with his sad eyes, his thin lips, his red and broken veins. He was dressed in white from head to toe: all white were his waiter's vest, shirt, and bow tie. The cabaret was empty, the light harsh; waiters were yanking off the tablecloths, stacking the tables and stools.

I stared fixedly at the man, as though he were an apparition. I was sure he'd recognize me. I let myself slip back against the banquette.

With vague, extraordinarily slow movements, staring at him all the while, I pulled whatever bills I had left from my wallet. That should pretty much cover it. The man pocketed them without even counting, then shrugged and shook his head.

"You have any idea how much you drank? At your age! In one night!" he said, more sad than stern.

In my mind's dark disorder, I cast about desperately for a lighted path toward my father, a password to open the door to my childhood.

"Saint-Gratien . . . in the Creuse, have you ever been there?" I mumbled in a thick voice.

Perhaps he hadn't even heard me? He grabbed me by the arm and helped me up. I could barely stand. He led me slowly to the door of the cabaret. It opened on a foggy alley.

"Don't you have a jacket?" he asked.

No, I had no jacket. I took a few steps forward at random, keeping to the walls of the neighboring buildings. I reached a triangular plaza, planted with spindly trees. I clung to one of them, then let myself fall to my knees and started throwing up.

I don't know how I made it back to Gagny. All I know is that in all my trips to Paris, I've never once been able to find that triangular plaza planted with spindly trees again, or the narrow door to that underground cabaret where I'd strayed that night.

I'd reached the age of wanting to travel, to see and do and learn, so I took a trip to Holland. It was a joy to discover the new museum devoted to Gauguin, whom I considered the greatest contemporary painter. At heart, I also believed that being far off, in a foreign land, beyond customs and borders, would save me from any fateful encounters this year.

The final morning of my solo trip, as I was leaning with my elbows on the railing of a footbridge, observing the traffic on the canal, the barges maneuvering on the still

> I clung to one of them, then let myself fall to my knees and started throwing up.

water, I spotted below, on a stone bench, ten feet below me, almost at my feet, the strange figure of a beggar, bearded and hirsute, wearing a filthy old sheepskin jacket and a rabbi hat. Lying across his knees, with its belly in the air and its legs spread out on a bundle of newspaper, was a hideous stray dog with a white and yellow coat, though the white was dirty and the yellow dingy.

This man, who didn't know he was being watched, seemed wholly occupied in stroking his dog's belly, and they both seemed to take an excessive, disturbing pleasure in it. This unusual scene of everyday Dutch life had commanded all my attention. I remained there for a long moment, watching him from atop the footbridge, when suddenly, as though he'd detected my presence, the man raised his head. Below his broad black hat, I saw his face, and our gazes met.

I remained frozen for a moment. I knew I should've gotten ahold of myself and found a way of reaching the bank of the canal. But after the initial emotion, a kind of filial instinct made me cry out with all my strength: "Dad! It's me! Fabien! Wait!"

My father had recognized me perfectly. He lowered his face, rose from his bench, and, carrying his hideous dog in his arms as one might a child, took off at a run.

The place was laid out such that he had to pass under the metal bridge where I was standing. I ran to the other side and saw his hat quickly growing farther and farther away. Once at a good distance, and knowing I could no longer catch up to him, Dad turned to me and shouted from far off, in a hoarse voice, in French, of course, "I'm not your father! I never had a son!"

I never saw him again after that terrible acknowledgment.

The law requires a period of seven years after an official missing persons report before that person can be declared legally dead by a civil court. My mother, recognized as a widow, was free to marry Frédéric Noche; the two had lived as man and wife since my father's departure. But on their wedding day, I remember shivering at the idea that he might suddenly appear and raise an objection, capital indeed, to the nuptials.

I was the only one who knew he was still alive, and that our paths had crossed, here and there, over the years. With the exception of the deli owner in Savoy, I'd never opened up to anyone about this heavy secret.

Shortly after their wedding, Frédéric and my mother sold the bakery in Saint-Gratien. They moved to Grau-du-Roi, where they still live today. They made a happy couple and brought me the joy of two little sisters—twins—named Marie-Ève and Marie-Marthe.

As for me, after training in education, I started out in the job I'd wanted so much, first as a teacher, then as principal of the school in Saint-Gratien. I moved back to the area and soon married a fellow elementary-school teacher. My mother and Frédéric came to our wedding with the twins. The next year, I ran for office in the municipal election and was voted deputy mayor of my township.

That same year, the highways department began construction on a major bypass to the national highway around Saint-Gratien, whose industry had significantly developed. The big-rig traffic that had resulted made getting around impossible. Excavators and other vehicles had already begun digging a vast trench along the edges of the former quarry right outside town.

One morning in January, the gendarmes came to see me at school, when class let out. They took me to the construction site where Setelec workers had just made an astonishing discovery: the remains of an adult male, buried in the sand for a good ten years. Nothing proved that this misshapen and contorted skeleton belonged to my father. But it could indeed have been his.

"I wanted to let you know, on the off chance," the officer said. "But surely you won't insist on reopening this old case?"

No, I wouldn't insist. 🛡

Adam Zagajewski

JOSEPH STREET

I often walk down Joseph Street, I enter Joseph's dreams,
always seeking to determine where that peculiar
street leads; it turns where
there is nothing, and I wonder what I am,
a passerby who won't last long.
The happiness and sorrow gathered here
will save no one, although the harvest may be abundant.
Years pass, I remain, memory is uncertain,
unheard prayers lie underfoot,
sparrows are eternity's frail emblem,
the rain is only recollection, the silhouettes
of unknown persons walk without casting shadows.
Toward evening the light grows feebler and death
rides swiftly on its high cart, laughing.

CLOUD

Poets build a home for us—but they themselves
can't dwell in it
(Norwid in the poorhouse, Hölderlin in a tower).

At dawn mist above the forest,
a journey, the rooster's husky call,
the hospitals are shut, uncertain signals.

At noon we sit in a café on the square,
we observe the azure sky
and a laptop's azure screen;

a plane writes out the pilot's manifesto
in clear, white script,
perfectly legible to the farsighted.

Azure is a color that happily
promises great events,
and then sits back and waits.

A leaden cloud draws close,
terrified pigeons rise
gracelessly into the air.

Storms and hailstones gather
in dark streets and squares,
and yet the light doesn't die.

Poets, invisible like miners,
hidden in the shafts,
build a home for us:

lofty rooms rise
with Venetian windows,
splendid palaces,

but they themselves
can't dwell in it:

Norwid in the poorhouse, Hölderlin in a tower;
the jet's lonely pilot
hums a lullaby; awaken, Earth.

I LOOK AT A PHOTOGRAPH

I look at a photograph of the city where I was born,
at its lush gardens and winding streets, at the hills,
the Catholic roofs, the domes of Orthodox churches,
where on Sunday the basses sing so mightily
that neighboring trees sway as in a hurricane;
I gaze at the photograph, I can't tear my eyes away,
and suddenly I imagine that they're all still alive
as if nothing had happened, they still scurry to lectures,
wait for trains, take sky-blue trams,
check calendars with alarm, step on scales,
listen to Verdi's arias and their favorite operetta,
read newspapers that are still white,
live in haste, in fear, are always late,
are a bit immortal, but don't know it,
one's behind with the rent, another fears consumption,
a third can't finish his thesis on Kant,
doesn't understand what things are in themselves,
my grandmother still goes to Brzuchowice carrying
a cake on her outstretched arms and they don't droop,
in the pharmacy a shy boy requests a cure for shyness,
a girl examines her small breasts in a mirror,
my cousin goes to the park straight from his bath
and doesn't guess that soon he'll catch pneumonia,

enthusiasm erupts at times, in winter yellow lamps
create cozy circles, in July flies loudly celebrate
the summer's great light and hum twilit hymns,
pogroms occur, uprisings, deportations,
the cruel Wehrmacht in becoming uniforms,
the foul NKVD invades, red stars
promise friendship but signify betrayal,
but they don't see it, they almost don't see it,
they have so much to do, they need
to lay up coal for winter, find a good doctor,
the unanswered letters grow, the brown ink fades,
a radio plays in the room, their latest buy, but they're
still wearied by ordinary life and death,
they don't have time, they apologize,
they write long letters and laconic postcards,
they're always late, hopelessly late,
the same as us, exactly like us, like me.

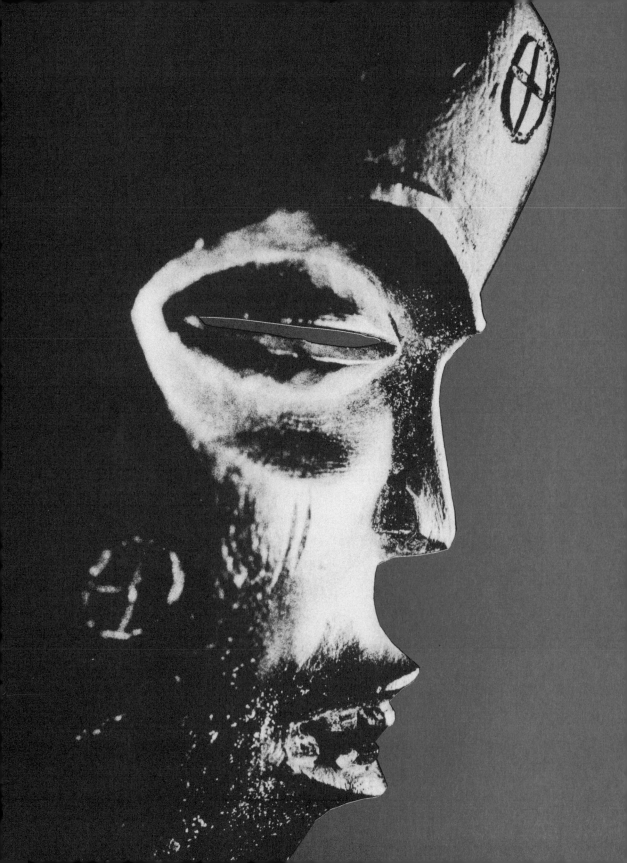

Volcano

Six months after she divorced her husband, Martha Fink packed her bags and flew to Honolulu to attend a lucid-dreaming seminar at the Kalani resort on the Big Island of Hawaii. She had discovered the faithless Donald in the same position that the wife of Samuel Pepys had discovered the London diarist three hundred years before, copulating with the family maid. "I was deep inside her cunny," Pepys admitted that night in his diary, "and indeed I was at a wondrous loss to explain it."

Lawrence Osborne

Martha filed for divorce. She collected the apartment on Central Park West and a considerable sum of money, then went to counseling. Lovers did not materialize to replace the discarded husband. She became yet more enraged, went on Zoloft, and finally decided that her eighteen years of therapy and dietary rigor had not, in the end, helped her very much to face the endgame of biology itself. Growing older had proved a formidable calamity.

Nothing saves you from it, she realized. Not irony, certainly, or dieting or gyms or drugs or the possession of children and priceless friends. Nothing saves the declining human from the facts of her decline except the promises of work. And that had not saved her, either, because, unluckily, she hated her work. She detested it more and more. A lawyer, she now realized, should always maintain extracurricular passions, and she had not. Her lifelong practicality and good humor had not sustained her, either, and her fine skin and aristocratic profile felt to her increasingly insufficient, if not wasted. There was now just Hawaii and dreams. The resort, run by two gay dancers, was next to an active volcano.

She spent a night on Waikiki in a high-rise hotel called the Aston. The city seemed compressed, airless and suffocating. A nightmare of dullness and saturation, of Burberry and Shiseido, of families braying on the far side of thin walls. Her room was filled with red neon.

She wept all night, strung out on sleeping pills. In the morning, she went to the old Sheraton for coffee in a courtyard of banyans and squabbling pintails. It was now called the Manoa Surfrider, and there was Soviet-looking architecture all around. She sat there for some hours. She felt herself coming apart. The sun did not cheer her up; there was no charm whatsoever in the colonial affect of her surroundings, a style that could be called New Jersey Tropical.

She went to Pearl Harbor in the afternoon. Sappy music played, and the crowd was hustled along like cattle. "Each visitor can contemplate his innermost responses and feelings." In the bus back to Waikiki, she saw a poster for Dr. Rosa Christian Harfouche, a preacher selling Signs, Wonders, and Miracles. The streets were full of federal detention centers and ukulele stores. Not a single attractive human. Suddenly she felt years older than forty-six.

She waited tensely for her flight to Hilo.

From the air, the islands regained their beauty. They seemed far-flung again, imposing, like sacred statues lying on their sides. The sea was immense, like a visual drug that can calm the most turbulent heart. Not

America, then, but Polynesia, though it was difficult to remember. She slept, and her tears subsided into her core.

A driver from Kalani was there to meet her. They drove down to Pahoa through a landscape of lava rock and papaya groves. In town, they had a milk shake in a "French café" and sat outside for a while, looking up at silver clouds shaped like anvils, static above the volcano. The driver told her, as if it were a detail she might relish, that he had transported fourteen people so far from the airport to Kalani for the Dream Express seminar. Most of them, he said cattily, were middle-aged women who looked like they were having a bad time.

> The sea was immense, like a visual drug that can calm the most turbulent heart.

"A bad time?" she said tartly. "Do I look like I'm having a bad time?"

"No, ma'am. You look real eager."

Eager, was she that? In a way, she was. A wide freeway swept down to the southern coast and lava flats and cliffs, above which Kalani stood in its papaya woods. As the sea appeared, she felt a keen relief. The road dipped up and down past affluent hippie resorts, yoga retreats, and fasting centers. A few flabby joggers shot by, all ponytails and tattoos. At the gates of Kalani, lanterns had been lit for the evening.

The resort was a considerable estate made up of groups of traditional spherical Hawaiian houses raised off the ground. In the thatched communal meeting place, everyone ate a macrobiotic, vegetarian buffet dinner, courtesy of the resort. The owners and the dancers were dressed in Hawaiian skirts and performing a votive dance to the volcano goddess, Pu'ah. They danced and clapped to welcome the new residents, jiggling their hips, rolling their fingers, and hailing the volcano itself, which lay only a few miles distant and had become active only two weeks before. At sundown, a dull, red glow stretched across the horizon.

Kalani hosted four different seminars at any one time. The Dream Express group was indeed, she saw at once, highly populated with middle-aged women wearing tense and confused expressions. Her heart might have sunk right then if she hadn't determined not to let it. She braced herself for these sad, bewildered specimens, who were likely capable of comradeship and kindness. Her eyes sorted through them, but she was unable to keep from disapproving. The seminar leader, Dr. Stephen DuBois, was a Stanford psychiatrist who supplemented his academic income with dream seminars in alternative health centers. It was he who had devised a way to "wake" the dreamer inside her dream and make her conscious of it, through a daily routine of herbs and nightly use of a special pair of goggles that shot regulated beams of light into the eyes during the deepest periods of REM sleep. With these methods, one could enter a state of "lucid dreaming" and consciously direct the flow of the dream itself. It was a common technique of dream therapy, but rarely used in such a controlled environment as Kalani, a context from which normal reality had been almost entirely subtracted. DuBois claimed to be able to alter each participant's relationship to her own dreams by the use of the herb galantamine. Aside from being a popular treatment for Alzheimer's, polio, and memory disorders, galantamine, derived from Caucasian snowdrop flowers, was said to induce exceptionally intense and memorable dreams by deepening REM sleep. It looked like a white powder, like very pure cocaine.

> People are what they are and they were no more broken down by life's disappointments than she herself was.

DuBois introduced them all to one another: a psychiatrist from Rome at the end of a long nervous breakdown, a married couple from Oregon working through their difficulties, a female stockbroker from London who already possessed a "friend" inside her dreams who flew with her across vast oneiric landscapes. There were a few Burning Man types from the Bay Area who came every year, young and wide-eyed, and two New York basket cases fleeing their catastrophic jobs and marriages. All in all, they were what she had expected. Bores and beaten-down shrews in decline and kooks. She didn't mind, particularly. People are what they are and they were no more broken down by life's disappointments than she herself was. She was sure that half the women had faithless husbands who had run off with younger women. They had that archetypal event inscribed upon their faces.

"It's very simple," DuBois explained from the head of their trestle table. The volcano dance had wound down, and a group of new-age square dancers arrived at the adjoining table. "Every night we'll take a capsule of galantamine and go to bed at a reasonable hour. We'll put on our goggles before we go to sleep. If the infrared beam wakes us up, we'll leave the goggles on and go back to sleep. Hopefully, though, we won't wake up at all. We'll simply become conscious inside our dreams."

"Really?" said the Italian psychiatrist.

"Certainly. When that happens, you all have to remember a few basic things. To change your dream, simply reach out and rub a rough surface. A wall is perfect. The dream will change immediately, and you can enjoy the next one. If you want to fly, simply start turning on the spot. You'll start flying."

They all began to smile, to nod. It would be like hours of entertainment every night. Like cinema inside their heads. And, because of the powdered snowdrop, they would remember it all.

"Every morning, we'll tell each other what we dreamed. It'll help us remember everything, and it'll help us write our dream journals. The dream journal will be a book we can take back with us when we have finished here. Something permanent and life-changing."

Now they would get acquainted and then return to their thatched cabanas and prepare for the first night of lucid dreaming. It seemed to Martha a simple enough plan, and she was still tired from the long flight. The resort owners stopped by the table, still in their skirts: handsome, tanned, muscular gay men whom you could imagine vigorously fucking in hot tubs and saunas. Shaking their hands gave her a twinge of arousal.

"Look over there," one of them said. He pointed to the glow visible above the tree line. "Looks like lava on the move."

Across the smooth, rolling lawns, Martha could see naked men strolling down toward the hot tubs surrounding the swimming pool. The resort was nudist after 9:00 P.M. After a cup of chamomile tea and a few desultory chats, she said good night to the group and walked back to her cabana. A high moon illumined the edge of the jungle.

She took the galantamine capsule, lay under the mosquito nets of her bed, and attuned herself to the rhythmic chirping of the tree frogs. She put on the cumbersome goggles and adjusted the strap so that it did not squeeze her face too tightly. Then her exhaustion took over. She was too tired to care that the goggles were uncomfortable or that the frogs were loud because the windows had no glass. She slept without thinking about sleeping, and soon the REM cycle had swept her up.

She began to dream at once, but later she could not remember it as clearly as she had hoped. She did recall that in this dream she was standing in a hotel bar, drinking a glass of port. Rain was falling outside, and behind her there seemed to be a roaring fire. When she turned to look at it, she felt the fire's heat touch her face, and the piercing red beam of the machine inside the goggles flooded her consciousness with its color. Unused to this intrusion, she awoke immediately and tore off the goggles.

The first thing she heard was the frogs. The moon had moved position and shone directly into the room, touching the foot of the bed. She was drenched in sweat. She got up and went to the screened window. Nightjars sang in the papayas. She felt intensely awake and therefore restless. She put on her flip-flops and a sarong and climbed down the steps of her cabana into the long, wet grass. At the end of the lawn shone the pool, wreathed with steam from the all-night Jacuzzi. She made her way to the hot tub, tiny frogs popping out of the grass around her feet, and when she reached the pool she disrobed again and sank into the water, naked. Tall palms stood around the pool. The moon shone between them.

As she floated on her back, she could feel that something in this idyllic scene was not quite right. It was too serene. Then, from far off, she heard a wild whoop of male voices. She sat up. A group of naked men was running down the lawn toward her. They ran in a line, their erections flapping about, and they headed straight for the pool. Startled, she leaped out of the water, grabbed her sarong, and darted into the dripping papaya trees on the far side of the footpath. The men, impervious to her presence, jumped en masse into the pool and filled it with phalli and noise. She reached out and touched the rough bark of one of the trees, and as she did she found herself back in her bed, the goggles still fixed to her head. Rain was pouring outside the window.

She tore off the goggles, gasping, her body drenched with sweat. The rain was so heavy that the frogs had fallen silent, and all she could hear was the mechanical dripping from the edge of the window frame and the rustle beyond, in the forest. She got up a second time, and her bewilderment made her reach out and touch the insect screen to see if it was real. She wrote down her dream straightaway.

In the morning, the sun returned, but there was a taste of burned wood on the air, born from afar, and a reddish dust that seemed to linger over the tree line. In the cafeteria, the group was eagerly discussing the eruption of the volcano during the night—one of a series of eruptions, it seemed.

"It kept me up all night," the London broker said, eyeing Martha up and down. "Didn't you hear it?"

"Nothing," Martha said. "Did it rain all night?"

"It rained, but there was one hour when it was pure moonlight, peaceful as can be. I went down to the pool." The broker lowered her voice. "Unfortunately, it was occupied. Men are strange, don't you think?"

The woman had bossy, aggressive green eyes that possessed a knack for mentally undressing other women.

"I slept badly," Martha admitted, rubbing her eyes. "The rain woke me up."

"Personally, the galantamine does nothing for me. You?"

Martha shrugged. "I have nothing to compare it to."

During the day, they listened to DuBois lecture in one of the rotunda meeting halls, and Martha dozed in a corner, feeling that she had not enjoyed enough sleep. It was a hot day, and after lunch, she went for a walk by herself along the coast road where the woods were thicker. She walked for miles, until she came to a gray beach under the cliffs, where sundry hippies and half-stoned locals sat drinking kava and smoking reefers. Beyond the beach lay flats of black lava that reached out into the sea. She went down onto the beach and lay in the roasting sun for a while. Her grief welled up inside her until tears flowed down her face. No one could see them there. She emptied herself out and breathed heavily until her body was reoxygenated.

> She sat up. A group of naked men was running down the lawn toward her.

Later that night, she walked down to the lava again with some of the other dream women. One of them was a mosaic artist from Missoula, Montana, and another sold hot tubs for a living. Makeshift kava cafés made of driftwood had been set up on the rock shelves, and wild travelers on motorbikes appeared out of nowhere, racing across the lava with their lights blazing. The women drank kava and seaweed honey out of small paper cups and watched the red glow of the volcano in the distance; three divorced women, two of them long into middle age, waiting for improbable turns of events. Aging European hippies in feather earrings, with names like Firewind and Crystal Eye, tried to pick them up. Martha felt supremely detached from everyone. She didn't want to talk about the love lives of the other women. Everyone's love life, she thought, was more or less the same, and to be disgusted one only had to remember that seventy million women were saying exactly the same things to their friends at that very same moment.

"I only left him six months ago," one of the women was saying, as if they had all known each other for years. "He never gave me cunnilingus, either. I know he was sleeping around—"

"They're *all* sleeping around."

"Does a fling every two years count as sleeping around?"

"Maybe we could fuck one of those filthy hippies. Firewind is quite sexy."

They drank the kava and became more stoned.

"Mine never gave me cunnilingus, either. They get lazy after a while. No one stays with anyone, ever, unless they're Christians."

"I wouldn't sleep with Firewind. He has blue fingernails."

"You wouldn't notice in the dark."

"Yes, but feather earrings?"

To Martha, the red glow in the night sky was more compelling than the conversation. It seemed incomprehensible that a volcano was active so close to them and yet there was no outward concern. The more distant molten lava must be moving down to the sea. The scene must be one of terror and grandeur, yet no one saw it. She thought about it as they licked salty seaweed honey off their fingers.

> **He looked up at her with watery, slightly bloody eyes in which there was a faint trace of lechery.**

She dreamed of her husband that night. She was cutting his toenails in a sea of poppies, and his toes were bleeding onto her scissors. He laughed and writhed as she ripped his toes with the blades. The galantamine made her remember it vividly. In the morning, she skipped the dream seminar, in which she no longer had much interest, and rented a motorbike from the front desk. She took a night bag and some money and decided to play the day by ear. She drove to Pahoa and on through Kurtistown until she reached Route 11, which turned west toward Volcanoes National Park. Soon she was rising through the Ola'a Forest.

At the top of the rising road stood the strange little town of Volcano. It was a cluster of houses on the edge of one of the craters, lush with rain forest. She parked by a large hotel and walked into a wonderful old lobby with a fireplace and oil paintings of volcanic eruptions on the walls. There was no one there. She wandered around the room for a while, admiring the Hawaiian native artifacts, then noticed a spacious bar on the far side of the reception desk. She went in.

Enormous windows wrapped around the room. Through them, the entire crater could be seen. It was a pale charcoal color, a vast field of uneven rock scored with ridges from which a glittering steam rose hundreds of feet into the air. A pair of antlers hung above the bar itself, next to a "volcano warning meter," a mocking toy with a red arrow that pointed to various states of imminent catastrophe.

At the bar sat an elderly gentleman in a flat-cloth cap, dipping his pinky into a dry martini. He looked up at her with watery, slightly bloody eyes in which there was a faint trace of lechery. He wore a windowpane jacket of surpassing ugliness and a dark brown tie with a gold pin in it. The barman was the same age, a sprightly sixty or so, and his eyes contained the same sardonic and predatory glint of sexual interest in a forty-six-year-old woman entering their domain unexpectedly.

"Aloha," the barman said, and the solitary drinker repeated it. She echoed the word and, not knowing what to do, sat down at the bar as well.

"Going down to the crater?" the capped man asked.

"Yes. I just wanted a stiff drink first."

"A good idea. I recommend the house cocktail. The Crater."

"What is it?"

"White rum, pineapple juice, cane sugar, Angostura bitters, a grapefruit segment, a dash of Cointreau, a cherry, dark rum, a sprig of mint, an egg white, and a hint of kava," said the barman.

"I'll have a glass of white wine."

"The Crater'll set you up better."

She looked at the volcano paintings, the flickering fire, the inferno landscape smoldering beyond the windows, and finally she noticed that the man in the cap was halfway through a Crater. Oh, why the fuck not?

"Okay," she said, "I'll have one."

They all laughed.

"Try walking across that crater after one of those," the drinker said. "The name's Alan Pitchfork. No, it's not my real name, but, hey, we're at the Volcano Hotel in Volcano, so who the hell cares?"

She took off her scarf and sunglasses.

"I'm Martha Prickhater. That is my real name."

"Oh, is it now?"

Alan leaned over to touch her glass with his. Her eyes strayed up to the ancient clock underneath the antlers, and she was surprised to see that it was already 2:00 P.M.

"Are you a local?" she asked politely.

"Moved here from Nebraska in 1989. Never looked back. Retired geologist."

"How nice. Did you come here with your wife?"

"Died in Nebraska, 1989."

"Ah, I see. I'm sorry."

"Long time ago, not to worry."

"Well, cheers."

She sipped the amazing brew. It tasted like the effluent from a chewing gum factory.

"Cheers," the man said, and did nothing.

"Staying at the hotel?" he went on, eyeing her. "Nice rooms here. Traditional style. African antiques in some of them. Views over the volcanoes."

"I hadn't thought about it."

"Well, you should think about it. You get a good night's sleep up here in Volcano, if a good night's sleep is what you want."

"I'll bear it in mind," she said testily.

"You should. Bear it in mind, I mean. There's no better spot for watching the sunset."

She finished her drink, said her farewells, and went back into the sunlight of the parking lot, where her bike stood, the only vehicle there. She drove down the lonely road to the trails that led to the crater. She chained up the bike and wandered down, through the rain forest dripping with water from a shower she apparently had not noticed. The trail led to the edge of the lava crater, which smelled of sulfur. She walked out into the middle of the stone plain.

In the sun, the wreaths of rising steam looked paler, more ethereal. She lay down and basked, taking off her shoes and pushing her soles into the slightly warm rock. Looking up, she could not see the hotel at all. To the south, the sky was hazed by the continuing eruption of the neighboring crater and soon, she could tell, that haze would reach the sun and eclipse it. She was tipsy and slow and her body ached for something. A man's touch, maybe. The touch of a rogue.

It was early evening when she got back to the hotel. The fire was roaring high and yet there was still no sign of other guests. She hesitated, because she was not quite sure why she had come back at all. The barman was on a ladder, dusting one of the oil paintings. He stepped down to welcome her back.

"Want a room?" he said hopefully.

"Not exactly."

"I can give you thirty percent off."

It was clear the place was empty.

"Dinner?" he tried, stepping gingerly around her. "A drink at the bar? Two for one?"

She peered into the bar and saw that the same drinker was still there, a little the worse for wear but still upright on his seat, another Crater in front of him. He caught her eye and winked. Behind him, the windows had dimmed, and only the outline of the crater could still be made out, illumined by the red glow that never seemed to diminish. The men told her the hotel's clientele had vanished after the volcano warnings had been issued two nights earlier.

"Volcano warnings?" she said, sitting down again at the bar.

"Red alert." Alan smiled, raising his glass.

The barman began to prepare a Crater without her asking for it.

"Yeah," he drawled. "They run like ants as soon as there's a red alert. But Alan here and I know better. We've seen a hundred red alerts, haven't we, Alan?"

"A thousand."

> The eruption had intensified, and it was easy to imagine the flows of lava dripping into the sea.

"See?" The barman served her drink with a yellow paper parasol. "It's perfectly safe to stay the night if you so wish."

"I wasn't thinking of it."

"It's a long ride back to Kalani," the geologist remarked. "In the dark, I mean."

She let it go.

I can do it, she thought.

They turned and watched the firework display outside for a while. The eruption had intensified, and it was easy to imagine the flows of lava dripping into the sea only a few miles away. The glow cast itself against the walls of the bar, turning the room a dark red. She gripped her drink and tilted it into her mouth, watching the geologist drum his fingers on the bar. Who was he and where did he live? He never seemed to leave the hotel bar. He asked her how she had found the crater, and he added that he had watched her cross it from this same window.

Soon, she was tipsy again. Something inside her told her that a motorbike ride back to Kalani at this hour would be suicidal. That "something" was simultaneously a desire to cave in, to book a room upstairs with African antiques and a view of the eruption. But it seemed, at the same time, inexpressibly vulgar to do so. To be alone in a hotel like this with two decrepit old men. She tossed back the dregs of her disgusting drink and ordered another.

"That's the spirit," the barman said. "It's on me."

Alan disputed the right to buy the drink and soon she was obliged to thank him.

"Shall we go sit by the fire?" he said.

In the main room, where the fire crackled and hissed, the Hawaiian masks had taken on a lurid uniqueness. They stared down at the odd couple sinking into the horsehair armchairs. The geologist put his drink down on a leather-surfaced side table and told her a long story about the last major eruption, when he had spent a week alone in Volcano smoking cigars at the bar and enjoying the view. People were cowards.

> **What was arousing to her was that she was alone and no one could ever discover what she was doing.**

"Personally, I'm not afraid of lava. It's a quick death, as good as any other, if not better."

"That's philosophical of you."

"I'm a geologist. You have beautiful legs, by the way. If I may say."

She started with surprise and displeasure and instinctively pulled her skirt down an inch or so.

"No, don't cross them," he went on. "Don't feel awkward."

Instead of feeling awkward, she felt warm and insulted. Her face began to flush hot and she wanted to throw her drink in his face. She controlled herself, however, and tried to smile it off.

"Thank you, if that's a compliment."

He said it was, and he wasn't going to apologize for it. His scaly, wrinkled skin seemed to shine under the equally antiquated lamps. After a while, she heard a quiet but insistent pitter-patter against the windows that was not rain. The man smiled. It was ash falling.

"Sometimes," Alan said, "I swear it's like the last days of Pompeii."

As the evening wore on, it became obvious that she would have to stay overnight. The barman told her that she could have the Serengeti Suite at half price. She agreed. He served them sandwiches with Hawaiian relishes, and more Craters. Martha began to see double. Eventually, she decided to go up to her room and lock the door. It was safer that way. She got up and staggered to the stairwell, while the geologist sat back and watched her radiant legs take her there. They said good night, or at least she thought he did, and she pulled herself up the squeaky stairs with a pounding head.

The suite was cold, and she left the main light off while she lit the glassed-in gas fire. Then she opened the curtains and let the red glow invade the rooms. On the horizon, beyond the extinct crater's rim, globs of white light seemed to shine behind a frazzled line of trees. She lay on the damp bed and kicked off her shoes. There were Zulu shields on the walls and pictures of Masai spearing black-maned lions under the suns of long ago. The chairs looked like something from a luxury safari lodge. She lay there and grew subtly bored, discontented with her solitude. She wondered what they would be doing at Kalani right then. Dancing in skirts to the volcano goddess, around a fire drinking their kava with marshmallow, or doing Personhood Square Dancing in the woods with paper hats. She lay there for an hour, fidgeting and feeling her emptiness and loneliness well up within her, then got up again and went to the bathroom to rebrush her hair. The antagonizing red light filled her with restless anxiety, but also an itching desire not to be alone. She looked at herself in the mirror and saw, for once, what was actually there: a lean, pale, frightened-looking little girl of forty-six. She put some salve on her lips and dusted her face with powder.

The hotel creaked like an old ship. Wind sang through empty rooms. She went out into the corridor with its thick, red carpet and felt her way along the hallway, listening carefully. She could hear a man singing to himself in one of the rooms, no doubt the repulsive geologist. She thought of his slack gray skin and his leery eyes, and she felt a moment's quickening lust-disgust. What was arousing to her was that she was alone and no one could ever discover what she was doing. She ran her finger along each door as she passed. As if responding to her telepathic signal, one of them finally opened and the familiar face, with its leprechaun eyes, popped out.

"So there you are," Alan said. He put a finger to his lips so that she wouldn't reply.

His room was exactly the same as hers, but it was plunged in complete darkness, as if he had been prepared to go to bed. She sat down on the bed. Soon his hands were all over her, the scaliness visible only by the light of the volcano. His dry, slightly perfumed skin was against hers, though she refused to look at his face. Instead, she kept her eye on the red glow and on the Zulu shields on the walls. He told her they were alone, as he put it, "on a live volcano," and the thought seemed to make him smile. All these years sitting in that damn bar, he said, and hoping that a beautiful woman like her would walk in. Up to then she never had. No sir, not until then. She had walked into the bar and he knew, he said, as soon as he laid eyes on her, that she would sleep with him.

"You did?" she whispered.

"I saw it in your face. You would sleep with an ugly old man like me."

He gripped her shoulders and kissed them slowly, as if there were kiss spots arranged in a predetermined line along them. His mouth was dry and papery, but not untitillating, precisely, because it was a human mouth. She could accept it in the dark. From behind, he slipped a hand between her legs, and she let herself roll to one side, sinking into sheets scented by contact with an inferior cologne. He pulled her arms behind her and, perhaps for the first time in a year, she forgot that her treacherous ex-husband existed. The geologist closed greedily around her, and before long he was inside her, desperate and voracious and relaxed at the same time, and although she knew it was a dream, she was not sure how to terminate it or change it. She reached out and stroked the wooden surface of the bedstead, then the cold surface of the wall, but still the old man held her pinned down and pumped away at her. *The goggles*, she thought. When was the beam of red light going to wake her? And soon she heard rain, or was it ash, pitter-pattering on the windows and tinkling like falling sand on the sills. The man gnawed her neck, her shoulder blades, and told her he was going to penetrate her all night long. His perspiration dropped onto her face. She flinched, but still she didn't wake up.

LADIES
OF THE HERMITAGE

photographs by Lucia Ganieva

E xperiencing rapture when encountering artistic masterpieces like the kind described by Stendhal in nineteenth-century Florence is well documented, but there aren't any explanations about how people who guard great art begin to resemble that art. If you look at the photographs of the ladies who guard the exhibitions at the State Hermitage Museum in St. Petersburg, Russia, shown here, you will note something mysterious is afoot: the resemblance of the guards to the ladies in the paintings is uncanny.

For their photographer, Lucia Ganieva, the similarities are not a coincidence but part of her artistic vision. She first searched for interesting faces among the guards, chose twenty-five, and then set out to find paintings within the exhibition halls that share visual similarities with those faces. "In each case I've looked for paintings that interact in some way or another with the person portrayed," Ganieva says.

Ganieva, born in Russia but now living in Holland, says that, like many Russians, she was hugely influenced by the Hermitage Museum and has had a long fascination with the guards—all three hundred and sixty of them. "When I came to St. Petersburg at the age of sixteen, I visited the museum often and was intrigued by the ladies working as guards in the exhibition rooms," she says. "Somehow they touched me and that feeling never went away."

The State Hermitage Museum in St. Petersburg, founded in 1764 by Catherine the Great, is one of the premier museums in the world, with over three million items and the largest collection of paintings of any other museum. Recently, the Hermitage has opened a satellite museum in Amsterdam, where Ganieva's photographs of the guards were exhibited from September 2010 to March 2011.

—LEE MONTGOMERY

NEW GHOSTS AND HOW
TO KNOW THEM

John Crowley

Literary ghouls and goblins galore

1. The Ghost Goes West

I was very young when I proved to my own satisfaction that the ghosts described in stories or appearing in movies didn't really exist. It was their *clothes*. I could entertain the idea that our spirits might live on after the death of the body, and appear as spectral selves before the living, but how do they come to be wearing clothes? It's usually by their clothes that we know them: the faded wedding dress, the bloody shirt, "my father in his habit as he lived." So how do they come to be dressed in clothes—often not even the clothes they were interred in? Are the clothes ghosts, too? What about the armor and swords and crowns and other things they bear? No, it was clear to me that such apparitions are not spirits of the departed but the guilty imaginings or irrational fears of the living made visible. Or they could be lost memory traces, images of the past recurring in time gaps into which we stumble; or else they are just made-up stories. Anyway, that sort of ghost is not, I concluded, a dead person, as aware of itself as I am aware of me.

Of course, that logic doesn't eliminate all kinds of other ghostly phenomena, vague wraiths in white drapery, eldritch whisperings and cold shudders in dark places, the certainty that one is observed by unseen presences. And the definition can expand—we can be haunted by the dead in a nonliteral sense that's just as powerful in its effect as any see-through fellow in a moldered tuxedo standing at the foot of the bed. Nonliteral hauntings are also harder to dismiss as story, bound up as they are in the consciousness of the observer, in the fragility of time, and in the ambiguity of perception.

This progressive evaporation of ghostly manifestations, from solidly extrinsic to internal and subjective, has of course been modeled in literature. Over the last couple of centuries, ghosts in stories and on stage lost a lot of their autonomy, along with their winding sheets and rotted cerements, and became projections of characters' minds, metaphors of guilt or hope or loss, symptoms of derangement—in short, psychologized. The older ghost types came to be restricted to frank fantasy or to genres in which they are accepted as entertainments, not instances of a real or general possibility, like marriage or war, as they are in Shakespeare. The culminating text of this long trend is Henry James's *The Turn of the Screw*, wherein it is impossible to decide whether the ghosts are "real" in the old sense of autonomous spirits, or products of the distraught governess's imagination.

In 1994, *The Norton Book of Ghost Stories* appeared, with a substantial introduction by Brad Leithauser that neatly sums up the nature and effects of the Jamesian, or standard modern, ghost story. "We are meant at the denouement of most supernatural tales to feel relief," Leithauser writes. "In its essential form the tale undertakes a careful sortie into a landscape of terrors—a cyclical journey (from the natural world to the supernatural and back again) that promises to release us, chastened but intact, at its close." A central concern of a ghost story, in Leithauser's view, is how a character comes to believe that the presences he apprehends are in fact departed persons, who often want justice or retribution. (Simple people—and dogs and cats—perceive ghosts in such stories sooner than proud rationalists, who are often the ones who Go Too Far.) Leithauser has, he says, a "good deal of patience with ghosts that are other than malign," but the frisson of dread, spookiness, and Freud's *unheimlich* are pervasive in his selections.

Recently, though, new ghosts have been appearing in fiction—ghosts not at all like the modernist ones we've come to know. They're perhaps companionably related to the old-style ghosts still haunting horror and genre romances, but they're not those, either. They come from new afterworlds or underworlds; they have different ways to haunt the living, and the living have new ways of dealing with them. They're usually wearing clothes. I have come (like an old ghost hunter) to recognize one when I catch it, and I'm trying here to taxonomize them, an effort that science recognizes as a first step toward understanding.

> Over the last couple of centuries, ghosts in stories and on stage lost a lot of their autonomy.

The first thing to observe about new ghosts is that the reaction of the living to their presence is often not disorientation, terror, or an inability to believe one's eyes. Matter-of-fact acceptance is more usual. This quality of new ghost stories became clear to me when I first read George Saunders's "CivilWarLand in Bad Decline," a story that announced a new style and matter in American storytelling that even now resists a label—"mall Gothic" is one miss; nor is Saunders really a "satirist," as some have said. But one distinct feature of his stories has been the ghosts. In "CivilWar-Land," they are the ghosts of the McKinnon family, who once owned all the land on which a crappy and failing theme park has been constructed, a dozen faux-old buildings. "They don't realize we're chronologically slumming," the narrator guesses, "they just think the valley's prospering." He encounters the spirits of the whole clan "wandering around at night looking dismayed."

Tonight I find the Mrs. doing wash down by the creek. She sees me coming and asks if she can buy my boots. Machine stitching amazes her. I ask how are the girls. She says Maribeth has been sad because no appropriate boy ever died in the valley so she's doomed to loneliness forever.

He does well with the Mrs. but can't get anything out of the Mr., which is too bad, "because he was at Antietam and could be a gold mine of war info." Saunders's story—like many of his—is certainly funny, but it isn't simply comedy, and the ghosts can be impressively dreadful. Mrs. McKinnon, murdered along with her daughters by the Mr., sits in a tree above the narrator: "Tears run down her see-through cheeks. She says there's been a horrid violent seed in him since he came home from the war . . . Then she blasts over my head elongate and glowing and full of grief and my hat gets sucked off."

We are never told how the narrator came to see ghosts, what he thinks of their presence in his life, or what he makes of them; his judgments about them are as shot through with fatuity ("It occurs to me that the Mr.'s a loon") and flashes of good sense as are his judgments of the outlandish humans living around him in the park. He certainly isn't afraid of them. Saunders's story rises, at the end, to a kind of sublimity powered by hilarity as the narrator is killed by a crazed park security guard and becomes a ghost himself. "Possessing perfect knowledge I hover above him as he hacks me to bits"—a triumph of the New Ghost mode.

The same unalarmed acceptance of the dead among us is a feature of Kelly Link's stories. Link has always described herself as a genre writer, and there is science fiction and fantasy matter in many of her stories, but there is no amalgamating her work with the mass of genre work. In "Louise's Ghost," from Link's first collection, *Stranger Things Happen*, Louise has come to be haunted by a ghost:

Louise woke up. It was three in the morning. There was a man lying on the floor beside the bed. He was naked . . . He was large, not fat but solid. Yes, he was solid. It was hard to tell how old he was. It was dark, but Louise doesn't think he was circumcised.

The man vanishes, reappears elsewhere; he shrinks, grows hair all over. He's never able to sit or stand—he only creeps across the floor or appears in the closet or under the bed—and he never speaks. Louise's best friend, another Louise, who is a lover of cellists, devises a plan to rid Louise of her ghost. Louise-the-friend will invite the eight cellists of the symphony orchestra—all of whom she has slept with—to come and play at Louise's house, and the ghost will be drawn into one of the cellos. "Apparently it's very good for the music," she tells Louise. The cellists all gather and play like mad, but Louise suddenly doesn't want her ghost to go. "He pulls himself up, shakes the air off like drops of water. He gets smaller. He gets fainter. He melts into the cello like spilled milk." The lucky cellist "holds onto his cello as if it might grow legs and run away if he let go. He looks like he's discovered America." At a concert, Louise glimpses her ghost within the body of the cello, squirming happily.

"Louise's Ghost" illustrates another variance of the New Ghost from the old: what the dead demand from the living they haunt, if *haunt* isn't a word too purposeful to begin with. Saunders's ghosts tend to persist, as the older ghosts often did, because of the unresolved, violent, sudden way they died; often, they are forced to reenact or reexperience their terrible deaths over and over until they are at last somehow freed, usually by a spasm of compassion on the part of a living person. This is familiar, but the actual interactions of dead persons with the living in New Ghost stories are riddled with comic misunderstanding and well-meaning inadequacy. In Saunders's "The Wavemaker Falters," a little boy, Clive, whom the narrator has, by an error, allowed to be sucked into an amusement park wave machine and chewed up, comes into the narrator's room at night to sit by his bed. "Even though he's dead, he's still basically a kid. When he tries to be scary he gets it all wrong . . . He's scariest when he does real kid things, like picking his nose and wiping it on the side of his sneaker."

> Saunders's ghosts tend to persist because of the unresolved, violent, sudden way they died.

He tries to be polite but he's pretty
mad about the future I denied him.
Tonight the subject is what the Mexico
City trip with the perky red-haired
tramp would have been like . . . Wistfully
he says he sure would have liked to have
tasted the sauce she would have said was
too hot to be believed as they crossed
the dirt road lined with begging cripples.

"Forgive me," I say in tears.

"No," he says in tears.

The unsatisfied dead in Link's story "The Hortlak" are less interpretable by the living. Technically, the people who come up out of the Ausible Chasm at night and wander through the aisles of the all-night convenience store that stands on its brink aren't ghosts but zombies—that is, they are not wandering spirits so much as dead bodies, crumbling and smelly, but ambulatory:

> The zombies didn't talk at all, or they said things that didn't make sense . . . "Glass leg. Drove around all night in my wife. Did you ever hear me on the radio?" They tried to pay Eric for things the All-Night didn't sell . . . Things the zombies tried to purchase were plainly things they had brought with them into the store—things that had fallen or been thrown into the Ausible Chasm . . . The zombies liked shiny things, broken things, trash like empty soda bottles, handfuls of leaves, sticky dirt, dirty sticks.

The store owner regards the zombies as "just another thing you had to deal with in retail." Eric "hoped they found what they were looking for. After all, he would be dead someday too, and on the other side of the counter."

Most ghosts in classic posthumous fantasies can't interact physically with the living—it's a great trial for them.

But it would be wrong to say that New Ghosts always arise in blandly wacky or surreal circumstances. Nick Antosca's *Midnight Picnic*, though it passes through some comic moments, is darkly gripping from the start and gets only more dreadful as it progresses. A drifter named Bram uncovers the bones of a young boy murdered decades before in the woods, and the boy's ghost along with them. The boy, who was killed by a man hiding from the law, wants vengeance, and his touch is enough to draw Bram into his world. Unlike Saunders's Clive, the boy, Adam, is fearsomely determined:

> "You don't want to help me anymore!" Adam starts crying. His face turns red and crinkles. "You can see me. I'm a person too. I'm just a little kid."
>
> "You keep saying that," Bram says, "but you don't always seem like it."

Adam and Bram embark on a journey that, without the explicit crossing of a boundary, takes them into the land where the dead are. They drive there in an ancient Buick abandoned by Adam's murderer. The dead land contains a mall of dead children, with a poster store that sells hundreds of film posters, all for the same film: *The Martian Chronicles*, with Rock Hudson. There is a Roy Rogers restaurant, with drive-thru, where there is no payment, and where the eaters don't eat. A "long, wide highway empty of cars." The dead and their land somehow coexist with the living and theirs; dogs see the dead but can't recognize them—they have no smell. "In the distance an outlet mall glows dimly. It seems like there is always an outlet mall glowing dimly in the distance."

Antosca keeps his strange realm in delicate balance, horrific, weird, puzzling. His ghosts are conflicted, capable of pain and harm. Adam is monstrous, but also just a kid. Bram, a bewildered Dante, sins and is sorry, is trapped and, at last, we hope, escapes that dead land—for now.

2. Afterlives

The critic John Clute, in his perspicacious *Encyclopedia of Fantasy* (1994, online version in preparation), identifies some subsets of the ghost story. Clute terms *posthumous fantasies* those stories in which dead people who don't realize they are dead must come to understand their condition—Charles Williams's classic *All Hallows Eve* is one example, M. Night Shyamalan's *The Sixth Sense* another. What distinguishes a posthumous fantasy is locus, or point of view: whereas the usual ghost story takes the point of view of a living person encountering the dead, posthumous fantasies describe the experiences of dead people from their own point of view. (Vladimir Nabokov's *The Eye* is narrated by one such.)

New Ghosts know they're dead, though sometimes they forget. Most ghosts in classic posthumous fantasies can't inter-

act physically with the living—it's a great trial for them, trying to get the attention of a living person, whether to harm or help them (see, for instance, Audrey Niffenegger's *Her Fearful Symmetry*). But New Ghosts aren't forbidden this kind of interaction. Roberto Bolaño's recent story "The Return" tells of a ghost witnessing his own freshly dead body being fooled with by a necrophiliac; the ghost has a lengthy conversation with the man, eventually taking pity on him and his sad desires.

Clute once named another sort of posthumous fantasy the *afterlife fantasy*, a term he now finds somewhat hairsplitting, but which I like, maybe for just that reason. Afterlife fantasies (as I would use the term) take place not on the earth that the point-of-view ghost formerly inhabited but in the realm to which the dead are remanded. These realms can involve Dantesque divisions between the saved and the damned, or they can be a lot like our world, though more labile, as in the afterlife that Alice Sebold posits in *The Lovely Bones*, where earthly life can be perceived by the dead, and possibly altered.

The New Afterlife story, though, is not usually about learning or transformation or redemption, nor about judgment or punishment, but simply further existence—though sometimes with the possibility of a deeper death, a lapse into nothingness or into a persistence without qualities. (Adam in *Midnight Picnic* dies a further death.) Kevin Brockmeier's *The Brief History of the Dead* derives its scheme for an afterlife from African beliefs that the dead remain alive to themselves for just so long as someone on earth remembers them; after that they're gone for good. Brockmeier's dead, after a "Crossing" different for everyone, find themselves in a vast, nameless city of monuments, suburbs, parks, slums, bridges: a triumph of New Ghost technology, where no judgments are made and the unsurprised souls carry on as before (get jobs, eat at diners, fall in love, have hobbies) until they vanish—thus the brief history. The delicious trick of Brockmeier's book is to imagine an apocalyptic virus released on earth that eventually kills everyone but a lone researcher stuck in the Antarctic who struggles to stay alive while everyone in the dead city wonders why whole districts are becoming depopulated, and why everyone left is somehow connected to a single living person.

This life and the afterlife—or "earthside" and "airside," as Alison, the professional medium in Hilary Mantel's acerb and complex novel *Beyond Black*, calls them—can commonly be bridged in New Ghost stories, with traffic in both directions; and mediums, as the name implies, can be the bridge. Alison seems, at first, to be no different from the mediums we know in reality, her practice a compound of showmanship, hit-or-miss guessing, and generalizations that could suit anyone; the difference is that Alison's spirit guides are present to the reader, active in her earthside life, and quite sinister. They are, we learn, men now dead who tormented Alison when she was young, the neglected and abused daughter of a part-time prostitute; they were thieves, tricksters, and sadists, and Alison was subject to them, and fought back, too. That one with the missing eye, the other with the missing testicles—that was Alison's doing. These horrid lowlifes are, we come to see, not out to help Alison but to punish her for her resistance back in the day.

There are things you need to know about the dead, she wanted to say . . . For instance, it's no good trying to enlist them for any good cause you have in mind, world peace or whatever. Because they'll only bugger you about. They're not reliable . . . They don't become decent people just because they're dead.

Alison's earthside, an England in decline into falsity, fear, ugliness, and disorder, is as bleak as Antosca's dead land, and more thickly textured. The afterlife she describes to her audiences isn't much better:

. . . that eventless realm neither cold nor hot, neither hilly nor flat, where the dead, each at their own best age and marooned in an eternal afternoon, pass the ages with sod-all going on . . . There's a certain nineteen-fifties air about the dead, or early sixties perhaps, because they're clean and respectable and they don't stink of factories . . . No wind blows here, only a gentle breeze, the temperature being controlled at a moderate 71 degrees Fahrenheit; these are the English dead, and they don't have centigrade yet.

But out of this flavorless afterworld come Alison's former tormentors, now fiends personally trained by the Boss, called Nick—and if they fail to please Nick, punishment awaits: you can be eaten, "and you don't get another round."

Alison knows that if she can do one selfless, good act she can defeat her pursuers, and although her good act has awful unintended consequences, it succeeds: her fiends are sent packing. That kind of moral arithmetic doesn't seem in the New Ghost mode, really, but the futility of most bargains that can be made in Mantel's world (where there's a devil but no God), and the longing for hope and resolution versus the blackly comic offerings from "airside" one gets instead, makes *Beyond Black* a strong and unique New Ghost work.

3. Out of the Past

Of course, new literary and artistic modes, unlike scientific paradigms, don't replace older ones. The matter-of-fact acceptance of the dead among us and an easy (though sometimes inconsequential or muddled) interaction with them are also a feature of magic-realist fiction now a half century old. There's a difference, though. Latin American magic-realist tales like *100 Years of Solitude* or *Doña Flor and Her Two Husbands* treat as fact those things that the characters in them, living with at least one foot in an animistic

world, naturally believe to be so. The former slaves and their troublesome ghost relations in Toni Morrison's *Beloved* are an example from a different continent and century, in which the near presence of the dead and the other world are daily realities. New Ghosts, though, mostly interact with people who have no such cultural receptivity; they're just the plain, postindustrial, postcolonial, deracinated people around us now.

A story that adopts ghost traditions that aren't the author's own might have to be listed under a different heading: Christopher Barzak's *The Love We Share Without Knowing* has its locus in the pervasive thinness of the modern Japanese urban cultural experience that even Japanese writers describe in which transitional worlds—sleep, death, afterlife, dream—seem equivalent to waking life; in their sadness and vacuity, the living (young people, particularly) can seem like ghosts, one easy step away from evanescence, an evanescence they sometimes long for. In Barzak's story, a "suicide club" of differently saddened and disappointed people dies together by burning charcoal briquettes inside a closed van and inhaling the fumes—apparently a common modern method. A Japanese character has to explain to an American how a rite or act that Americans would generally regard as the most solitary you can undertake is naturally communal in Japan. One of the

New literary and artistic modes, unlike scientific paradigms, don't replace older ones.

group survives, but remains in the company of the others, who are now dead. Suffocated longing is the central emotion throughout the book; the American visitors are overcome by it, too, drawn to Japanese lovers as characters in Japanese folktales are drawn to spirits.

Barzak's long menu of marvels might have been treated in extravagant postmodern mash-up mode, but he chose the bare and allusive tone and style of such writers as Haruki Murakami (*Kafka on the Shore*) and Banana Yashimoto (*Asleep*); his Japanese world also carries a whiff of that special delicacy and fragility that certain Westerners, like the Japanophile American Patrick Lafcadio Hearn, have perceived in Japanese culture. By the time the tale reaches the festival of Obon (a Day of the Dead that Hearn also described), Barzak has created the conditions for a lovely and truly ghostly mingling of living and dead, farewells and reconciliations, remembering and forgetting.

Writers, of course, still have the modernist or Jamesian doubtful ghost to return to if they choose, and Sarah Waters, in *The Little Stranger*, does so with a thoroughgoing conviction, even placing her tale in a richly rendered past time (1949) and place (a crumbling British country house populated by impoverished gentry). The vengeful something that inhabits the house, the little stranger, is never seen, and every manifestation of it or her (is it Madame's long-dead first child?) can be explained away, or almost away. The skeptical doctor who narrates never quite capitulates to an otherworldly explanation of the haunting, though, of course, we readers do. Waters's realism is not the magical kind; her constant, careful building up, over many pages, of social moments or shifting feelings, as an illusionist painting is built up by hundreds of minute brushstrokes, is so convincing (and so convincingly of its purported time) that what is essentially a standard family-curse story, which in the past would have fit nicely into twenty pages, emerges as unfamiliar, and newly chilling.

> The double vision tickles; the right response is a delighted gasp of laughter.

In fact, the more ghost stories I read, the more variety I find: ambitious stories and standard ones, noirish and punkish ones, sentimental and somber ones. *Twenties Girl*, by Sophie Kinsella, author of *Shopaholic*, is a ghost *comedy*, among the many descendants of Thorne Smith's deathless *Topper* (1926). Ghosts are also crowding into popular films and television, from corny romances in which a mischievous dead spouse upsets the applecart of a living one to the very New Ghost–like ghosts in *Six Feet Under*.

Criticism strives to note real distinctions, not invent false ones. In trying to taxonomize the New Ghost story, and distinguish something that's in New Ghost stories and not in other kinds, I have come to see not a break with past masters so much as a *clinamen*, to use Harold Bloom's term: both an appropriation and a swerve into new meaning.

Freud theorized that, as modern people, we no longer believe in ghosts in any literal sense, and thus lay ourselves open to certain attacks of fear and dread that we can ascribe to no cause. So the New Ghost—so frankly put forward, so easily accepted by the living persons in the story—might be a renewed assertion of the possibility of palpable ghosts, and of congress with them, perhaps making our resolution of fear and dread more achievable. But I think not. I think that the New Ghosts can arise in fiction now just because we absolutely *don't* believe in walking spirits anymore, not even down deep. The indistinct but shuddery possibilities that power the modernist ghost story, which Waters still deploys, do not require belief, but they do require the temporary suspension of disbelief, which the author promotes by a careful ambiguity, maintained until the story's done. New Ghost stories ask for no suspension of our disbelief at all: disbelief is actually central to their effect.

It's said that when Akira Kurosawa was making his early samurai films, he tried to figure out how John Ford, in his Westerns, had given such power and affect to scenes in which a character, having been gun-shot or arrow-pierced, fell slowly to the ground. *Very* slowly. Somehow, such moments seemed to be prolonged beyond what was possible for an actor and a camera. Unable to figure out how Ford achieved the effect, Kurosawa shot his own falling dead men *in slow motion* to reproduce it. The first audiences for those films, both in Japan and America, were familiar with the Ford films, and would have felt—even if unconsciously—a kind of double vision in Kurosawa's slow-motion trick. But Kurosawa wasn't trying to fool us. Though the story of his working it out might imply so, his solution wasn't a failure. It was a success. Kurosawa was showing us the Ford moment, emptied of its original life-and-death power by becoming an obvious yet subtle gesture, a gesture in an art of his own making. In Russian formalist criticism this is called *baring the device*. It's not supposed to go unnoticed. By brilliantly reminding us of what it is *not*—its great predecessors—a work of art makes something new. The double vision tickles; the right response is a delighted gasp of laughter. It's a response that seems proper to New Ghosts, one of the signs by which we may know them. Link, Saunders, Antosca, and Mantel use the matter of an earlier, more sincere, and purposeful art, and their use of it has to be *insincere* at bottom; but that insincerity is their stories' signal virtue. There's nothing in it of camp, or simple jokiness, or snarky irony; even less of nostalgia or wishful thinking. Stories of that sort can be defined out. The insincerity of New Ghost stories is instead at once a salute to the old and an assertion of new mastery. 🏮

FICTION

Bright Before Us

Katie Arnold-Ratliff

As I drove to school, I realized that the only way to survive whatever came next was to retreat into my own head. I considered feigning a sore throat, pretending my voice was gone; no one asks questions of those who can't answer. I thought about tasks that would take the kids all day and accomplish nothing. Here, sort these lima, pinto, and kidney beans; here, write down all the animals you can think of. I would create a baseline of normalcy and wouldn't attempt to better it. I downed two Vicodin; not enough to put me out, but plenty to accomplish the spaced-out order of the day.

I parked outside Hawthorne, walked carefully up the hall, and found the door open. I stepped into the classroom, expecting to see the janitor.

Mr. Mason, the principal said gently. She was one of several adults in the room: Six or seven parents stood along the walls or crouched beside their children. Mr. Noel was sitting at my desk, holding his son, Caleb's, backpack.

Mr. Mason, the principal said again.

The clock's second hand was deafening. The few children who had come with their parents were silent, curious about why the grown-ups were present. Some of the parents stared in my direction, below my line of sight. I followed their gaze to my hands, which were thrust downward, clenched into fists.

Our task that morning was to learn to sing in a round, and I said a prayer of thanks that I had scheduled something easy. The parents were concerned. This I understood. I knew their children must have been overflowing with questions, spouting them in little bursts of alarm whenever an image from the field trip returned—the body's bloodless skin against the sand, the sight of me sobbing, the unsmiling policemen. It made sense to me that the parents had come; they were offering their support, making my job easier—there were so many children and just one teacher. We would need to work together.

The principal pulled me aside and confirmed this. *Frank,* she said gently, *nothing to worry about, just—the kids had a rough weekend, as I'm sure the parents told you last night . . . I know I got several calls—*

No, I said. *No one called me.*

She nodded. *Well, they just want to ease the kids back into the classroom, and so they're all going to stay as long as they can today, and maybe tomorrow . . .*

An excerpt from *Bright Before Us,* forthcoming from Tin House Books May 2011.

PREVIOUS PAGE: © PHOTO BY PAUL BURNS/GETTY IMAGES

I must have been frowning, because she started speaking faster. *But I really doubt they'll be here past then*—she put her hands up defensively—*and they'll stay out of the way, obviously.*

There was a pause, and I imagined her retracing her steps. She was realizing this was a breach of etiquette; it was dawning on her that she should have discussed it with me. She tried another approach, her face softening. *And how are you doing, in all of this?* She placed her hand on my shoulder. I looked down at it.

An image from the field trip returned—the body's bloodless skin against the sand, the sight of me sobbing.

Okay, I think we should probably get started now, I said, turning away. I heard myself speak in a higher pitch than normal, like something was pressing on my throat, choking off my air. *Mr. Noel, maybe you can give me a hand moving these tables?* The class needed to divide into two groups— one to begin the song, another to come in seconds later. Mr. Noel stood slowly, his eyes bugged, and lumbered toward me. I saw the principal walk over to the parents, nodding and shaking hands and being gentle with them like they were children who had fallen down. I was aware of the eyes watching me as, with a pealing squeak against the floor tiles, Mr. Noel and I dragged the tables to the perimeter of the room. I could hear fragments of the principal's quiet speech to the parents. *The important thing to remember . . . difficult time, certainly.*

Frank, Mr. Noel said, *I just want to mention that I've done some work in schools.*

I strained to hear the principal. *. . . . Just up the hall if it seems like . . . my eyes and ears, here.*

Pardon? I said to Mr. Noel.

Some of us guys from the fire department go to schools and talk about what it's like. You know, to the kids.

. . . Don't hesitate to alert me to . . . benefit of the doubt . . .

Oh, I said to Mr. Noel. *That's great.*

So, Mr. Noel said, *if you need me to take over at any point, just holler.*

I frowned at him, struggling to stand up straight.

Greta was scheduled for a sonogram that night. She had made the appointment for the evening, having taken the night off, and it was disconcerting to drive to a hospital in the dark. It was something I had only ever done in an emergency: slicing off part of my thumb chopping garlic, breaking my collarbone falling from a bike.

Is this a checkup ultrasound, or a particular kind of ultrasound, or what? I asked.

She shrugged. *What do you mean?*

Are they checking for something? A defect?

She rolled down the window, spitting out her gum. *The baby is doing great,* she said. *I can feel it.*

Good, I said, looking for parking. *That's good.*

Inside, the doctor confirmed her intuition. *Everything is a-okay,* he said. Greta's expression bore a whiff of petulance, as if she had won a bet.

I bought her an ice-cream sandwich at the gas station, and when we got home, we lay down on the bed to listen to an old CD on the stereo. She rested her head on my shoulder, and I combed her hair with my fingers.

Are you doing okay? she asked me.

Of course, I said, my eyes clenched.

I know this is new to you.

It's new to you, too.

No, Frank—I mean that you've never lost anyone before.

She tensed, waiting for my response.

I'm fine, Gret.

We can talk about it if you want.

I sighed.

I know she meant a lot to you.

Stop, I said. *Please.*

She lifted her head from my chest and turned away. When I heard her breathing go ragged for long, difficult moments, and then slow finally into a distinct rhythm, I knew that she had cried herself to sleep.

The first time Greta miscarried, she waited only a few days to pack away the contents of the nursery. Everything had been yellow, her one nod to the unknown. A yellow wall hanging with a quilted sun; a yellow set of curtains. Yellow clothes, yellow blankets. A yellow liner for the bassinette. By then all of the pregnancy books had been read, the suitcase packed, though it wasn't yet necessary. Greta had collected an array of pants with elastic waistbands, had made lists, charts, budgets. We hadn't decided on names.

> We hadn't decided on names. She had been eleven weeks along.

She had been eleven weeks along.

I made the mistake of looking in a pregnancy book to see what a fetus looked like at that stage. *Your baby may soon be able to open and close his fists,* the caption said.

The second time, the hospital called me at Hawthorne, about two months after school started; a morning in November when I had given my students a photocopy of ten clocks and asked them to write the time below each. I came around to measure their progress.

Simon, how's it going? He had filled in only twelve o'clock.

What I don't like, he began, his voice edged with irritation, *is when the little hand is between the numbers.*

Okay, I said, *you have to see which number the small hand is—*

Am I just supposed to guess? he asked, exasperated.

The phone rang, and I patted Simon's shoulder, setting my pen down on his desk before walking away.

Mr. Mason, a woman said. I understood immediately—from the familiar sounds behind her, the discomfort in her voice, the fact that the classroom phone almost never rang.

You're from the hospital, I said.

Yes, she began.

But I cut her off. *Has something happened to my wife?*

I watched Simon squirrel my pen away, slipping it into the plastic tub under his desk.

Your wife will be fine, the nurse said.

Give IT! one of the kids said, somewhere behind me. *I said give it!*

The baby's dead, I said.

The children closest to me looked up.

Your wife has miscarried, sir, yes. You'll need to come pick her up. She paused only a moment before she asked, *Sir, did you hear me?*

Yes, I said flatly. *I heard you.*

The principal covered my class. I drove down the street beneath the elm trees that lined each side, their branches meeting above in a canopy. The world looked different—when I left school in the afternoon, the streets were always crowded with children walking home. But with class still in session, the school looked abandoned, the swings moving in the breeze. I had the uneasy feeling of playing hooky, like when I stayed home sick as a kid and got carted around on my mom's errands, suddenly privy to the workaday world. I turned on the radio absentmindedly, whistling to an upbeat tempo, tapping the rhythm on the steering wheel. I caught myself and shut the radio off, sitting at a red light, disgusted by my still-pursed lips.

———— •-• ————

That Tuesday night, the favorable sonogram behind us, Greta went into an upswing, cleaning the house with a fervor she pretended had been there all along. *This is how you're supposed to do it,* she said. Her actions took on a frantic, repentant quality, as though any show of capability would stave off what had come to feel inevitable.

As she cleaned, I slipped into the garage through the hallway door, telling her I would tidy the boxes of Christmas decorations, old school papers, other unnecessary shit we kept out of obligation. But then I snuck out through the retractable garage door, walking down the driveway to retrieve a bottle of whiskey from my trunk. I drank, among the Christmas lights and mildewed boxes, until my belches were accompanied by wet trails. I spun my wrist, cracking it: click, click, click, the tendons vibrating like harp strings. I continued drinking until I couldn't stand.

I woke up on the cement a few hours later, walked back into the house, brushed my teeth, and was happy to find Greta silent, perhaps even sleeping, when I got into bed. I slept deep and heavy, like something was pressing on top of me. But at the sound of some nocturnal animal rustling outside I stirred, my hand going to my head. I turned toward Greta. Her eyes were open. *It's okay,* she said. *You had a nightmare.*

I did?

It's okay, she said again, brushing her hand across my temple. *What are you so scared of?*

I ran my dry tongue over the ridged ceiling of my mouth. *I'm not scared,* I said.

You're terrified, Greta said. In the dark, it was hard to see. Her expression shifted with the shadows.

I didn't have a nightmare, I said. *Why did you say that?*

I can tell, she said.

There was a knock at the bedroom door.

Come in, Greta said.

A massive stroller, its seats lined up in a row, rolled forward and into the room, and around us swelled an awful, searing light; the paint on the walls began to blister. I looked down into the stroller. Three faces stared placidly back.

Oh, good, Greta said.

When I woke a moment later, Greta was standing in front of the mirror.
It's okay, she said flatly. *You were having a nightmare.*

Wednesday morning, I skipped the shower and instead rose from bed, walked to the bathroom, ran the tap, and dunked my head. I was so hungover my lips trembled, my tongue still numb from the alcohol. My neck was destroyed—a familiar injury from a car accident, reawakened now and again by a hasty turn or an incorrect angle to my pillow, had this morning limited my mobility to a sickening degree: I wasn't sure I'd be able to look over my shoulder when changing lanes. I popped the last of the Vicodin as I made my way to work.

> I was so hungover my lips trembled, my tongue still numb from the alcohol.

I waited for her arrival, but the principal never showed. As the moments ticked past and she remained absent, I felt ever lighter, slowly filling with relief, bathed in chilly sweat.

Oh my God, I thought. It's going to get better.

There were a few parents still present, and once again I felt I understood their presence for what it was: not about me. They were here for their kids.

Good morning, Mr. Mason, Mrs. Stone said.

Good morning, I said back.

They were there because they wanted to give their children one extra boost of support; they wanted to ease them back into life's inevitable trajectory, the parent-ectomy—*you go here during the day, and I go there*—before quietly backing out of the room, confident that their kids had readjusted. I just need to keep repeating this, I remember thinking. Just keep on believing this.

Take your seats, take your seats, I sang out, rallying every ounce of my strength to say the words, to do this small thing, to exist. *I'm counting to five and anyone still standing is last to go to afternoon recess . . .*

I mounted my stool before the wall of windows, legs bowed like a cowboy. *Time to play Description, gang,* I said. *Who's ready with an object?*

Amber's hand shot up. *Apple,* she said: a perennial, predictable favorite.

Okay, apple. Who's ready with a description word?

Amber's hand went skyward.

Let's let someone else have a turn, I said. *Who's ready?*

Me! Jeff said. *Apple is round!*

No it ain't! yelled Mariana.

Jeff looked at me helplessly. *It's almost round?*

I had my mouth open to speak when someone else did: *Hands raised, I think, is the rule,* Mr. Noel said. The kids all turned to stare at him, dumbfounded. Before I could stanch it, I felt my face smear with snide shock. The words spilled from my mouth before my drowning brain could catch up:

Do you mind? I said.

> I'd gotten away with one sharp remark; if I stayed, I knew I'd make another.

The three or four seconds that followed had a high-pitched whine about them, barely audible, like a teakettle seconds from a full-on wail. I could feel each instant teetering on some kind of awkward fulcrum, deciding which way to go: all-out confrontation, as is always imagined in those sorts of moments in the corner of the brain that governs fight or flight—or what actually happened, which was absolutely nothing. Mr. Noel pretended I hadn't spoken; I turned back to the kids and smiled insincerely, and a few somebodies called out—without raising hands—*Red! Green! Shiny!*

We got through six nouns—I was so exhausted that the final one, *pillow,* drove me to distraction—and I said I had to visit the restroom and then carry out another small errand: *I'm just going to run up the hall to the copier to make a few . . .* I paused, delaying the stupid, inevitable final word: *copies,* I finally said. I had to get out of there. I'd gotten away with one sharp remark; if I stayed, I knew I'd make another.

After the final bell rang, most of the parents escorted their children outside to begin the car or bus or cab rides home. I planned on staying late to correct the children's reading responses from the week before. Rebekah needed to stay, too—we had just begun double-digit addition, carrying numbers, and she was one of the many who was struggling. Her father often let her linger after school, until she could finish her reading or confidently spell *CALIFORNIA.*

I'd be happy to walk her through the math again today, I told her father that afternoon.

I should get her home, he said.

It's no trouble, I said. *I'm always glad to help her.*

He grimaced. *I'll come back at 4:30.*

Great, I said, trying to ignore his reluctance. *We'll have her caught up in no time.*

We went over it and over it, and then Rebekah returned to her chair; though I knew she still didn't understand, I let her. And then, sure enough, at quarter to four she finally caved in and walked back over, frowning. *Mr. Mason, I don't get it,* she said. Her paper was translucent, worn thin by erasure.

Here's how it works, I said, beginning again, repeating verbatim what I had said already. *The number is two digits long. There's only one spot for a number, so the other number gets carried.*

Okay, she said, not comprehending.

Rebekah, I started to say, *I think we should—*

The classroom's phone rang, startling me. I set her paper down, watching the receiver tremble in its cradle.

Shit, I said aloud. I told her, my mouth dry, *Just a sec, okay?* before hesitantly answering the phone. *I can finish helping you in just a second.*

I spoke into the receiver. *Is this about my wife?*

A male voice cleared its throat. *This is Officer Buckingham.*

We took turns exhaling.

Mr. Mason, have you got a minute? I tried you at home, but—

I'm with a student.

This won't take long.

Rebekah watched me. I mouthed again, *Just a sec.* She ignored me, holding her paper up.

I'm wondering if you've been able to remember more about the time line that day, Buckingham said.

Is that my dad? Rebekah said.

Sorry, I said to Buckingham, shaking my head at Rebekah. *The time line? What does that mean, exactly?*

I was just going over what happened, he said. I heard him sip something, heard the mug being set back down on his desk. I heard the faint air of irritation in his voice. *Just filling in the blanks in my report, really. I was wondering how long you and your class were at the beach beforehand.*

Mr. Mason, Rebekah said, *is my dad coming soon?*

Bek, can you sit at your table for just a minute? I said, holding my hand over the receiver. *I'll be right there.* Into the phone, I said, *I think we were probably there twenty minutes before she jumped, maybe thirty, but I—*

Buckingham was silent. I felt my spine snap taut as a tripwire.

*I—I didn't—*All I could manage was a whisper.

He scoffed. *You saw someone jump off the bridge?*

No, I said, scrambling. *I didn't.*

You didn't bother to tell me this?

No, I didn't mean to say—

He cut me off again. *Christ,* he said. *Start over. Tell me whatever it is you're not—*

I think I interrupted you, I said, interrupting him. *What did you—you needed to know something. What did you need again?* I hastened to cover my tracks, erase what I had said with new words; I talked so fast I doubted he could understand me.

He said nothing for several moments. I knew he was sorting through our interactions, evaluating my motives, gauging my veracity.

Start over, he said again.

I took a deep breath. Rebekah fidgeted in her seat. Outside, a motor-cycle bellowed down the narrow street.

I know I should have said this sooner, I said carefully. *But the body on the beach . . .*

Rebekah looked up. I turned my back on her.

. . . The woman on the beach . . .

Yes? He sounded spring-loaded. I pictured him leaning forward in his chair. This time, I didn't feel the usual quickening, the lightness of a lie being borne out of my body—as I spoke what came next, it seemed pure, definitive, clear as water. Real and whole and impregnable.

. . . The woman on the beach was my wife.

Your wife, he said.

My first wife. I got confused when I said I saw her jump. I was just confused.

And why's that?

Because I had nightmares about it all weekend, I said. *I kept dreaming that I saw her jump. My ex-wife.*

There was a harsh little beat of silence. *Why didn't you tell me this at the scene?*

I wasn't certain then, I said.

And what's made you certain now?

I sorted through things. Evaluated my motives. Gauged my veracity.

I was in shock, I said slowly. *You saw me at the beach. I didn't understand why I was so upset, and then over the last few days I've . . .*

I turned around. Rebekah was standing at the window, watching the cars pass.

. . . I've had a chance to process.

Have you tried to call this woman—what's her name?

Nora Lucas, I said. *No, I haven't called her.*

Well, look, I can't just—

I stopped by her house, I said. *She wasn't there. She hadn't been there in a while. Look, isn't there any evidence you can, that you can divulge?*

I don't know what's going on here, Mr. Mason, he said. *But I can't share anything with you about this case until identity of the deceased can be established.*

I tensed. *But you know the identity, I'm telling you who . . .*

As my voice rose, Rebekah turned to watch me.

This is my wife, I said, weighting the final syllable.

So you said.

My chest tightened.

I need you to come down to the station, Mr. Mason. You said you're with a student—can someone else take over for you?

I sputtered. *You're just going to ignore what I told you?*

There was a long pause, and when he spoke again his tone had shifted. In place of his anger was something new; he held it back enough that it took a finely tuned ear to discern its presence, but it was there: pity.

Frank, listen, I'll be honest with you . . .

I don't understand, I said. I felt a helpless, hiccupping laugh rise in my throat. *It's the truth. She jumped from the bridge.* I stared out the window, trying to collect my thoughts. *I didn't see her jump, I didn't mean to say . . . you could probably tell from the autopsy that—*

When he spoke again it was deliberate, slow. *Why do you think this woman is*—here he paused, presumably to look at his notes—*Nora Lucas? The deceased wasn't in a state in which—*

I grabbed a piece of chalk from the chalkboard's rim. *Not with any accuracy.*

He sounded perturbed. *Right.*

She was unhappy. I waded through my reasoning. *She told me, "This is where people come to die." I saw the body, and it was her. Her house was abandoned. The strands of red hair.* My fingers ground the chalk into an ashy dust.

His voice was quiet, compressed. *Mr. Mason, I think you've—*

I haven't, I said.

Outside, a car rolled past, blasting its radio.

I'd like it if you would come to the station right away, he said.

I replaced the receiver without another word. Walking over to Rebekah, I sat in the miniature chair beside her. We looked at each other for what seemed like a long time. *Here's how it works,* I said again. *There's only a place for one number. Only one number can go there. So the other one gets carried.*

She looked at the paper, and then back at me. *Why?* she said. 🖋

THE LIFE
HE LEFT HER

Douglas Bauer

The dark shadows of family secrets

My father died in August 2001, roughly seven years before my mother would. Some months after his death, while visiting her, I walked from her apartment at the edge of the village to the cemetery, a distance of two blocks. It was my first look at the gray marble gravestone they were to share. Reaching it, I saw that its polished face was relatively plain; their names were, of course, carved next to each other, and there were touches of scrollwork in the upper corners, but it had none of the beveled filigree distinguishing many of the neighboring stones.

When I returned to my mother's apartment, she was waiting eagerly for my opinion. Did the stone look too bare? I said no, its simplicity was exactly right, which was true. But I could tell my words did little

to reassure her. She said she wished she'd ordered a marble base. She was worried that the stone's sitting directly on the ground made it appear unfinished, incomplete.

The nature of her fretting seemed to me to betray a concern that its design might reflect poorly on her taste, and maybe even more on her generosity. I suppose I imagined her worrying that, in the judgment of her self-scrutinizing little Iowa town, the spareness of the stone showed she'd scrimped on the cost. Although her name was next to his, I'm sure I saw the stone as something *she* had bought for *him*, as something marking *his* life and its end, not, ultimately, hers, too, and not their life together. She was, after all, quite vibrantly alive, which partly explains my assumption. But only partly.

In my parents' nearly sixty years of marriage, there were no outlandish public treacheries, no flagrant adulteries. There was no drama at high volume. Instead, their marriage was a long narrative of quiet erosion, their years together marked by the slow wearing away of her respect for him. In reaction, he retreated more and more into a silent obduracy. He seemed to be a person who met the world deferentially, to a fault, reflexively submitting to the preferences of others.

> My mother bristled whenever she heard some East Coast wag on radio or television make a crack about a hick farmer from Iowa.

Running beneath, however, was an enormous stubbornness; often his way of getting what he wanted was simply not to do what he'd said he would when it went against some stronger, private wish.

My mother was an almost comically ardent Midwest chauvinist. She bristled whenever she heard some East Coast wag on radio or television make a crack about a hick farmer from Iowa. I remember her once standing in the kitchen at the ironing board, shaking her head at the radio and muttering, "Oh, good lord," as she listened to an interview with one of the state's long-serving senators, a man with the perfectly Dickensian name of Bourke B. Hickenlooper.

I believe she lived in a kind of mortal terror of my father doing something that would reveal him, and therefore her, to be a hick farmer from Iowa. Once, in Boston, they took my partner, Sue, and I to brunch, and at the end of the meal my father got the check and put down his credit card. But he'd not tucked the card into the leatherette folder's little plastic pocket so the waiter could see it. Noting this, she made a sound of complete exasperation, a prosecutorial near syllable, moist and mean, at the back of her throat. Then she opened the folder and, rolling her eyes, put the credit card into the plastic pocket.

Imagine the aggregate effect of such relentless monitoring, of his knowing she was waiting for him to make his next mistake. He invariably chose the wrong spot in a parking lot, arranged suitcases in the trunk the wrong way. He chose the wrong shirt to wear, the wrong living-room lamp to turn on, the most inconvenient time to come in from the fields for the midday meal.

What a merciless lens to put on the daily tedium of a marriage. The result was a kind of silent-film sped-up jumpiness as he offered the wrong hand or rushed to open the wrong door.

The day after his funeral, I went with my mother to their bank to search the contents of their safe deposit box. The bank manager led us into a room with the box, offering condolences along the way.

At first, we took the time to pause and reflect on the letters and contracts as we removed them from the box. If I asked a question, she let her memory take as long as it wished in answering. Soon enough, the various documents started to pile up on the table, and the more they accumulated, the more the nostalgia left her voice. We'd yet to find what we had specifically come for—the life insurance policy my father had taken out some years ago.

I had no idea how much it was worth, but it was clear that her mind was greatly eased in knowing it was there, remembering his assurances to her that she needn't worry, that when he was gone she'd be taken care of. It would hardly make her wealthy, but, along with Social Security, it would take the edge off her deep anxieties about money. She'd be able to live in an apartment of reasonable size, maintain the 1998 bottle-green, boat-sized Buick she drove, and go with a friend after church for Sunday dinner at her favorite franchise restaurant, all without having to ask herself whether she could afford it.

At the bank, we sped up into a rhythm of alert cooperation—reach in, withdraw, quickly examine, and discard, her turn, my turn, her turn, my turn. It became like one of those children's games, Crazy Eights or Pick-up Sticks, which requires no skill and involves no strategy. There was no skill or strategy in our game, either, just an increasingly anxious need for one of us, either of us, to win.

When, at last, I spotted the policy, I said, "Ah, here it is!" I handed it to her as though I was presenting a much overdue award.

My mother looked at the policy, with its tissue-thin pages in a light blue cover, and immediately said, "No. That's not it." When I looked again, I saw that it was a policy she'd taken out herself, for two thousand dollars, naming my brother as the beneficiary.

So we returned our attention to the safe deposit box. We found several contracts tracing the ownership of the farm, one a handwritten abstract from 1890, its perfect, ornate cursive a beautiful calligraphy. Others, from the 1930s on, documented the maneuverings of my kind, deeply shy Grandfather Bauer, a man deceptively shrewd about the commerce of land, with ten acres acquired here, six acres sold there.

And as we continued, I felt my worry building, building. Could she be wrong? Had she misunderstood? I kept glancing at her. I simply couldn't believe where this moment seemed to be going. Her eyes squinted with every document she reached for. Her face was growing increasingly pinched, looking as if she were trying to draw a badly frayed thread through a needle's eye.

Until we'd finished emptying the box.

We sat back, subsiding into a wrenching quiet. I fought the urge to lean forward again and peer down into the box, to run my hand along its bottom and feel its sides for the hidden compartment that held the policy, to turn the box upside down and shake it.

I've tried many times to imagine her feelings as she sat there—not her thoughts, but her feelings. But the best I can do is an image of a solar eclipse, darkness drawing swiftly across the terrain of what she'd thought her coming years would be.

We sat for what was probably not very long. My mind was frantically alive with questions. Had she ever actually seen a policy, or had he simply said there was one when there wasn't? Was there a chance it had been taken from the safe deposit box? Maybe packed with other papers when she'd moved from the farm?

Was it possible he'd actually cashed it? And was that even legally permissible without the presence and signature of its beneficiary? If it wasn't, this meant he *had* to have invented the whole thing, safe in his assurance that she'd never ask to see it. But if that's what he'd done, why?

I had no idea what to offer her, whether consolation, indignation, or disbelief. Any and all of these seemed both appropriate and not remotely enough. She appeared stunned, naturally, and in pain. But when she finally spoke, her voice sounded calm, her tone conclusive.

"It's my own fault," she said. "When it came to the money, I just let him handle it. I should have kept track of what was going on, but I didn't. I never paid attention." It was as if she'd already answered for herself all the questions that had come to me and some that had not. The only one left for her was not if or how or why but *when* he'd cashed it in.

All I could think to say was hopelessly inept. "I'm really sorry, Mom. I'm sorry."

Lines in her face converged at her puckered mouth like tightened netting. But even as she fought tears, she continued to give

off that particular calm when the terms of a grief are acknowledged and accepted.

She said nothing more. We sat a few minutes further until she'd composed herself, then she gathered up some papers and put everything else back in the box and locked it again.

In the lobby, as she was handing back the key, one of the tellers came around from behind the long counter and took her hand. "I'm so sorry," she said. "He was such a great guy. It was always fun when he came in. He was so friendly, so easy to talk to."

Mom managed a weak smile that the teller doubtless saw as sorrowful affection. "It's true," she said, "he could talk to anyone. When we went to the mall in Des Moines, he'd wait for me on a bench outside a store and I'd come out and he'd be having a great conversation with some total stranger."

"We'll miss him," said the teller.

We stepped outside and met the August day's sodden heat. I felt a need to fill an even more freighted silence and offered stupidly, "You know, Mom, there are two sides to all of us. The way we are in private and the way we are in the world. And they're both real. I mean, what I'm saying, his public self, the friendly guy who could start a conversation with anyone, that's who he was, too."

She'd been nodding regularly as I spoke, as if my nonsense had a meter. "Yes," she said, "they *were* both in him. They're in all of us, I know that. The trouble was, in Dad, those two ways you're saying . . . the talker you got the feeling he'd do anything for you, and the one who wouldn't budge when he didn't want to . . . they were too far apart."

Seven years later, the day after *her* funeral, I drove into the village past the cemetery where my parents' gravestone was one of hundreds rising up out of a January snow in long straight rows, like a bumper winter crop. I'd checked out of my motel and was headed for her apartment, where I would spend the next two days beginning to clear out her belongings.

She'd been a militant cleaner and keeper of rooms in my youth, so the velour of dust on her shelves, the shadow of scum ringing her bathtub, the few small balls of wadded-up Kleenex that lay on the carpet next to her bedroom wastebasket started a particular sadness in me. It was not so much for her death as for her life, for *life* itself, which seemed just then a dismal playing out of unremarkable diminishment.

It was late afternoon and growing dark when I began work in her bedroom. I turned on the bedside lights and opened a bureau drawer filled with scrapbooks and photo albums and envelopes stuffed with snapshots. I sat down on the floor and spread them out before me. There was a powerful fascination in seeing people I'd known so well for so long—my many aunts and uncles, my parents' friends—growing older or younger, depending on the image: becoming steadily heavier or increasingly gaunt, balder, flesh looser, faces more lined. But what really made me linger were the dozens of photos of my parents from the years my father was a soldier in Cheyenne, Wyoming.

They were newlyweds when she joined him there. For nearly four years they lived what I believe was far and away their happiest time. Growing up, whenever I heard them speak of it, their voices *lifted* on their memories: their landlords' son, Carl, a simple young man who spoke with a lisp and never learned to drive and rode his bicycle everywhere; the Valencia tavern, a downtown dive where my mother and her fellow clerks from the Montgomery Ward department store gathered after work; the night my father smuggled bottles of pure alcohol out of the dental lab to take back to the apartment to make bathtub gin.

Their achingly young faces in the snapshots were just the faces I pictured whenever I heard them recalling those years. There was one photo of them with their arms around each other, my father's lips pursed as if ready to whistle wolfishly. There was one that showed them flanking another man in uniform, a pipe jutting at a jaunty angle from his mouth, the three sitting on the concrete steps of the state capitol, their expressions conveying a happy slyness. Again and again, in photo after photo, their smiles suggested that life's pleasures could be sometimes bold and sometimes subtle,

> Had she ever actually seen a policy, or had he simply said there was one when there wasn't?

sometimes plain and sometimes intricate, and always deliciously close to illicit. In Cheyenne, they lived in a permissive present, a great, freeing distance from their past and their future. So that, whatever they thought they were, they knew—and especially, I suspect, my mother knew—that they were not hick farmers from Iowa. And, for all that she could tell, might never be.

Many times since the day I sat with my mother in the bank I've been tempted to see the missing life insurance policy as melodrama—my father's revenge from the grave. But that makes his mind Machiavellian, and it wasn't. To the extent he got revenge, it was accidental. He was a man who lived in dread of her caustic disapproval—*that* part of him was real, too; *that* was who he was, as well—and I believe his wish to elude it was simply too strong to let him tell her whatever he'd done that brought the need for money. Or what he'd done to get it. Which leaves the unanswerable questions of exactly what he did. And how heavily he suffered in living with it. And for how long.

Among all these questions, the only one I know the answer to, thanks to the lawyer who helped me settle the estate, is that the purchaser of a life insurance policy is its owner, and has the right to cash it in without the knowledge of its beneficiary.

The second morning of my stay, I sat at her kitchen table, sorting the contents of her wallet. There were various business cards

> Every week she wrote God a check for as much as she could give Him.

from companies and agencies I needed to call. There was a credit card I needed to cancel. I picked up her checkbook and began to scan the register. It felt too intimate an act, almost a violation. Here, somehow more nakedly than anywhere else, was her life revealed; what it cost her to live it.

She'd written checks to her landlord, by far the largest ones, and to the drugstore and the little grocery on the town square. She'd written checks to the telephone company and to a service, Lifeline, which provided her with a button on a necklace that she could push in an emergency to alert the hospital. Then, with little variance—an occasional check to Wal-Mart for around twenty dollars—she'd written these same few again.

For everything I'd known about how little she had, it was this stark arithmetic of her expenses, their unwavering recurrence dated and recorded, that brought home the remarkably spare commerce of her life, and with it the particular thought that *of course* she'd scrimped on the cost of their gravestone. What choice had she had?

There were two other regular checks, these written weekly. One, "Hair," was to the Colfax Beauty Parlor. It was usually for $12.84, though now and then she paid a few dollars more for something extra.

The other weekly check, recorded just below "Hair," and always for twelve dollars, was to "Church." At first it was the amount that caught my interest: twelve dollars a week—how had she arrived at that figure? I pictured her sitting down with the sums and long division of her life, compiling a list of its clear necessities and coming up with the figure she could afford to give without risking the embarrassment of a Sunday when she couldn't.

But as I thought further, it was not the amount of the check but the weekly writing of it, regular as a healthy pulse, that impressed me. Seeing "Church" repeatedly entered with her shaky, once-perfect Palmer-method penmanship was as though I'd come on a contract she'd signed and signed and signed. Every week she wrote God a check for as much as she could give Him. It seemed a statement of fidelity, of final conviction, of confirming an alliance.

The question for me is whether some parallel sense of fidelity, conviction, alliance shaped her feelings about my father at the end.

For here's the thing: to to my immeasurable surprise, in the last couple of years of my mother's life, something like that buoying Cheyenne lightness came into her voice when she spoke of him. Her tone grew warm. Her descriptions were fond. His foibles were recast, becoming ingrained quirks and not the behavior that had maddened her for decades. His recalcitrance became the constitutional resolve of a "stubborn German." This was a description she seemed weirdly prideful in awarding him, and she did so frequently. It was as if she were recalling a scampish renegade, shrugging her shoulders as if to say, *What was a gal to do?*

Given what I'd witnessed of their years together, and what I knew of his final betrayal, it was incredible to me that such seemingly genuine affection could appear, or resume. I'm not speaking here of memories, of her liking to recall the years when they were young, though she did that, too. Nor am I describing an old woman whose mind had become susceptible to confusion or nostalgia. Hers, to put it mildly, had not. Her *feelings* for my father, her attitude toward him, sounded young, her voice having found that Cheyenne timbre, and she seemed wholly untroubled when she invoked his name, except for her sadness that he was gone.

So I picture her in Cheyenne, with all her varieties of smile, and again at the close of her life, talking of my father in a spirit of fresh infatuation. I see the span of her years and these replicate emotions at their beginning and their end. At the start, her innocent excitement for the life they had and, she thought, *would* have. At the last, her grand alteration of the life they in fact had.

Sometimes, thinking about the life of their marriage, I've remembered Willa Cather's great novella, *My Mortal Enemy*, in which Myra Henshaw is filled with a bitter resentment that her long marriage has not continued the mythically romantic moment—a thrillingly scandalous elopement—that began it. Dying, she's asked why she's treated her husband so severely, and she replies, "Perhaps I can't forgive him for the harm I did him."

Perhaps my mother forgave my father for the harm she did him. Which is to say, she came to see that the person she was as a wife contributed vitally to his deceit. Perhaps she was then able to forgive herself—enough to sit down one day with her checkbook to worry about money, which was surely *every* day, which was surely constantly, and not resent the consequences of what he'd done. And so she was perhaps also able, another day, to visit the gravestone and see it as finished, and tastefully simple, and theirs.

In the bank that day, I saw her expression as one of eerie calm, her discovery more confirming than confusing. But now I wonder if she wasn't as shocked as I was; if what looked like dark calm was actually her attention turning inward to an unprecedented fear moving wildly through her.

How could she not have spent hours and hours in her last years trying to imagine his actions? Picturing him, maybe, defeatedly shaking his head, having spun some tale of woe for the insurance agent, as he signed the necessary papers in his office. Envisioning him taking a check to the bank for its deposit. Hearing him charming the tellers, as always, with his small-town, schmoozy patois.

It seems to me the only way she could have placed him convincingly in any of these scenes was to imagine him as someone else, not my withdrawn, domestically bumbling father. I could believe that unconsciously— not delusionally—over time, she might have explained his great deception to herself by letting a kind of hybrid emerge—the handsome young rake of the snapshots in Cheyenne with his mischievously puckering lips and his ate-the-canary grin, but turned devious and scheming. To do what he did, and yet receive her valedictory adoration, he would have needed to possess a boldly devious impulse. He would have needed to be a guileful version of the man she loved as a young newlywed. That man, that rascal, that stubborn German, would possess the lawless spirit willing to lie to save his own ass.

So she forgot or ignored or forgave his betrayal, which let her take her feelings for him all the way back to Cheyenne. In the end, *at* the end, that's where she needed them to be. And who am I to say it wasn't just the place for them? 🌢

Patricia Smith

BABY OF THE MISTAKEN HUE

Baby of the mistaken hue, child of the wrong nose
with its measure unleashed, baby of the nappy knot,
I am your mother. Mad at your whole damned face,
I swear to the task of torching the regrettable Delta
from your disobeying braids. I pinch your breathing
shut to reteach the bone, smear guaranteed cream
on your pimpled forehead, chin, and cheeks. I am
the corrector. Soaking a kitchen towel with the blaze
of holy water, I consider just what you are naked,
recoil at the insistent patches of midnight blanketing
your skin and I scrub, scrub, push the hard heel
of my hand deep into the dark, coax cleansing
threads of blood to the stinging surface, nod gently
in the direction of your *Mama, don't!* I command
you to bend, to turn, to twist in the wobbly dinette
chair and reveal what hides from me, those places
on you that still insist on saying Negro out loud.
Remember how the nonbelievers screeched their
nonbelief at Jesus even as He laid His giving hands
upon them? One day you will comprehend the torch
I am. You will be burned smaller, lighter, ever closer
to the whiteness of my God, who loves you as you are.

IT CREEPS BACK IN

And before I can focus, before I can remember
my exercises, I'm gulping gin and warm water,
I'm standing in front of an open Frigidaire spraying
butter into my mouth. In the bathroom, I brush
dead hair into the sink, stare hard at blackheads
and bleeding gums. I thought this had been healed
every Tuesday: *And are you still sleeping all day?*
Taking your pills on schedule? The blue ones?
They say depression can't be ignored, so I nurture
the drunkenness, say hello to pink rituals of throat.
Wiggling a finger inside myself, I'm wooed by the ghost
of current. September whispers *I still need you.*
It lies in the voice of a mother.

JOHANNESBURG
UNDERGROUND

Richard Poplak

The suitcase murder that stunned South Africa

Hillbrow is Johannesburg's central suburb, its dark heart. Lift a manhole cover, and you will find piles of clothing and books—a clandestine network of souls living below ground. By night, this dense, twenty-block stand of apartment buildings belongs to white men looking for black flesh, junkies after a fix, otherwise respectable men out cruising. By day, it belongs to businessmen, shopkeepers, black domestics pushing white kids in strollers. It is October 1964, the height of Apartheid. Hillbrow, like all of Johannesburg, has an underworld and an overworld, and only rarely do they meet.

In a block of flats called Groot Drakenstein, a black maid enters a third-floor apartment. A typical home of a lower middle-class white couple. She blinks in the low light, tasting iron in the air, as if in an abattoir. At first,

she thinks she sees great splotches of black paint, but soon she realizes otherwise. She hurries downstairs and tells the superintendent that Master Burch's place is covered in blood. She doesn't want to touch it. The super looks up from her knitting and—in a gruesome version of the domestic pageant that plays out across the country hundreds of times a day—tells the maid that there is no blood up there, and if she wants to keep her job, she'd better stop being so lazy.

The maid shuffles back up the open stairs, sucking in hunks of dry Highveld air, and goes to work. She spends hours on her knees, scrubbing the flat clean to the last microbe.

A week later, a young teacher named Robert Bekker stands on the western shore of Boksburg Lake, ten miles or so from Hill-

brow. Two dusty swans make lazy turns in the water. Boksburg is one of the mining towns strung like tarnished pearls along the main reef, linked to Johannesburg by gold. It is a quiet place of empty boulevards, centered by staunch brick churches.

Bekker notices a suitcase washed up on the shale. He opens it and finds a hock of water-logged meat wrapped in plastic, butcher paper, and a filthy sheet. The flesh is pocked with knife marks. He removes the sheet. A woman's breast, areola dark against a pallid mound, falls from of the suitcase. An arm follows. Organs spill out like a chicken's giblets.

> A woman's breast, areola dark against a pallid mound, falls from of the suitcase. An arm follows.

Scores of police arrive. Forensic specialists fingerprint what's left of the mutilated hands. They sift through backdated missing-person reports. Nothing matches. The coroner says that the torso spent between twenty-four and forty-eight hours in the water. It belongs to a white woman in her forties. He says, "The abdominal wall has been incised from the xiphisternum to the pubis, and the heart and lung have been removed from the thoracic cavity. There are numerous superficial stabs wounds in the thorax, heart, lungs, liver and arms. Almost the entire small bowel is missing." The coroner suspects that the woman was alive when much of this butchering took place. There are no signs of legs or a head.

The news that day, and for weeks and months thereafter, screams of the "Suitcase Murder." No one talks about anything else. "A KILLING AS JOBURG AS JACARANDAS," reads one headline, referring to the trees that carpet the city in purple flowers every spring.

Johannesburg is a mining town, a frontier post, and a perfect iteration of the Calvinist ethos that fashioned South Africa. Ambition and avarice are the presiding values. Prostitution, gambling, alcohol, gunrunning, stabbing, shooting, strangulation, horse whipping, abduction, rape, sodomy—in Johannesburg, the sheer cumulative scale of such activities is remarkable. Over the years and into the twenty-first century, the city has embraced violence with an esprit that prompts one to revise one's notions of human nature.

No surprise, then, that Johannesburg has produced an incredible and prodigious cast of villains. In 1914, the maniacally violent Foster Gang was cornered and killed in a cave in Bertrams, but not before the legendary Boer War general Koos de la Rey was accidentally shot at a roadblock meant for them. Daisy de Melker, a nurse who poisoned two successive plumber husbands for their life insurance (and her own son out of pure spite), has long stalked the collective consciousness. Some used to say that a door closed by a gust of wind is the work of her poltergeist. Elias Xitavhudzi, the second-most prolific of at least six serial killers from the Pretoria township of Atteridgeville, killed sixteen white women with a machete in the 1960s. Johannesburg has produced 1.3 serial killers for every decade of its history, with a cumulative tally of about 450. Yet no single act of violence—certainly nothing until the infant rapes of the post-Apartheid years—gripped the nation as relentlessly as the so-called Suitcase Murder.

The case presents white Johannesburgers with too many open questions. They see their own limbs dredged up from the water. It is a press-ready mystery, with no clues other than a few body parts of a white "everywoman," and thus stokes conflagrations of the very hysteria that motivated Apartheid in the first place: an embattled white minority, surrounded on all sides by bloodthirsty black hordes. "We must remember that we here in this country are under siege," says a parliamentarian. "Segregation is the only way we can be safe. It is not just our country that they will tear to pieces." Who "they" are does not need to be said.

Ten days after Bekker's discovery, yachts dot Wemmer Pan for the Saturday regatta. The pan, on the southern fringe of the city, was once a quarry, and the remains of a brickworks rust among blue gums by the main jetty. The wind smells of rain, and of meat cooking on dozens of barbecues. A suitcase bobs up against a yacht. This time, no one opens it.

> There is blood in the trachea, which means that the victim was beheaded while still breathing.

Inside, wrapped in plastic, are two severed legs, "the skin edges . . . grossly irregular and ragged," according to the forensics report. There are no further clues. The cops sift through hundreds of tips and even more hoaxes. The country's obsession with the case compounds the cops' frustration. "Is this the death knell for our country's morality?" asks a church leader. "No," thunders a politician. "This is the black man rising up to exercise the murder we know lurks in his breast." The missing head is a form of collective torture, an absence that becomes a suffocating presence.

December 17, the height of summer in South Africa. Two boys fish under a Japanese maple by the Zoo Lake boathouse. The area is a miraculous remnant of the colonial civilizing impulse. In 1886, it was dust and shrub. Eighty years later, it is lush with jacaranda, acacia, blue gum, birch, oleander, and oak, the roots of which drink deeply from the groundwater rushing underfoot. A fountain was pledged in King George's honor, and on this glorious December day, two ten-year-old boys watch it spit up water while they wait.

When their bite comes, it's a big one. They fight to reel in their catch, a tangled mass of sodden plastic. They hastily unwrap it and discover a human head, its skin the wrinkled consistency of a rotting baseball mitt. Crabs have eaten away the eyes and the nose. The mouth is agape in a panto-mime of stupid, toothless surprise. It is several hours before the boys think to mention their find to anyone. They were planning on taking it to school the following day.

Forensics gets to work. There is blood in the trachea, which means that the victim was beheaded while still breathing. Dentures and artificial eyes are fitted. Papers run a picture of this mummified head on front pages. A medical artist makes a reconstructive drawing, also widely circulated. Now there is a face to fit the myth. She could be someone's mother, perhaps, and someone's daughter. Her neck is stout, her lips wide, her eyes open and bright. She looks like a farm girl—the kind of woman on whose back this country was made. The cops expect an early break in the case.

They are wrong. There are too many variables; too much gets trampled under-foot. In early 1965, a woman named Catherine Cronje visits police headquarters and tells the police that the body parts cooling in the mortuary fridge must belong to her estranged mother, whom she has not seen in years. She says a botched gynecological procedure left her mother with a livid scar that ran from her belly button to her pubis. But the murderer, wielding a harsher blade, was careful to hack away such identifying marks. Cronje has nothing but intuition to go on. Where, she wonders, is her stepfather? Raymond Burch: ladies' man, dandy, scumbag.

The police pay a visit to her mother's last listed address in Hillbrow. Dry and airless as an abandoned museum, the flat displays no evidence of a crime. An inquest

is held—cause of death goes on the books as "unascertained." The remains are buried in a pauper's grave, and the Suitcase Murder becomes part of Johannesburg's collective nightmares. When a door is blown shut by a gust of wind, people now say it is the Suitcase Murderer.

In 1960s Johannesburg, there is acceptable violence: barroom corpses, shivved hookers—hallmarks of any mining town; institutional bloodshed visited upon an occasionally restive black population; domestic servants beaten to death by their employers. But the Suitcase Murder is something different. It suggests, by way of the murderer's corporeal poetry, that the republic's unstated aim—to maintain a Canaan for its white population—is a bankrupt promise. There is this sense, motivated by the fact that there are so many unknowns, that this is not a random act of brutality, but a tribal warning of sorts—like a severed head on a fence-post. And that the monster is not so much among us, but *of* us.

Three years later, Catherine Cronje returns to the station. It's 1968. A young captain named James Beeselaar has been assigned to the open file. For a couple of years, he has pushed papers, chased leads, busted myths. Cronje is still no less convinced that the victim is her mother. Beeselaar decides to follow up. What he learns about Cronje's stepfather, Raymond Burch, he does not like. There's an Immorality Act conviction—Apartheid's defining law, making it illegal for whites and blacks to have sexual relations—and the fact that four years ago, Burch cashed his wife's final paycheck and then disappeared. Beeselaar believes he finally has his murderer and, no less significantly, the name of his victim. Mrs. Catherine Burch, forty-one, late of Hillbrow, Johannesburg.

He puts out an all-points bulletin. The papers release a picture of Catherine Burch. She is a brunette who wears her hair in the bouffant style of the day, and has high cheekbones, horn-rimmed glasses, and an upturned mouth that reminds one of Doris Day. She stares into the camera, on the other side of which stands Raymond Burch. There is something in her eyes, a deadness that one cannot help interpreting as terror. The papers do not modify the hysteria, but rather turn it up a notch. "We are all at risk," states one editorial. "Something has changed in Johannesburg." They give no indication of what that might be.

Captain Beeselaar has tea with Burch's mother. The house in Bertrams—Johannesburg's oldest suburb—is quiet, with frayed lace curtains drawn against the sun. Mrs. Burch says her boy is overseas, visiting friends. Beeselaar presses, but she does not waver. I don't know where he is, she says. I am not his keeper.

Beeselaar broods for a month or so and, on November 26, makes a return visit, this time with a detective sergeant named Post-humous. Mrs. Burch's composure cracks. She shakes and weeps. She tells Beeselaar and Posthumous that she has locked Ray-mond in the small backyard cottage at his request. She begs them not to hurt her boy.

The two policemen fiddle with the lock. There's nowhere for Burch to run now. And Beeselaar is resolute. He will not leave empty-handed a second time.

He draws his revolver. Posthumous slides the deadbolt clear. Inside, a pale white man stands at the windows, rusted gardening implements cluttered around him. The cops stop and stare. He wears several homemade bracelets fashioned from tin, connected to a modified electrical socket by a filigree of wires. Without a word, Burch calmly reaches over to the switch. He flips it on and his shoulders jerk, his mouth locking in a ghastly rictus. *Hy het soos spek gerook*, Beeselaar says later. *He smelled like cooked bacon.* Burch's singed corpse hits the floor like a toppled statue, rigid with current. The fuse blows. The body goes limp and leaks fluids into the dirt.

In the end, it appears as if the Suicide Murder was nothing more than a domestic dispute resolved with a hacksaw, and not the millenarian racial upheaval suggested by the press and promised in parliament. Beeselaar is, however, a policeman, and doesn't like all the open questions. He'll never know definitively why Burch murdered his fourth wife, why he butchered her, why he scattered her remains across the city, and how he was able to get away with it for so long. The charred mess the captain has on his hands will take those answers to a murderer's grave—an unshaded, untended plot in a dusty prison yard on the outskirts of Africa's greatest city.

LIFE-ELIXIR SOUP:
HISTORY AND RECIPE

Jake Wolff

Living forever, one serving at a time

"Scientists find elixir of eternal life—in a worm,"
—THE DAILY TELEGRAPH, 2007

"A naturally occurring substance that can create 'immortal cells' could be the key to finding a real elixir of youth, scientists claim,"
—THE DAILY TELEGRAPH, 2008

"An 'elixir of life' biochemical has been discovered in the soil of Easter Island . . ."
— THE DAILY TELEGRAPH, 2009

My antler juice arrives on a Saturday. It has been shipped from a wapiti farm somewhere in Ontario, and, presumably to avoid scrutiny as it crosses the border into Wisconsin, the product description on the padded envelope says "Children's Toy." But this is not a toy. This is the elixir of life.

The concoction is made from the harvested antlers of adult wapiti. The antlers are severed clean from the head and then processed with a combination of natural and unnatural ingredients: water, concentrated apple juice, and "fragrance," to name a few. The primary determinant of an antler's quality is its blood content, and the antlers are processed quickly to preserve this content before it, I don't know, leaks out. The harvesting of antlers is not fatal to the wapiti and is said to be painless, though this last point seems conveniently difficult to prove.

The juice is held in fifteen plastic tubes about the size of my index finger—"Now in vials!" exclaims the box. The liquid itself is a light, muddy brown, the color of beer, and my first thought when I see it is *blood content*. I snip the tip of a vial with a pair of scissors and hold it over my mouth. Nothing comes. If I want to drink this stuff, I'm going to have to squirt it.

So I try again, this time squeezing at the vial's edges until I feel a stream of antler juice hit the back of my tongue. The first notes I taste are from the apple juice—sweet, a bit sharp—and for a moment I think this might not be so bad. But then the antler kicks in, and a heavy, bitter taste floods my mouth. It's like the aftertaste of cough medicine, but with antler.

I finish off the vial and then listen to my body for the sounds of new energy. So far, nothing. In order to achieve a "more rapid effect," the instructions suggested holding the elixir in my mouth for thirty seconds before swallowing. That would be much, much harder than it sounds.

It's nearly impossible to trace the precise origins of the elixir of life—it seems every culture in every century tried to find it, and it has been known by thousands of names. One of the earliest and most popular stories involves the First Emperor of the Qin Dynasty, who sent the sorcerer Xu Fu to search distant islands for the secret of immortality. Xu Fu was convinced that only the spiritually pure could find the elixir, and so to bless his journey, he brought one thousand virgins along for the voyage. It was, in its own way, the first and worst Semester at Sea.

Xu Fu never found the elixir. A decade later he showed up on the mainland and requested a small army of archers to help hunt the giant sharks he claimed had stolen the elixir and were hiding it in their bellies. One gets the sense he was just killing time at this point. The First Emperor of Qin died soon after.

The search really got going in the late Middle Ages, when the alchemical arts were in full bloom. In 1516, the German monk Trithemius is said to have passed along a recipe for the elixir that involved some combination of mercury chloride and cinnamon. The fact that Trithemius dictated the recipe from his deathbed may have weakened his followers' enthusiasm.

Perhaps the great-grandfather of my antler juice was Louis XI of France, who tried to restore his fading youth by drinking the blood of children. In 1667, Denys of Paris transfused the blood of a lamb into a sick child, and later the blood of a calf into a maniac. According to *Knight's American Mechanical Dictionary*, a sort of history of inventions published in 1876, Denys carried out similar experiments with dogs, birds, and horses. Depending on the source material, the patients were either miraculously cured or suffered terrific, painful deaths.

I first became interested in the elixir of life when I discovered a lump in my breast that I was sure was cancer. I wasn't so much worried as embarrassed. Old people—old *women*—are supposed to find lumps, not young men in their twenties. As a child, my trips to the doctor were nothing more than confirmations of my youthfulness—for acne medication, for example, or after I jumped my bike off a homemade ramp. But this time, as I sat in the breast doctor's waiting room surrounded by century-old women with huge, sagging breasts and huge, sagging purses, I could feel the youth draining out of me.

I went online. I typed "cure for cancer" into a search engine and quickly found myself reading about mysticism and the occult, about blood transfusions and medieval recipes for immortality. I was dumbfounded by the energy and persistence of the search, the sheer amount of ingredients that had been suggested as the foundation for an elixir of life, among them aloe, saffron, ginseng, solar dust, green tea, red tea, red wine, chocolate, sugar, milk, love, and, in a 1916 article in *The American* magazine, golf.

I didn't have cancer, it turned out, and was well enough to go out for sushi the same day the lump was removed. (Another suggested elixir of life: fish oil.) But the search for the elixir lingered in my mind long after the stitches were removed and the scar began to heal. My interest fully returned a year or so later, when I came across an article in the *Scientific Monthly* written in 1928 by Professor A. C. Eycleshymer, a retired dean of the College of Medicine at the University of Illinois. I was employed as a medical editor at the time, and the company I worked for had a small, dusty library of old medical literature tucked into the back of the warehouse.

"Growing Old and the Search for an Elixir of Life" is an unusual piece for a scientific journal, combining a history of life elixir with Prof. Eycleshymer's personal thoughts on aging and medicine. Before retirement, he discovered that injecting the sperm of a young rat into an old rat would increase the liveliness of the old rat's sperm. But the effect was like the jolt of energy from a strong cup of coffee: not meant to last.

At the end of Prof. Eycleshymer's article, a footnote explains that he died before he could finish the manuscript. The published version was completed by a friend. This shook me. I always liked to think that when old age came, I'd be ready. When my grandmother died of ovarian cancer at seventy-three—my first encounter with death—she went with such peace that it seemed almost strange to be sad about it. I thought the fear of death was just another thing I'd lose over time, along with my hair and my sex drive. But Prof. Eycleshymer was scared to die and said so: "The cold, dark clouds of life's winter are gathering; the ghastly image of old age is ever near and haunts us through the long restless nights." As I sat on the floor of the warehouse, reading among the disordered stacks, I was forced to admit that what I'd been calling an interest, a hobby, began to seem a lot more like fear.

After I finish off the antler juice, immortality next arrives in an alchemical potion, "an extract of colloidal ocean minerals," that I order off eBay for over seventy dollars. The potion is mixed and bottled by a mysterious but affable Australian alchemist, whose blog posts offer many small gems: "Hello Sorry I Have Been A Little Busy Studying The Properties Of Dew Water." He doesn't say much about his credentials, but the eBay posting claims some elite Hollywood connections: "My clients include Linda Evans (actress), Jennifer Aniston, and Gwyneth Paltrow." Those parentheses make me sad. Poor Krystle Carrington. What's the point of living forever if the world forgets us by the time we turn sixty?

This elixir arrives in a twenty-five-ounce plastic bottle that has been wrapped entirely in tin foil, giving it a distant, alien appearance. Unwrapping it reminds me of the week after the surgery, when I first removed the bandages from my chest. There was anxiety, even fear, but also a kind of giddiness at the prospect of being surprised, of being out on a ledge. Giddiness and then dizziness, when I saw how my chest looked—bruised, scabbed, with a black-stitched scar running in a roller-coaster loop. "I look like Franken-nipple," I said, before I had to sit down.

I hold the bottle up to the light. The instructions say to have a few teaspoons a day, though the Australian told me via e-mail that those are just guidelines, and that I should follow my own intuition when it comes to dosage. My intuition is to have less. The liquid is thin, eggshell white, and not quite uniform in color. Eighty-four sea minerals go into the elixir, and you can see these many components interacting on a micro level, creating a layered sort of swampiness. I tip the spoon into my mouth. The elixir is essentially saltwater, and as such tastes more familiar than the antler juice. But there's a depth to it that is unnerving—more of my taste buds are involved than I anticipated. I've heard that every ocean tastes a little different than the others, and I wonder if all of them bottled together might taste something like this.

There was anxiety, even fear, but also a kind of giddiness at the prospect of being surprised.

My first impulse is to spit it out. But there's a difference between this and the antler juice, which with its artificial flavoring and questionable ethics tasted somehow phony, false. The Australian, for all his silliness, strikes me as completely sincere. This life elixir feels *cared for*, and in its own way, food that is cared for always tastes good.

After I finish the potion, I take a few weeks off my search for immortality to consider my next move. So far, nothing has made me feel especially vigorous. More surprising is that nothing has made me sick. Still, ordering mysterious liquids off the Internet and forcing myself to drink them is beginning to lose its charm. When a new package arrives in the mail, my wife has started to ask "What now?" with the doleful, defeated tone she normally reserves for her mother. The next logical step is clear. I'm going to make my own elixir of life.

The market for life elixir began to change in early-nineteenth-century America. Where once only the wealthiest classes pursued the elixir, now it was the poorest population who heard the call. The advent of the democratic system promised prosperity, and yet the country lacked the health-care system to support such promises. Thus an entire profession of quackery arose to take advantage of America's sick, working poor.

Victoria Woodhull, the suffragist who is best known as the first woman to run for president, spent many years traveling with her sister, Tennessee Claflin, to sell psychic readings and an elixir of life. The elixir, "Miss Tennessee's Magnetio Life Elixir for Beautifying the Complexion and Cleansing the Blood," was little more than cheap alcohol. Known as "patent medicine," such elixirs were prevalent throughout the next century. Most potions, like Claflin's, focused on the immediate health benefits rather than on eternal life. Consumers were more concerned with the common diseases of the times—cholera, diphtheria, small pox— than with immortality.

In 1905, after receiving a pamphlet for an elixir, an angry Mark Twain penned a letter in which he referred to the salesman as an "idiot of the 33rd degree," and concluded:

> A few moments from now my
> resentment will have faded and passed
> and I shall probably even be praying
> for you; but while there is yet time
> I hasten to wish that you may take a
> dose of your own poison by mistake,
> and enter swiftly into the damnation
> which you and all other patent medi-
> cine assassins have so remorselessly
> earned and do so richly deserve.
> Adieu, adieu, adieu!
> Mark Twain

By then, Twain had lost his son to diphtheria and his daughter to spinal meningitis. Nearly all life elixirs would have claimed to cure both.

I assemble my list of ingredients. I want everything in my potion to have been linked, at one time, to the elixir of life—ginseng, avocado, nutmeg, et cetera. I don't care about simplicity or elegance. If previous attempts at an elixir have been akin to aiming for the bulls-eye with a single dart, my attempt will be closer to a shotgun fired at close range.

The centerpiece of my elixir is *Boschniakia rossica*, a rare parasitic plant that grows primarily in mountainous regions of Asia. Legend holds that a fairy descended on a dying village in the Changbai Mountains and used the herb to heal the sick and elderly. One interpretation says the village was dying of cancer. I order mine from a seller in China who refers to it as the "Immortal Herb."

The herb's healing properties are not entirely based on myth. Studies in rats have shown that the Immortal Herb shares some qualities with the antioxidants commonly available in vitamin form. It limits the amount of free radicals—considered a primary factor in aging—and increases the production of proteins that help control them. In these preliminary, still inconclusive studies, rats treated with the Immortal Herb seem younger after treatment.

To search for the elixir is to believe in a grand solution to life's inescapable outcome.

The herb itself is long, purple brown, with rows of flaky knobs and a chunkier, knotted root. It looks a bit like a pinecone's gangly younger brother. The smell and flavor are mild, earthy but with a hint of sweetness, like dark chocolate. Just as in the pamphlets of snake-oil salesmen from the nineteenth century, the company selling the *Boschniakia rossica* provides a list of conditions you might treat with the herb, including impotence, knee pain, "womb coldness," nephritis, depression, "trance," and—the silent killer—"wet dream." The instructions suggest soaking the herb in wine or tea, using it to braise chicken, or—and here inspiration strikes—putting it in a soup.

I give my wife the list of ingredients and break the bad news that she's gone from spectator to participant. She attended culinary school in Chicago and has worked in some of the best restaurants in the Midwest, so it's not long before she turns my ramblings into the framework of a workable recipe. We make the soup on a Saturday night; it takes a little over an hour. The Immortal Herb turns out to share some biological properties with catnip, and as we cook, our cat tries to bury his face in the brittle combs.

In 1934, the first multivitamin was introduced to the American market. In many ways, the magic of life elixir was officially gone.

These vitamins may be the closest we have now to an elixir of life, right down to the vague, unsubstantiated medical claims. No one believes vitamins will make you live forever, but, like so many people, I take one every day. The many beauty creams available on the market provide an even more cynical approach to the modern elixir of life—you'll still die in your seventies, but you'll look fifty when you do.

The less obvious but no less prevalent progeny of life elixir are energy drinks. I intended to sample a number of these energy drinks along with my more exotic purchases, but after tasting a few I simply couldn't take it. I tried Red Bull, which tastes like Skittles, except that Skittles are delicious. I tried Monster Energy Drink, a fruity, carbonated abomination that came in a can the size of my head. I tried 5-Hour Energy, which tasted like Sour Patch Kids and made my heart race. I preferred the antler juice.

The soup tastes like a mild curry, though brothier, and with a slightly grassier tone from the *matcha* powder. Sitting down to eat, I found myself thinking differently about the searchers who came before me. The more I'd learned about the history of life elixir, the more I'd begun to view those who looked for it as desperate, fearful, deserving of pity. But that night I started to appreciate their hopefulness. To search for the elixir is to believe in a grand solution to life's inescapable outcome. It's to believe there's nothing that can't be cured. For a few hours—for the duration of dinner—I almost believe it myself.

And it tasted great. The soup has a relatively complicated preparation, and some of the ingredients are expensive, but compared to the price paid by Xu Fu, by Trimethius, an evening spent cooking with a loved one is not a lot to ask for immortality.

We eat the leftovers for a week. Some-
times when I carry the soup from the
refrigerator to the stove—the pot pressed
high against my chest—I feel a pang along
the old incision. The scar is still there,
curved across the breast like a small smile.
I don't mind it now; it only makes me nos-
talgic. I began searching for the elixir of life
because I was scared I was dying, but the
only reason I can give as for why I've kept
looking is that there's something in that
fear worth recapturing. It was, after all, an
adventure—the adventure of not knowing.

I think of that fear now. I think of Prof.
Eycleshymer, poring over his life's work
and scrambling to finish his final paper. I
think of Louis XI, a silver goblet of child's
blood trembling in his grasp. I think of Xu
Fu, many years at sea with his armies of
archers and virgins. And then I think of
that moment, after the surgery, when the
doctor told me I didn't have cancer. I had
returned to his clinic to hear the results of
the lab work. He told me to sit down and
then turned his back to me, rifling through
some papers. "It was a fibroadenoma," he
said over his shoulder. Then there was
silence as I sat wondering if I'd been given
good news or bad. *Fibroadenoma*. He turned
around and must have seen me frowning,
searching. "It's fine," he said, and I'll never
forget how he said it: as though I should
have known all along. 🛡

LIFE-ELIXIR SOUP

FOR SOUP:

1 shallot, minced
2 garlic cloves, minced
¼ cup olive oil

3 ounces *matcha* powder
2 teaspoons curry powder
1 teaspoon ground allspice
½ teaspoon ground ginger
1 tablespoon ground coriander

10 ounces + 4 ounces coconut milk, divided
2 cups vegetable stock

¹⁄₁₀ ounce Immortal Herb
20 cardamom seeds

¹⁄₁₀ ounce ginseng root
¼ teaspoon fresh nutmeg, grated
2 tablespoons basil, chiffonade
2 tablespoons cilantro, chopped
1 cup raw spinach, chopped

Salt to taste
White pepper to taste

1 avocado, small dice
1 mango, small dice
2 tablespoon minced jalapeno
¼ teaspoon lime zest

1 lime, juiced
Olive oil
Salt to taste

Steam ginseng root for 5 minutes, or until the root becomes slightly softened. Peel the outer skin of the root and grate the entire root using a microplane (it should yield about 2 tablespoons).

Mix the 4 ounces of coconut milk with the *matcha* powder to make a slurry. Whisk until there are no visible clumps of powder. Set aside.

Wrap the Immortal Herb and cardamom seeds in a small sash of cheesecloth and tie with thread. Set aside.

Heat the oil in a heavy-bottomed pot over medium heat. When the oil is warm, add shallots and garlic. Stir for 3 to 4 minutes, until the shallots start to turn translucent and the oil becomes highly fragrant. Add the curry powder, allspice, ginger, and coriander seed. Heat spices in pan for one minute, stirring constantly. Add 10 ounces coconut milk plus the vegetable stock and bring to a boil. When the soup has come to a boil, lower the heat and allow the soup to slowly simmer.

As soon as the soup has stopped boiling, place the sachet of Immortal Herb in the soup to infuse for 20 minutes to half an hour.

Add ginseng and nutmeg to soup. After 30 minutes, lower heat until soup is hardly simmering. Add the coconut milk and *matcha* slurry to the soup and whisk vigorously to help it emulsify. Add the basil, cilantro, and spinach and stir to combine.

Prepare the garnish. Place avocado, mango, jalapeno, and lime zest in a bowl. Pour lime juice over garnish, season to taste, then toss to combine. Finish with a drizzle of extra virgin olive oil. Garnish each bowl of soup with a tablespoon of the avocado mixture and serve.

Yield: 4 servings

CONTRIBUTORS

Raphael Allison is a poet and literary scholar. He has published numerous essays on figures as diverse as James Schuyler, Muriel Rukeyser, and David Antin. Currently, he is writing a book on recorded poetry. He teaches writing at Princeton University.

Katie Arnold-Ratliff received her MFA from Sarah Lawrence College. She is on the editorial staff of O, *The Oprah Magazine*, where her writing appears regularly. Her first novel, *Bright Before Us*, will be published by Tin House Books in May 2011. She lives in New York.

Andrea Barrett is the author of six novels, most recently *The Air We Breathe*, and two collections of short fiction, *Ship Fever*, which received the National Book Award, and *Servants of the Map*, a finalist for the Pulitzer Prize. She lives in western Massachusetts and teaches at Williams College.

Douglas Bauer's books include the novels *Dexterity*, *The Very Air*, and *The Book of Famous Iowans*, and the nonfiction books *Prairie City, Iowa* and *The Stuff of Fiction*. He's received grants in both fiction and nonfiction from the National Endowment for the Arts. He's currently a professor of English at Bennington College.

Kenneth Calhoun's fiction has appeared in the *Paris Review*, *Fence*, the *St. Petersburg Review*, *Quick Fiction*, and other publications. His story "Nightblooming" will be included in *The PEN/O. Henry Prize Stories 2011*.

Clare Cavanagh is a professor of Slavic languages and literatures at Northwestern University.

Paul Collins teaches creative writing at Portland State University. His book *The Murder of the Century*—an account of rival yellow journalists covering a sensational 1897 crime—will be released this summer by Crown Books.

John Crowley published his first novel, *The Deep*, in 1975, and his eleventh novel, *Four Freedoms*, in 2009. Since 1993, he has taught creative writing at Yale University. In 1992, he received the Award in Literature from the American Academy and Institute of Arts and Letters. His criticism has appeared in the *Boston Review*, the *Washington Post*, the *Yale Review*, and other venues.

Colin Fleming writes for *The Atlantic*, the *New Yorker*, *Slate*, and *Rolling Stone*. His fiction has appeared in the *Iowa Review*, *Boulevard*, *Black Clock*, the *Hopkins Review*, and *Pen America*. He can be found on the Web at colinfleminglit.com.

Writer and translator Edward Gauvin (edwardgauvin.com/blog) has received fellowships and residencies from the Centre National du Livre, Ledig House, the Banff Centre, and the American Literary Translators Association. His work has appeared in *Conjunctions*, *Subtropics*, *World Literature Today*, the *Southern Review*, and the *Harvard Review*.

Cheston Knapp is managing editor of *Tin House* magazine. He lives in Portland, Oregon, where he does the probing.

Eddie Muller, aka "The Czar of Noir," is an internationally recognized authority on film noir and founder and president of the Film Noir Foundation, which raises funds to rescue and restore vintage noir films. He's a familiar voice on dozens of film noir DVD commentaries, and the prize-winning author of the novels *The Distance* and *Shadow Boxer*.

Lawrence Osborne has written for the *New York Times Magazine*, the *New Yorker*, and other publications, and is the author of nine books. Born in England, he has lived in France, Italy, Morocco, Mexico, and Thailand, and now lives in New York City.

Benjamin Percy is the author of two novels, *Red Moon* (forthcoming in 2012), *The Wilding*, and two books of short stories, *Refresh, Refresh* and *The Language of Elk*. He teaches creative writing in the MFA program at Iowa State University and is a faculty member of the low-residency MFA program at Pacific University. His

honors include the Whiting Award, the Plimpton Prize, the Pushcart Prize, and inclusion in *Best American Short Stories*.

Actor, writer, and translator Maurice Pons was born in Strasbourg in 1927. His first book of stories, *Virginales*, won the Prix de la nouvelle de la Société des Gens de Lettres, and his collection *Douce-amère* won the Prix de la nouvelle de l'Académie Française. This is his first short story to be translated into English.

Richard Poplak is an award-winning journalist and author, most recently, of *The Sheikh's Batmobile: In Pursuit of American Pop Culture in the Muslim World* and of the journalistic graphic novel *Kenk: A Graphic Portrait*. He splits his time between Toronto and Johannesburg.

Hugh Ryan is a vagabond with a predilection for activities that get him dropped on his head. He's currently working on an anarchist kid's book. He holds an MFA in nonfiction from the Bennington Writing Seminars, and his writing has appeared in the *New York Times*, *Details*, the *Advocate*, and other venues.

Robin Beth Schaer is the recipient of fellowships from the Saltonstall Foundation and the Virginia Center for the Creative Arts. Her poetry has appeared in *Denver Quarterly*, *Barrow Street*, *Prairie Schooner*, and *Washington Square*, among others. She has taught at Columbia University and sailed as a deckhand aboard the HMS *Bounty*.

Patricia Smith is the author of five books of poetry, including *Blood Dazzler*, a finalist for the 2008 National Book Award, and *Teahouse of the Almighty*, a National Poetry Series selection. Her work has appeared in *Poetry*, the *Paris Review* and *TriQuarterly*, among other publications, and she has received a Pushcart Prize.

Justin Taylor is the author of the novel *The Gospel of Anarchy* and the story collection *Everything Here Is the Best Thing Ever*, both out now from Harper Perennial. His Web site is www.justindtaylor.net.

Tonaya Thompson is a senior editor at *Tin House* magazine. She earned an MFA from Bennington College and was the managing editor of the student anthology the *Bennington Review* and of Bennington's alumni newsletter, *From the Far Side of the Vortex*. She has poetry forthcoming in the *Dos Passos Review*.

Natasha Trethewey is the author of *Beyond Katrina: A Meditation on the Mississippi Gulf Coast* and three collections of poetry, *Domestic Work*, *Bellocq's Ophelia*, and *Native Guard*—for which she was awarded the Pulitzer Prize. She is the recipient of NEA, Guggenheim, Bunting, and Rockefeller fellowships. At Emory University, she is a professor of English and holds the Phillis Wheatley Distinguished Chair in Poetry.

Luis Alberto Urrea has published extensively and is the critically acclaimed and best-selling author of thirteen books, including *The Devil's Highway*, which won the Lannan Literary Award and was a finalist for the Pulitzer Prize, and *The Hummingbird's Daughter*, which won the Kiriyama Prize in fiction. Urrea lives with his family in Naperville, Illinois, where he is a professor of creative writing at the University of Illinois-Chicago.

Sarah Weinman reports on the publishing industry for *Daily Finance*, writes Dark Passages, the *Los Angeles Times*'s monthly crime-fiction column, and contributes to publications such as the *Wall Street Journal*, the *Daily Beast*, *Maclean's*, and the *Guardian*. She blogs at *Confessions of an Idiosyncratic Mind* (at www.sarahweinman.com), hailed by *USA TODAY* as "a respected resource for commentary on crime and mystery fiction."

Jake Wolff holds an MFA in creative writing from the University of Wisconsin-Madison, and is now pursuing his PhD in creative writing at Florida State University. His work has appeared in *Redivider*, *Fiction Weekly*, *Word Riot*, *Sou'wester*, and elsewhere.

Adam Zagajewski was born in Lvov in 1945. His previous books include *Tremor*; *Canvas*; *Mysticism for Beginners*; *Without End*; *Solidarity, Solitude*; *Two Cities*; *Another Beauty*; *A Defense of Ardor*; and *Eternal Enemies*—all published by FSG. He lives in Chicago and Kraków.

Adam Zagajewski's poems are excerpted from *Unseen Hand: Poems*, translated from the Polish by Clare Cavanagh, to be published in June by Farrar, Straus and Giroux, LLC. Copyright 2011 by Adam Zagajewski. Translation copyright 2011 by Clare Cavanagh. All rights reserved.

Color photographs on pages 161-168 ©Lucia Ganieva, courtesy Schilt Publishing.

COVER CREDITS
Front cover: *Agnostic II*, by Julie Heffernan.

220

Missed the First Forty-Six Issues?

Fear not.
We've hidden a limited number in our closet.

Premiere Issue: David Foster Wallace, Ron Carlson, Stuart Dybek, Charles Simic, C. K. Williams, Rick Moody.

Issue 2: Yasunari Kawabata, Faiz Ahmed Faiz, Walter Kirn, David Gates, Jean Nathan.

Issue 3: Amy Hempel, Yehuda Amichai; interviews with John Sanford, Dawn Powell.

Issue 4: Aleksandar Hemon, Derek Walcott, Daniel Halpern, Stéphane Mallarmé; Sherman Alexie interview.

Issue 5: Kevin Canty, Nancy Reisman, Bei Dao, Donald Hall, Jane Hirshfield, Sylvia Plath, Ann Hood; Ha Jin interview.

Issue 6: The Film Issue, starring Russell Banks, Todd Haynes, Bruce Wagner, Barney Rosset, Jerry Stahl, Jonathan Lethem, Rachel Resnick.

Issue 7: SOLD OUT

Issue 8: Elizabeth Tallent, Paul West, Jennifer Egan, Jerry Stahl, Josip Novakovich, Billy Collins, Barney Rosset interview.

Issue 9: Richard Ford, Mary Gaitskill, Jim Shepard, Czeslaw Milosz, David Shields, Mark Doty, Nick Flynn.

Issue 10: The Music Issue, with Jonathan Lethem, Francine Prose, Rick Moody, C. K. Williams.

Issue 11: SOLD OUT

Issue 12: Jo Ann Beard, Lynn Freed, Andre Dubus III, Diane Ackerman, Charlie Smith; Ron Carlson interview.

Issue 13: Dorothy Allison, Richard Powers, Olena Kalytiak Davis, Helen Schulman; Francine Prose interview.

Issue 14: SOLD OUT

Issue 15: The Sex Issue, featuring Francine Prose, Denis Johnson, Mario Vargas Llosa, Charles Simic, and a bunch of bad sex.

Issue 16: Summer Fiction, with Stuart Dybek, Joy Williams, Charles Baxter, Melanie Rae Thon, Pablo Neruda; Marilynne Robinson interview.

Issue 17: SOLD OUT

Issue 18: Julia Slavin, Dale Peck, Anthony Swofford, Inger Christensen; interviews with Paul Collins and Jim Shepard.

Issue 19: SOLD OUT

Issue 20: Robert Olen Butler, Steven Millhauser and Elizabeth Tallent; Interview with Chris Offutt

Issue 21: Stacey Richter, Amanda Eyre Ward, Seamus Heaney, Adam Zagajewski, Lucia Perillo; George Saunders interview.

Issue 22: Emerging Voices, Daniel Alarcón, Nami Mun, Jung H. Yun; James Salter interview.

Issue 23: SOLD OUT

Issue 24: SOLD OUT

Issue 25: SOLD OUT

Issue 26: All Apologies, with Casanova, Donna Tartt, Ken Kalfus, Robin Romm.

Issue 27: International, with José Saramago, Seamus Heaney, Ismail Kadare, Bei Ling, Binyavanga Wainaina, Anita Desai.

Issue 28: SOLD OUT

Issue 29: Graphic, with Lynda Barry, Marjane Satrapi, Zak Smith, Todd Haynes.

Issue 30: Milan Kundera, Anthony Doerr, Jillian Weise, Etgar Keret, Anthony Swofford, Rick Bass interview.

Issue 31: Evil, with Nick Flynn, Chris Adrian, Sam Lipsyte.

Issue 32: Rick Bass, Ann Beattie, Antonya Nelson, Elizabeth Strout.

Issue 33: SOLD OUT

Issue 34: Charles Baxter, Joshua Ferris, Yiyun Li on William Trevor; Deborah Eisenberg interview.

Issue 35: Off the Grid with Ron Carlson, Marie Howe, Charles Simic, George Makana Clark, Roberto Bolaño.

Issue 36: Allan Gurganus, Adam Johnson, Chris Adrian, Mary Jo Bang; plus Frank Bidart interview.

Issue 37: Politics, with Eduardo Galeano, Thomas Frank, Nick Flynn, Francine Prose, José Saramago.

Issue 38: Anne Carson, Christopher Sorrentino, Ron Hansen, Arthur Bradford, Matthew Dickman; Daniel Menaker interview.

Issue 39: Appetites, with Pasha Malla, Stephen Marion, Ann Hood, Charles Wright; Catherine Millet interview.

Issue 40: Tenth Anniversary, with Dorothy Allison, Anthony Doerr, David Foster Wallace, Jim Shepard; Colson Whitehead interview.

Issue 41: Hope / Dread, with Karen Russell, Matthea Harvey, Ander Monson; Lorrie Moore interview.

Issue 42: Ben Marcus, Antonya Nelson, Karen Shepard, Michael Dickman; Roy Blount interview.

Issue 43: Games People Play, with Tom Bissell, Jennifer Egan, Matthew Zapruder, Karen Russell, plus David Mamet.

Issue 44: Per Petterson, Lydia Millet, Rawi Hage, Daniel Handler; plus Etgar Keret and David Shields interviews.

Issue 45: Class in America, with Lewis Hyde, Benjamin Percy, Luc Sante, Lydia Davis's Madame Bovary.

Issue 46: Kevin Brockmeier, Dan Chaon, Rebecca Makkai, Adrienne Rich, Eileen Myles, Paul Bowles's letters, plus Karen Russell interview

Seventeen dollars each issue, including postage. Make checks payable to Tin House and mail to Back Issues, Tin House, P.O. Box 10500, Portland, OR 97296-0500.

Stay tuned for **Summer Reading** (#48) and **The Ecstatic** (#49)

Log on to **www.tinhouse.com**

Best American Short **Stories**

Best **American** Poetry

Best American Essays

Best American **Science**

& Nature **Writing**

the **Pushcart**

Prize anthology

Since 2006 ecotone is the only publication in the country to have had its work reprinted in all of these anthologies. Find out why **Salman Rushdie** names us one of a handful of literary magazines on which "the health of the American short story depends."

REIMAGINING PLACE

ecotone

ecotonejournal.com

GET YOUR LIT FIX

Separate Kingdoms
Stories by Valerie Laken

"[Laken] takes aim at the human experience, and does not shoot. Instead, she steps forward, into places we wouldn't dare, and lays them bare for the reader. This is life-changing work."
—Laura Kasischke, author of *In a Perfect World*

The Gospel of Anarchy
A Novel by Justin Taylor

"A beautiful, searching and sometimes brutally funny novel. Justin Taylor writes with fierce precision and perfect balance."
—Sam Lipsyte, author of *The Ask*

You Don't Love This Man
A Novel by Dan DeWeese

"The story has left me in that strange place between emotional exhaustion and raw, refreshed excitement for life. This amazing novel is why novels exist."
—Patrick Somerville, author of *The Cradle*

A Fierce Radiance
A Novel by Lauren Belfer

"A love story and murder mystery rolled into panoramic family saga and industrial-espionage thriller.... Belfer's prose is heartbreaking... fuses fiction and history cleverly and seamlessly."
—*USA Today*

Russian Winter
A Novel by Daphne Kalotay

"A magnificent tale of love, loss, betrayal, and redemption...the author lets the truth ebb and flow until a final riptide of revelations leave the reader profoundly moved."
—*Washington Post Book World*

There is No Year
A Novel by Blake Butler

A wildly inventive, impressionistic novel of family, sickness, and the birth-wrench of art, from a "deeply promising young author" (*Time Out New York*).

ABOUT THE COVER

Elissa Schappell

Julie Heffernan's rococo-surrealist self-portraits represent the artist as, among other things, a bare-chested female girdled in dead beasties, a towering glass skyscraper, and a beguiling young man who offers us a peek beneath the landscape he's lifted up like an oriental rug. What unifies these lush, seductively enigmatic portraits is the sense of contained rapture as well as the tiny, ever-present tableaus—Boschian romps, domestic dramas—that exist within her paintings. With these windows into the alternate universes within, we see that we do indeed contain multitudes, if only we could access them. Mystery relies on our willful suspension of disbelief, and Heffernan is a master magician. No matter how absurd the conceit, her paintings possess a fevered dream logic that we can't help but embrace; we know it's impossible to remain upright and self-possessed when under attack by an avian mob in a grand ballroom, or when one's head has been set on fire by a tiny city burning inside the body, yet we are convinced—even once we've left that dream state—that the world we entered was real. How she does it is a mystery.